Endlessly

Andréa Kohalmi

Pronunciations

Aeterna Flamma: Ayterna Flahma
Anchises: Ann-kī-sees
Artemis: Ahr-teh-miss
Bellatori Dei: Bella-toree Day-ee
Cenweard: Keen-ward
Cynan: Keen-an
Gaap: Gahp
Hadrianus: Hay-dree-ahn-us
Mwnt: Moont
Qaletaqa: Kah-lay-takah

Cover Graphic Design by Chris Koutroulos
Copyright © 2015 by Andrea Kohalmi
All rights reserved.
ISBN-10: 0692461442
ISBN-13: 978-0692461440
*Library of Congress Control Number: [LCCN]
Veritas in Lumenum, Novato, CA

For
E

Trust in your heart for truth lies there.
Whatever rips you apart is healed by love,
Which mends the tear.

Hold tight, my angel, a new day is dawning,
A day without lonely pain and fear.
Dry your eyes, my little one,
We will always kiss away each tear.

One day you will see past the pain
And understand your destiny has been attained.
The torture that hurts so much today will be the hand
that helps others see the way.

Through the blackest of nights, stars still shine.
Wish on the moon and heal with the sun.
Your innocence and perseverance withstand all time.
And, someday soon peace will return, the battle won.

"When [God] expelled the man, he settled him east of the garden of Eden; and he stationed the cherubim and the fiery revolving sword to guard the way to the tree of life."

Genesis 3:24

Preface

Did you ever love someone so much that it hurt? I mean, physically cause you so much pain that you couldn't eat or drink?

Nausea becomes a daily part of existence and every thought of your special someone—no matter how fleeting—leaves you feeling queasy. The remedy is rather simple. Share your feelings and wait for his reply. With rejection your appetite returns immediately and is satisfied by a half-gallon of French vanilla ice cream drowning in chocolate syrup while you watch a sappy movie that becomes your excuse to cry all night. With acceptance, the butterflies already dancing in your stomach start a marathon, which keeps you running non-stop for months.

I'd take queasy over food any day.

There was one complication in my current nauseous state. Yes, I was in love, but the love was wracked with guilt. With all of my being I loved CJ, but the sick tremors of infatuation craved Rick.

Cringe.

Then again, I couldn't escape Rick even if I wished it. Being a world-famous celebrity, who disappeared mysteriously a year ago, the media and paparazzi still kept him front-and-center in the public eye. His heart-stopping face was plastered on the cover of every teen mag and every Hollywood-fed website.

I tried to walk by the grocery store magazine racks without looking at him, but I couldn't avoid him at the checkouts. Every time I glanced at his handsome face, guilty dread sunk like a ton of bricks from my head to my toes. After all, I was the reason for his disappearance.

In a lightning-fast flash, the memory of Rick saving me from the grip of his evil vampire father, Hadrianus, filled all of my senses—the smell of the sleepy Welsh countryside, the cool breeze blowing through my hair, the feeling of warm blood streaming down my cold, white skin. Shudder. I shook my head to fast-forward the all-too-real memory.

Of course, I didn't return the favor when two of our good, Bellatori angels captured him and disappeared with him to some undisclosed prison.

And why was I wasting my time thinking about Rick? He was here—well—somewhere on this plane of existence anyway. I was terrified that our paths would cross again sooner than later, but my worries were based on so much more than that. His goodbye haunted every minute of every day since last year's battle against Aeterna Flamma, an evil group of fallen angels and demons running a vengeful rampage to spite God for being banished from heaven. The innocent look in Rick's captivating green eyes and his last kiss spoke to me on a level where words had no meaning. Our souls connected.

Double cringe.

At least this is what my fickle heart wanted to believe. My head was logically and incessantly reminding me of the facts. Despite Rick's suave words and to-die-for tall, dark and handsome good looks, he was a vampire determined to destroy humanity, not to mention that he killed CJ in a prior life and was determined to make me his against my will. He nearly accomplished his goal last summer in Wales. Thankfully, the Bellatori Dei's angels intervened before he could kidnap me after I stupidly rescued him from his father's murderous grasp.

Still, there was something nagging about him that I couldn't wrap my conscious thoughts around. Of course, this shameful obsession betrayed my love for CJ. So, I was stuck somewhere between feeling horrible and despicable.

The balmy, summer, mid-day sun baked my face as I lay on the empty expanse of Salem Common. The warm, lush, green grass tickled my neck and back. Fluffy white clouds floated aimlessly across their pale blue blanket. The scent of the gentle ocean breeze and freshly cut grass reminded me of all the reasons I used to love this time of year.

Notwithstanding the peace I felt externally, my insides still churned from last summer's events at Endymion Manor in Wales. Today was the one year anniversary of a battle that changed my life forever. The day I vanquished a foe with a five-thousand-year-old grudge. The day I found the strength to overcome my fears. The day I lost my true love to his inevitable fate a world away from me.

The year since then passed by in a blur. I found it somewhat easier to deal with the memories by ignoring my special powers and pretending most of it was just a nightmare. I walked through the motions of attending freshman year at Salem State College as an undeclared major. Nothing appealed to me. Actually, life didn't appeal much to me either, but I promised CJ I'd try.

In a sick twist of fate, he was doomed to the afterlife while I was stuck here. The only thing prohibiting my suicidal tendencies was the promise I made not to follow him. I knew I had a destiny here that still needed to be fulfilled, otherwise I would've died fighting the undead last June.

Still, that realization did nothing to alleviate the excruciating pain that ripped my insides to shreds every time I thought of CJ. True to his word though, his warm, unseen embrace encircled my body whenever I asked him, which was pretty much every morning, noon, and night. Having a ghost for a boyfriend wasn't ideal, but it was all I had and I wasn't about to let him go.

I'll readily admit I was a walking zombie for months and spent most of my days sitting beside Zach's grave. Not being able to talk to anyone about what happened was excruciating. As the cancerous misery ate away at me, my weight dropped drastically. That's when my mom forced me to see a psychiatrist. I truly respect their trade, but what could I say? Surely, not the truth. How would that conversation have played out?

Hi Doctor. My boyfriend, Zach, died last year, which led me into a desperate depression. Then, I spent a month in Wales only to discover that my life was at the center of the ultimate battle between good and evil. To top it off, I found out that my temporary guardian angel, CJ, was actually Zach, reincarnated for three weeks' time.

Throw in a few vampires, werewolves, and fallen angels and the shrink would've committed me instantly.

Actually, my mom did try to commit me, but I threatened to go back to Wales, so she backed off. Instead, my younger brothers and sister followed me everywhere. For their safety, I got a job closer to home at the Salem Witch Museum. I missed my new Wiccan friends, Sam and Cynan, and considering my mental stability, or lack thereof, my mom wouldn't let me visit them. This job bound me to them tangibly.

And so, there I was lying on Salem Common during my lunch break, wishing I was with CJ and my friends.

Oh, for all that's holy. What does she want? All *I* wanted was a few minutes of peace and quiet, but my mother text messaged me at least five times in the past ten minutes. I dialed her number furiously.

"What?!" I shouted harshly when she answered. Part of me felt sorry about the rude tone, but most of me was too angry and too miserable to care.

"I'm sorry to bother you, dear," she said evenly. I certainly didn't deserve this courtesy. She had an amazing knack for making me feel immensely guilty. "I know you're working and…"

"Spit it out, Mom," I interrupted, soaking in the sun's rays to pacify my irritability.

"Angie, there's a young man here waiting for you."

"A guy?" I huffed incredulously.

"I'm serious, dear. He insists that he knows you," she said, trying simultaneously to convince and calm me. Her voice dropped to a hushed whisper, "and he insists on staying here until he sees you."

"Who is he?"

"He said he's from a company with some sort of Italian name... Belladonna...Belarus... Barilla..."

My heart stopped. Blood drained from my entire body. I bolted upright. "Bellatori?" I asked cautiously.

"Yes, that's it!" she exclaimed.

I couldn't form words; then again, you need air to speak. I gasped trying to remember how to breathe.

"Angie? Honey, are you ok?"

The phone slipped from my ear and I shoved it into my pocket as my feet flew across the Common.

Were the Bellatori Dei really breaking their year-long silent treatment? Could it be CJ? *No.* I grimaced in disappointment—his hands were still wrapped tightly around me. The Bellatori I could handle, but the alternative is what made my heart screech to a halt and my feet run faster.

What if—just perhaps—maybe they didn't need a hundred years to recuperate? What if last year's battle was only a precursor to the real event? What if the guy in my living room right now—sitting with my mom and siblings—wasn't from the Bellatori? What if this was a trap?

And what if this wasn't just any Aeterna Flamma henchman? What if he escaped? My heart skipped a beat in ecstatic, masochistic enthusiasm at the thought. Guilt pierced it. What if he was forcing fate's hand? What if the angelic presence in my sanctuary was actually my five-thousand-year-old vampire stalker? What if Rick was going to make good on his promise to make me his? Was my destiny inescapable…and only a few minutes away from becoming a reality?

There was only one way to find out. Taking a deep breath, my seemingly disembodied hand slowly turned the front door knob. Despite the hazy, hot, and humid day, fear froze every inch of my body. I stepped through the threshold.

Shaking and terrified, I peered warily around the front door…

Chapter 1 – Lottery with a Catch

Like a star-struck fan ogling at a celebrity, my mom stared in awkward silence at our guest's radiant face. Like all others of his kind, a gold, white aura glowed around his perfect face and piercing blue eyes. The living embodiment of a holy Donatello sculpture, his gloriousness belonged in a church or art gallery. He stuck out like a sore thumb against the pale violet walls, drab ivory colored carpet and faded furniture in my living room.

Lurching to his feet a little faster than humanly possible, my mom shook her head, trying to process what she thought she saw.

"Ms. Kiss," he began in a melodic Welsh accent with pure innocence in his gaze. "My name is Adam Darius. Bellatori Bank of Southern Wales sent me to deliver an important message."

The cherubic angel with golden brown curls glanced nervously at my dumbfounded mother before turning his all-too-powerful eyes on me.

I nodded eagerly and motioned for him to follow me through the front door and down Church Street. My stomach flopped anxiously.

"You're here because…" I urged, avoiding his face partially because his beauty was distracting and partially because being in his presence reminded me too much of CJ. I didn't care that Adam was a stranger. He was from the Bellatori and that meant he had access to my boyfriend.

"The Bellatori would like to repay your bravery from last year," he started, sounding very official. "As you know, our organization would not have survived if not for the sacrifices you and Cenweard made on our behalf."

My heart squeezed painfully at the sound of CJ's name. At the same time, his invisible embrace clutched my arms to keep me from breaking apart. A strange and sudden surge of anger burst through my otherwise depressed state.

"It took a year for them to say 'thank you?' Are you kidding me? Where the hell have you guys been? Why have you ignored me? You used me last year and then once you won, you didn't care whether I lived or died!" I blurted lividly at his utterly surprised face.

Closing my eyes to keep from softening toward his peaceful expression, I stared straight ahead and hung a right on Washington Square West without waiting for my unexpected guest.

Easily keeping pace, he continued. "I understand your frustration with the organization, but you needed to live your life as if we never entered it. Our constant presence would only prohibit your rehabilitation into society," he said void of emotion.

"Too late," I scoffed. "I'll never be 'rehabilitated.' Every day gets worse. Why can't I just join the group? I'd do more good there than here, pretending to like college and my insanely boring life."

Not entirely realizing that I was almost running, I raced through the crowds and made a left onto Derby. We walked briskly for a couple of blocks in quiet, mutual irritation.

"Angel, I'm not here to argue with you," he began again, his tone almost pleading this time. He shook his head quickly at something I missed. "Not yet," he said firmly, under his breath.

"Who are you talking to?" A chill shot down my spine. "It's the Concilius Patri, isn't it?"

He nodded wordlessly, his face expressionless like smooth stone.

CJ told me the Concilius Patri—the head council of the Bellatori Dei—could see into our thoughts as if they were tuning into a channel on TV, so it was no surprise they were spying on me through Adam.

"Can I say something to them? I'd like to get a few things off my chest," I quipped belligerently. They had ignored every question I'd directed to them through my own thoughts.

"I don't think that would be a good idea. Whingers are unpopular with the Bellatori. Clearly, whining led you nowhere," he smirked, sounding very much like the 25-year-old he resembled.

"Humph," I pouted, arms crossed, my feet quickening their already frantic pace.

Adam followed in expectant silence.

We reached one of Zach's favorite places, The House of Seven Gables. I plopped into one of the white wrought iron chairs dotting the colorful garden beneath the wisteria arbors. Adam swept lightly into the seat across from me and stared deeply into my eyes.

There was something intriguingly familiar about him, but I couldn't put my finger on it. Growing increasingly unsettled by his searching gaze, I finally asked, "Why are you really here?"

"Do you understand why the Bellatori left you alone for so long?"

"Other than ungratefully ignoring everything I did for them, no." There was no stopping the year's worth of anger flooding my emotions.

He shook his head in slight exasperation. "First and foremost, they wanted to give you time to live a normal life with your family and friends. Secondly, your mind and body needed to heal. Thirdly, your heart needed to find peace."

"Great. Well, it would've helped if you could've clued me in, oh, I don't know, a year ago! I've accomplished none of the above," I waved my hand, dismissing his suggestions as I slumped back into the seat and stared beyond him toward Salem

Harbor.

"All of this was in hope you'd reenergize yourself and grow stronger," he dropped his eyes implying a hidden innuendo.

Now he had my undivided attention. "Stronger? How?"

He stared steadily into my hesitant gaze. "You have a gift, which is not meant to be wasted."

"That weird energy thing is no gift. It's freaky at best. Besides, it only works when I'm provoked."

In less than a blink of an eye, he hurtled the ceramic sugar holder from the table at me. In an even faster reflex, my hand swatted it away like a fly without ever making contact with it.

He smiled, knowing he had me. If he weren't so pure and holy, his grin would've seemed mischievously evil.

"Fine," I caved. "Did the Bellatori send you to rub this in my face?"

I spent a year avoiding my *powers*. I wasn't about to start messing with them again. What was the point other than feeling impotent at not being able to release the energy against any vampires or werewolves? A shiver of twisted excitement rushed through my veins at the thought. Apparently, I hadn't just spent the past year in solemn depression. I had a healthy case of denial too. I craved the high that the energy release brought with it.

He nodded at the unseen conversation playing out in his head.

"Unless you're going to share whatever they're saying, can you please stop talking to them?" I begged impatiently.

Resuming his business-like appearance and sitting perfectly upright, he said, "The Bellatori want to give something to you."

"What, exactly?" I asked suspiciously, raising my eyebrows.

"A bank account."

"A bank account? How's this going to differ from the empty one I already have?"

"If there was one thing you wanted to buy, what would it be?"

"I don't know—a new car for my mom maybe. Her van is ancient." I shrugged.

"Well, now you can get it for her."

My mouth dropped open.

"What?!" I jumped out of my seat, scaring a comely, middle aged woman passing nearby on the white gravel path beside the house's dark brown wooden siding.

Adam smiled.

I regained my composure and sat down again. "Ok. Well, thank you for the car, I guess." Why would the Bellatori let me buy a car?

Seeing my confusion, Adam added, "Not just a car. Whatever you want. Whenever you want. It's the Bellatori's small way of expressing their gratitude. It's not enough considering your sacrifices, but it should help."

I nodded blankly. I hit the angelic lottery—an endless supply of cash for one month's worth of work last year.

Then, instantly, my thoughts smacked into the brick wall of reality.

"This isn't for last year, is it?" My stomach sank with dread into my toes and I began to hyperventilate.

Adam's stone, poker face turned whiter than its already pallid hue.

"The bad guys are coming back for me, aren't they?" I choked.

Chapter 2 – Getting Drafted

Adam paused a moment, looking steadily into my eyes.

"Yes," he said simply.

"So, this is a bribe then?" I seethed. "Or is it a payoff to enjoy what's left of my life?"

He waited silently until I worked through the anger and betrayal in my thoughts.

"It's neither. However, there's a lot you still need to learn. The Bellatori is merely providing you with the means to do it."

"Learn what? Does the money come with instructions?" I sneered.

"You will know when the opportunities cross your path. As with all things on this plane of existence, you need to make your own decisions."

Pursing my lips in fuming disbelief, I muttered, "It's starting again. The secrets. The lies. Why can't you just tell me?"

"This time it's not about protecting you. You've proven you can take care of yourself for the most part. The experiences, however, have to manifest from your instincts."

"English, please," I sighed, knowing I had no way out.

"You need to learn to trust your instincts. They'll guide your lessons and growth."

I clasped my hands along my face trying to grasp the monstrous changes he just presented. My fingers dragged along my cheeks until they ended up clawing my neck. Incredulity and frustration numbed my fingertips. I wanted to destroy something…badly.

Breathing deeply, I stood and walked to the end of the purple and pink seaside gardens. Salem Harbor's dark blue depths looked so welcoming from this vantage point. The salty air fluttered through my layered auburn hair hanging long and loose along my back. The warmth of the summer sun's rays defrosted the icy indifference of my frozen heart.

I spun around to face Adam. Like a statue frozen in time, he stood steadfast ten feet away from me, hesitance plainly painted on his expression.

"What?" I asked, suddenly fearful Aeterna Flamma might not even give me the chance to enjoy my newfound wealth.

"Calm yourself, please," he ordered placidly.

"What?" I asked again, confused.

"I can't come closer until you calm yourself." The blue rim around his irises undulated softly and hypnotized my thoughts.

I collapsed into a white iron chair by the thick green hedges marking the garden's edge and stared emptily at the leaves fluttering in the light breeze.

Adam rushed to my side and propped my back upright against the seat. "Are you all right?" he worried.

My head spun groggily. "Yeah, it's not the first time."

CJ used the same technique to calm me last summer when I found out my whole life had been orchestrated by angels and vampires.

Rubbing my temples, I recovered, "Why couldn't you come closer?"

He cocked his head to the side, perplexed by my confusion. "Don't you realize what you're doing?"

I shook my head obliviously.

Adam smirked. "Your energy is so powerful. If I would've gotten any closer, you could've drained me."

"Huh?" I asked.

"My energy. My life."

"Yeah right," I scoffed and shook my head. "I didn't feel anything."

"Apparently not using your energy for so long increased your strength instead of diminishing it. You didn't feel it flowing from you? Don't you feel tired?"

"No," I replied innocently. "Should I?"

"Amazing," he muttered in response to the private conversation with the angels in his head. "I wonder if some of Hadrianus' energy conferred to her when she killed him."

"Wanna explain what's going on?" I snapped impatiently.

His responding smile was brilliant and enthusiastic.

"Your talents have far surpassed the Bellatori's wildest expectations and," his demeanor became serious, "you need to learn to control that strength. If you don't, it will have dire consequences."

"Does this make me an easier target for Aeterna Flamma," I worried, suddenly remembering the vampires' ability to smell my blood from miles away. They were all tuned into me then. They experienced my energy in the battle. Could my energy become a beacon too?

"It could."

Glancing toward the harbor, I gulped the fresh Atlantic winds to keep from going crazy. "So, what now?"

He nodded in assent to whatever the Concilius Patri told him. "They'll answer your questions now."

"Really?" my interest sparked. But what could I ask? I spent a year agonizing over everything that didn't make sense last summer wondering what I could ask if given this very opportunity.

"If everyone has auras, why doesn't Rick?" This wasn't my most important question, but it'd been bugging the hell out of me. I could see everyone's affiliation during last year's battle, simply by looking at their energy. The angels had a white glow around their bodies; the guardians had blue; the vampires were black-red. Rick had none. I worried about his immense powers, and wondered if I could identify him if he concealed himself.

"It's just part of who he is. Some people—very few actually—are able to hide their true selves from everyone else's perception," Adam answered simply.

Great. Just another thing to worry about. Then again, even if he'd change his appearance to trick me, he'd be pretty easy to spot being the only person without an aura.

Starting softly, I asked the one question which mattered most. "Before Zach died, did he know he was really CJ? Did he know who I was?"

Ever since last year's revelations, I speculated about every aspect of my life prior to the trip to Wales. If Zach would've known more about our alternate existence, then our relationship would've been a lie.

"No, he didn't know."

I sighed in relief but recoiled quickly at the next thought, which had to be asked. "Was Zach's death an accident?"

Adam hesitated and whispered, "No."

I trapped the anguished cry in my throat. I had shed enough tears for him, and now I knew the truth. Zach was alive and well as CJ. He just wasn't in the form I preferred…human.

"Who killed him?"

Adam looked away, focusing on the sailboats speeding across the harbor.

"Oh," I mumbled stupidly.

Of course Aeterna Flamma would've ordered and carried out his death if they figured out his true identity as CJ.

"If he was human as Zach, what was he as CJ? He definitely wasn't normal."

CJ's unseen hug shook my arms as if he was laughing. In spite of myself, I smiled. For a fleeting moment, it felt like he was actually with me.

Adam furrowed his eyebrows. "That's hard to explain. You see, most of us are one thing or another. I'm an angel. Sam is a witch. Rick is a vampire."

I shuddered.

"CJ and you are different. On this plane you're usually both human…with added abilities. Since the Bellatori needed him to come back, there wasn't time for him to return as an ordinary human. He was able to retain the human memories, but only those which the Bellatori wanted him to know."

"And me? What am I? Is it the goddess thing?" I rolled my eyes still finding it hard to believe I was the incarnated goddess, Artemis.

He smiled. "That's something you'll need to figure out on your own."

"Great," I frowned.

"You actually know the answer already. You just haven't pieced the puzzle together."

My mind raced. Goddess? No, not in the omniscient and omnipotent way anyway. CJ explained that ancient gods and goddesses were just humans who were more in touch with their spiritual abilities than other people. Angel? No. I wasn't pure enough. Vampire? Definitely not. I lacked the blood lust. Witch? Possibly. It's the only one that fit, but, if this was the case, I needed Sam to teach me because I was 19 years behind in learning the Wiccan Way.

"Any other questions?" Adam prodded.

"About a million." But I couldn't figure out what was most important to ask next.

Smirking, he stood and extended his hand politely to help me to my feet. "Ready to purchase a car?"

I nodded. The depression and anger from the past year seemed to dissipate as my new life path took shape. It was time to move on.

Adam escorted me home at sunset. Shopping and planning—or plotting—were arduous tasks. He stood beside me on the front porch wanting to say something, arguing with the voices in his head.

"Angel," he whispered, apparently wanting to escape notice by those eavesdropping—either on his side or mine, I couldn't tell which. "He'll always be with you." Adam smiled sweetly, bowed his head politely and vanished.

"CJ?" I assumed aloud. CJ's arms wrapped around me, warming my body against the chilly night air. I reached for the doorknob, but the door swung open before I touched it.

Startled, I gasped as my heart raced from the surprise.

"WHERE...HAVE...YOU...BEEN?" My mom's scream echoed down our street lined with old Victorian brick homes and white-blossomed pear trees.

Her furious gaze shifted from my face to the street behind me. "What's that?" she asked pointing to the cars in front of our house.

"Can we go inside?" I asked in a fearful whisper, wanting to hide from our neighbors' nosy ears.

I pushed my way past her and plopped onto the couch in the living room. My two youngest siblings were playing catch out back on our postage-stamp sized yard of green grass. My other brother was raiding the fridge.

"Explain, Angie," my mom demanded. The fear in her eyes was familiar. She was reliving my suicide attempt after Zach's death and the unintentional hunger-strike of recent months. Staring daily at my sunken eyes with deep black sleepless circles and emaciated cheeks, I was a constant worry to her.

My mom was beautiful once. Before my dad died, there was a contagiously happy presence about her. Everyone used her as a confidant and she had many friends. Over the past couple of years however, the friends stopped calling and she became a prisoner in her own home. The deep wrinkles creasing around her eyes and mouth formed a permanently sad grimace, which only made her boyish, too short, salt-and-pepper hair style seem all the more fierce.

"The guy from the bank had to deliver a private message." So far this was the truth. I hated lying to her. "Apparently, I won a lottery or something when I was there last year." Again, mostly true. "He spent a year tracking me down and finally found me today." Half-truth.

"Lottery?" she asked skeptically, her left eyebrow arched in disbelief. Standing straight with her arms crossed, I was going to have to come up with a darn good story if I had any hope of convincing her.

"Um, yeah," I agreed pathetically.

She furrowed her eyebrows and squinted at me trying to figure out whether or not she should believe me.

I might as well just lay my plans on the table. Why lie? I was going to do what I wanted anyway.

"So," I hesitated and closed my eyes before blurting, "I'm taking a year off of school."

She gasped and stopped breathing.

I leaned forward and took a deep breath. "I'm going to travel. I want to see things and experience things that I can't do here in Salem.

"Mom, I wasted over a year being depressed,

and it's kept me from living," I pleaded, not that she could argue with that statement. "It's time for me to move on and figure out what I want from my life."

And figure out what the Bellatori needs me to know before the fallen angels, demons and vampires get me.

"Is that what the car is for?" she asked uncertainly, processing my argument.

"What car?" Caleb, my eighteen-year-old brother, asked munching on a sandwich while looking unkempt with his dark brown hair in a tousled mess. He caught the guilty grin on my face and rushed through the front door.

"No, mom, the SUV is yours."

She gasped again, thoroughly shocked.

"I figure if I'm going away, you'll need a decent ride for the kids and Caleb can have your old car, since he's going to college."

Her eyes remained frozen on my face, while she tried to figure out if I was being honest or if I just concocted the most amazing lie. Although my day was spent with far greater concerns, I could see why she'd be in shock from the changes that took place in my attitude over the course of a few short hours. Her unsure, worried gaze drifted to my vampire 'tattoo,' an unpleasant, black-red scar in the shape of a crescent moon on the inside of my right forearm. She assumed it was a symbol of teenage rebellion from last summer. Unfortunately, it was a painful 'gift' from Hadrianus, the evil, head vampire.

Caleb burst through the front door, squeezing

the sandwich so hard it was turning into mush between his fingers.

"A six hundred horse power Viper in venom red metallic?!" he shrieked.

Snapping out of her dazed confusion, my mom's shock faded into a speculative grimace as she raised one eyebrow in distrustful speculation.

"Well, the SUV is for you and the Viper is for me," I rushed to explain. "I need a good car for where I'm going."

"And where exactly are you going that it would necessitate a car like that?" she asked, chiding me.

"I don't know yet," I muttered. I saw it and I wanted it. Now I felt guilty for the rash purchase. I'd make up for it somehow. I understood my mom's concern. It was an irrational and socially irresponsible purchase.

But it was so cool!

Though a small part of me felt bonded to the ancient, faded red Toyota Tercel because my dad bought it for my 16th birthday, the power pulsating beneath my fingertips as I clutched the Viper's steering wheel thrilled me to my core and helped ease the guilt in my transition from old to new. I finally understood why CJ, Rick, and Mark loved their sports cars.

"How much money did you *win* exactly?" she asked as her eyes narrowed judgmentally.

"Um, a lot." I looked at her sheepishly. "Does it matter? I paid for everything. You won't have a car payment and I won't need to worry about money while I'm away."

"Angie, any amount of money you have would be better spent getting an education and helping those who are less fortunate," she argued level-headedly.

"I will be getting an education—just not a traditional one." This was totally true.

"I don't know, sweetheart."

'*Sweetheart*.' This was a good sign I was on my way to being forgiven.

"Something doesn't feel right about any of this. I'd feel better if you stayed close by."

Cracks ripped through my heart.

"I love you, mom," I paused uncomfortably before resorting to begging, "but I *need* to go. I have a lot to learn and a lot to see and a lot I missed over the past year. I can't live my life from our couch here in Salem."

Speechless, she nodded. I seized the opportunity, "I'm gonna call Kelly." Jumping from my seat, I bounded upstairs to my room before she regained her composure and strength to argue with me.

"I still can't believe it," my best friend, Kelly, said an hour later, sitting across from me on my bed covered in a blue quilt with the crescent moon and stars. "I haven't seen you this excited about anything since—" she caught herself, "uh, in a long time."

I smiled. "Yeah. I'm not stuck anymore. I feel like my life is going somewhere finally."

"You know who'd love this?"

"Yeah, but he made it totally clear last year he never wanted to speak to me again."

My thoughts quickly shifted to my other best friend, Davey—the other 'musketeer' as my mom used to refer to him fondly.

"Why don't you try again?" Kelly urged, her blue eyes burning in encouragement while her short golden blonde curls made her seem angelic.

"Kell, I've been trying for a year. Voicemails, emails, texts—he's ignored everything. I just can't believe he'd throw our friendship away, just like that," I snapped my fingers.

"But you hurt him," she argued. "You chose Zach."

"I didn't even know he really liked me until it was too late," I said defensively. "He never said anything except that he didn't like Zach. I just thought he was upset because we didn't hang out as often anymore."

"Still, he liked you…"

"So what? Can't I choose who I want to be with? Maybe he should've made his feelings known before Zach and I started dating.

"Regardless, it still doesn't excuse the fact that after Zach died he moved away and never spoke to me again." I seethed, allowing the anger and betrayal of our friendship to run its course as it had so many times since Zach's funeral.

"Does he talk to you?" I asked curiously.

"He texts every once in awhile," she said.

Jealousy burned inside me. He and I were far closer friends than he and Kelly ever were. We knew each other better than we knew ourselves. And I was the only one who had the honor of calling him Davey. As much as I loved and appreciated Kelly, I wanted him in my life too.

"Why don't you call him now?" she suggested.

I pulled out my cell phone and typed a quick message to him wondering where in the world he was hiding. Maybe the Bellatori could hunt him down for me.

"What are you going to do with the money?" Kelly asked when I tossed the phone onto the bed.

"I don't know." I stared at the numerous pictures of Zach in a rainbow of odd shaped frames lining the long white dresser beneath my mirror. "I always wanted to travel, but I don't know where to start."

Reaching toward my nightstand, I grabbed my mom's yellowing, worn-edge map of the US and spread it out in front of us on the bed. "What do you think? Where should I go?"

She turned her head toward me, "Where do you feel like going? What's your heart saying?"

Her statement sounded like something Sam would say. I wondered momentarily if Kelly was channeling Sam or the Bellatori somehow. Of course, this only made me miss my Welsh witch friend all the more.

Annoying beeps from the cell phone

interrupted my thoughts, causing me to jump in surprise. My hands trembled from nervous excitement. I never handled rejection well. Considering he was one of my best friends, who I never would've hurt intentionally, I agonized over Davey's reaction.

"Read it!" Kelly urged.

I opened my messages. And there it was—a note from my best friend.

"You made your choice. I made mine. I won't take 2nd place to Zach or his memory."

My lower lip trembled. How could he hate me so much? How could he forget all the good times we had? How could he not care about how his words killed me?

Kelly wrapped her arms around me silently. At least I had one friend here.

Even though I wished he'd change his mind, I understood his anger and couldn't begrudge him that. I wrote one last message to Davey vowing never to think of him again after this day, knowing I'd carry the pain of his loss with me for this lifetime.

"Sorry that what I offer now is too little,

too late.☹"

Sudden rage bubbled in my veins. I chucked the phone across the room and it smacked the wall breaking into a thousand minuscule pieces. *Ooops,* I thought the second the phone left my fingertips. Kelly didn't know about my strengths. I'd done a fairly good job of hiding it from everyone since I returned, which wasn't that difficult considering I purposely didn't use them.

She raised her eyebrows at my outburst. "Listen, I know you're mad. Maybe you should let him go though. He's not worth having as a friend if he doesn't support you, right?"

I nodded, though the pain still pulsed in every fiber of my being.

"So, where are you going to go?" she pushed, turning her focus back to the map.

I closed my eyes, pointed my finger and let my unconscious feelings drag it across the map.

As if someone was pulling on it, my finger dropped sharply and nearly poked a hole through the paper.

Wide eyed with excitement, I blurted, "San Francisco, here I come!"

Chapter 3 – Plans, Worries & Goodbyes

"I'm gonna miss you," Kelly whispered downcast.

An idea popped into my mind. "Hey, why don't you come with me? This way my mom won't freak about me going by myself."

Kelly's face lit up like the summer sun. "Really? I wouldn't be in your way?"

"Nah, although…" I needed time to research whatever it was the Bellatori wanted me to find. She couldn't be a part of that. Actually, it wasn't so much that she couldn't be a part of it, but, for her safety, I didn't want her to be a part of it.

"Well, I'm going to be learning about some very specific things, which aren't exactly…normal," I winced, worried I'd said too much to my conservative friend.

Concern and fear crossed her face. "Is it illegal?" she worried.

"No!" I laughed at her assumption.

"Well then, who cares? Let's do it!"

The next two weeks were spent planning and coordinating the move. Kelly signed up for fall classes at UCSF while I spent most of my time familiarizing myself with finance. I set up trust funds for my siblings, donated money to charities, and wrote up a will. The hardest part was concealing the paperwork from my mom. She was never one to snoop, but I didn't want to get into the details of how these things were made possible and why I was doing them.

Adam showed up unexpectedly on my doorstep one morning fully aware of all of my plans—not a surprise since the Bellatori seemed to be inside my head whether or not I wanted them there. With his help I bought a house sight unseen. I trusted the Bellatori wouldn't put me in danger, so I knew whatever he picked would be just fine.

Aside from the frenzied preparations, I had one day, which was the highlight of the past few months. Yes, it was even better than finding out that I won the "lottery."

"Bellatori or not, I can't believe you're doing this, Ang," Mark said in disbelief as I slurped my Iced-Tea-with-no-ice in the Museum Place Mall. Arms crossed over his chest, he leaned back on the bench, shaking his head in disapproval.

Mark made good on his promise from last summer to visit as frequently as the Bellatori allowed. He drove up once a month and stayed for a weekend each time. He became a fixture at my family's dinner table, which isn't all that surprising considering his love of food. Still, it felt like I had an older brother watching out for me when he was around.

"How am I going to visit you three thousand miles away?"

"Fly," I quipped sarcastically, focusing on sucking out the last few drops of tea from the almost-empty cup.

"You know what I mean," he said morosely. "Driving from New York to here is a breeze compared to that trip. I thought you liked seeing me?" he asked with a sarcastic frowny face.

"Of course I do, but I need to do this. Besides the Bellatori is funding it, so why not?"

"It seems weird that they're doing this now, isn't it?" he asked doubtfully. "I don't like that they're letting you go so far away. What if something happens and I can't get to you in time?"

"Then something happens. You can't always be there to protect me."

"Uh, have you forgotten? That's my job."

"Come on. It's not like you're around 24/7

now. The Bellatori will have others looking out for me there."

He sighed deeply in defeat.

"Hey, why don't you come with us?"

"It's tempting, but I can't. Remember, I'm helping Matt's family. I promised him."

At the sound of Matt's name an instant flash of guilt crushed me. My slow reaction in battle last summer cost him his life—his mortal life anyway. Now he was a vampire struggling to survive in Sam's care. If she couldn't keep him from attacking people, the Bellatori would destroy him. They weren't keen on vampires to begin with but gave him a chance considering he served them well as my guardian.

Matt's little sister, Annabel, was about my age and struggling with the loss of her brother. His family was unaware of his double life and job with the Bellatori Dei. Mark told them that he was stricken with an overly contagious disease overseas. He didn't bother mentioning it was only contagious if Matt bit them.

"Hey, can I help them too?"

"How?" Mark looked at me curiously.

I rummaged through my purse and pulled out the checkbook Adam gave to me. I wrote a check in Mark's name and shoved it into his hands.

"What do you want me to do with a half a million dollars?" His eyes ogled at the number. "I can think of a car or two I'd like to buy," he smirked.

"Set up a fund for her and her family. Isn't Annabel supposed to start college this year? Maybe she can go to a better school?"

"And how am I supposed to explain this to them?" Mark asked.

"Just say you won the lottery," I grinned. "We should get going. I promised Mom we'd be back by six."

"Hold on. I need to get something. Meet me by Essex Pizza in twenty." He jumped off the bench and rushed off.

Preoccupied with the move, Annabel, and missing Mark from the opposite coast, I meandered through the mall window-shopping before arriving at the pizza place five minutes early.

A chorus of girly giggles and shallow conversation about the season's shoe trends caught my attention as I hoped beyond hope the source wasn't who I thought it was.

"Angel," cooed the doe-eyed, statuesque blonde.

Yup, it was just as I feared—and worse—since her elite clique of wealthy snobs followed close behind. "Still alone, I see," my high-school nemesis taunted.

"What do you expect, Steele? She drives guys away," Sahari jeered before turning her malicious glare on me, "or kills them."

Their teen groupies tittered in expected response. Sahari's smooth, flawless ebony skin complemented Steele's paper white complexion. They looked like living dolls dressed in expensive designer clothes and accessories. They were truly blessed with enviable looks and possessions; unfortunately, they lacked compassion and more simple things, like consciences. I could probably find a thousand vampires with more feeling than these evil, poor excuses for people.

"I bet she'd even scare strangers away," one of their mindless clones added.

"What about him?" Steele pointed to someone in the distance behind me.

"Yeah, Angel," Sahari goaded. "Why don't you walk up to that hot guy and ask him to be your friend? Let me guess, now that Dave is gone, you only have Creepy-Kelly?" she sneered.

*I wish…*I bit my tongue knowing my wishes had very real consequences these days. Instead, I clenched my fists, fighting the urge to throw her through the two-story glass entrance.

"Angel, why don't you introduce me to your friends?" Mark asked innocently, wrapping his arm around my shoulders.

Sahari and Steele's mouths dropped open in astonishment as the "hot guy" turned out to be my protector and steadfast twenty-two-year-old friend. Standing tall with a linebacker's build, his short brown, messy hair and golden brown eyes were kind and confident.

"This is Sahari and Steele—my backstabbing best friends from school," I added, relishing this moment of much-deserved and long-overdue vengeance. They made my life a veritable hell for four years.

"But you said they were gorgeous," Mark said matter-of-factly, appraising them with unconcealed disdain. "I guess your personality really does match your appearance sometimes. Let's go," he said, whisking me away from their awestruck, dumbfounded, and open-mouthed glares. For added measure, he kissed me on the cheek. The girls' collective gasps echoed in the mall's main stretch. He smirked at his accomplishment.

"Thanks," I said.

"Don't let people talk to you that way," Mark grumbled angrily, dropping his arm once we were through the front doors. "You deserve better."

"I was getting to the defending myself part, but you interrupted. Perfect timing, actually."

We paused at the mall's entrance on Washington Street.

"Before I forget, I have something for you," Mark offered sheepishly. "Just a little something to ward off vampires," he added with his usual sarcastic sense of humor.

His cheeks blushed as he pushed a little white box into my palms awkwardly, shoved his hands into his pockets, and turned to face the two-way traffic.

Flipping the lid open, a beautiful marcasite cross dangled from a delicate silver chain that sparkled in the sunlight.

"Wow," I breathed at its artistic exquisiteness. "Thanks, Mark!" I exclaimed in a surprised whisper as my fingers traced the pendant's detailed outline.

"It's just something to remember me by," he explained abashedly. "And something to keep the nasty vamps away."

"You're becoming a softy in your old age." My statement was heavily pregnant with uncurbed mockery. Mark was the toughest guy I knew and definitely anti-mushy. I threw my arms around him as a sudden sadness caught my breath.

"I'm going to miss you. Will you visit?" I asked as a pang of painful loneliness stabbed my heart. I should've gotten used to saying goodbye by now. "I'll buy your plane tickets," I added, hoping to sweeten the offer.

"We'll see," he said, crushing me in an inescapable embrace. "Let's get you home."

As the big day neared, the house was filled with conflicting emotions, which led to an odd array of residual energy weaving from room-to-room. In the living room I was overjoyed, but I cried every time I walked through the kitchen. My whole family seemed lethargic when I was around as if I'd sucked their happiness and will dry.

For the most part my siblings were happy for me primarily because they expected gifts from each of my destinations throughout my travels. My mom tried to hide her feelings, but every time she looked at me I saw pain behind her feigned façade.

The Bellatori's movers packed a truck with my meager collection of personal junk. Between the gloriously glowing angels and the massively muscular guardians, passersby stopped and gawked openly. As I stood guard with a cup of coffee in hand, it was a rather amusing sight to watch from my living room window.

With only a few hours left until my exodus from Salem, I couldn't sleep. Tomorrow would start a whole new chapter in my life—a chapter that for the first time ever didn't have someone—parents or Bellatori guardians—watching over me every minute of every day.

Heading back to my room with a glass of water well past midnight, my mom's anguished cries echoed from her room. Scared for her, I reached for the doorknob but paused when she spoke.

"Isaac, I need you. I need her. I can't do this on my own." Her words faded into muted wailing. She must've been crying into her pillow, trying not to wake the kids.

I wanted to rush to her, hold her, and tell her everything was going to be ok, but I couldn't lie. My dad was gone. She couldn't get him back no matter how much she needed him. I had to grow up despite the fact that she needed me. She had to experience whatever fate had planned for her.

Hearing her cry though tore me to shreds.

I missed my dad too, but losing Zach and CJ somehow overshadowed his loss. As my parent, I always expected him to die before me. That pain hurt like hell. However, losing my soul mate added a whole new aspect of sorrow and depression I didn't think possible. It was this pain that made me understand the torture my mom faced every day without my dad.

I leaned my back against her door and slid to the floor. I stayed there in impotent empathy until her intermittent sobs gave way to light snoring. Creeping to my room, I waited sleeplessly and impatiently for the pink-orange sunrise to erase the dark gloom and guilt suffocating me.

After a quick shower, I dragged my suitcase downstairs and set it by the front door. Nervous anxiety squeezed my stomach. Homesickness was sinking in and I hadn't even left yet. It didn't help that Kelly wasn't joining me on the opposite coast until next week because of a family reunion she had to attend.

The distracting smell of pancakes and coffee permeated the first floor; its heavenly aroma lured me to the kitchen.

Balloons and streamers covered the room. My siblings' beaming gazes met my surprise.

"What's all this?" I asked with a smile.

"Your goodbye party," my sixteen-year-old sister, Amanda, chirped. Bright-eyed with enthusiasm, she bounced over to me in the doorway and wrapped her arms around my waist tightly, her waist length light brown curls mimicking the spring in her step.

With her back facing me, my mom continued to flip pancakes in silence to avoid me.

Mason, a seventeen-year-old 'clone' of our brother Caleb down to the same brown eyes with green gleam, handed a flat package to me.

"We wanted to give you something," Mason

said excitedly.

Ripping the iridescent, pale pink wrapping from its contents revealed a hot pink framed picture of my mom and siblings.

"We all helped with this," Amanda added, handing a card to me.

Inside the generic card picturing a rainbow that wished me well in my travels was a note scrawled in Caleb's handwriting.

"From monoliths and sheer cliffs,
From Mediterranean to Pacific seas,
From gods and philosophers to simple seers,
Each of us is special, no matter what others see.
No matter who you become, No matter where you go,
We love you.
This you should always know."

A tear slipped from my lashes. "Thanks, guys."

They rushed to me and squeezed me in a family hug until the smell of bacon became too great for the boys to resist.

Not long after, a loud, long honk announced the arrival of the airport shuttle. After several rounds of hugs and kisses with my tearful siblings, I made it to my mom.

"I love you, sweetheart. Don't ever forget that," she gazed into my eyes trying to convey the deeper, unspoken sentiments that drove me to the brink of tears yet again.

"Love you too, mom." I hugged her tightly, wishing I could explain the supernatural insanity so she could understand why I was going away. I loved my family and I didn't want to leave them or the safety of their familiarity.

But I had a job to do. A new adventure was waiting.

Anxious energy tingled in my fingertips, itching to find release.

It was time.

Chapter 4 – Fresh Start

Adam met me at SFO in my hot Viper. The ride heading north from the airport was relatively uneventful and drab until we hit the outskirts of San Francisco and its colorful homes along 19th Avenue. Pastel pink, blue, green and yellow townhouses backed to the city's steep hills on our right side and glimpses of the Pacific Ocean to our left sped by between buildings and streets.

Aside from the fact that he was a holy angel, being in Adam's presence was comforting. I felt like I belonged here with the supernatural, because I surely didn't fit in with "regular" people any more. I knew too much and had experienced too much to feel satisfied with the ordinary.

As we wound our way through Golden Gate Park, the pungent aroma of eucalyptus trees ignited my senses. Like a shot of pure caffeine straight into my veins, I was on high alert and amazingly focused as Adam darted off an exit toward the marina along San Francisco Bay.

White sailboats and small yachts dotted the harbor and lined the marina where a flat expanse of lush green grass split the boat parking lot in two. Kites of all shapes and sizes danced high in the air. The sun peeked through the fog and clouds periodically to illuminate their bright and bold red, green, blue, and yellow hues. Children giggled gleefully as they chased after them.

Here and there, adults sunned themselves on the field, while reading novels or magazines. A group of teen boys was determined to play a pick-up soccer game around the more relaxed sky gazers, who didn't seem to mind. Muscular, shirtless, die-hard athletes (and those wishing they were) ran along the cement path lining the park. Timid tourists rode rented bikes down the path and street; their eyes focused on the bay and Golden Gate Bridge in the distance.

Adam slowed to a crawl along Marina Boulevard allowing pedestrians to cross the street.

The salty flavor of the sea hung lightly in the breeze. It was refreshing and nothing like the rotten fish smell of low tide back home.

To the left beyond the marina, the Golden Gate Bridge graced the entrance to the bay in its burnt red-orange splendor. Its magnificent architecture was a true testament to humanity's determination to conquer the impossible. Hidden by a thick layer of low-lying fog, the uppermost section of the bridge's two towers and the center of the bay remained in its frigid shadows. Straight across from the bridge centered in the middle of the bay stood Alcatraz in its formidable, dilapidated state.

Despite the sun's occasional presence, there

was no denying that summer in San Francisco was more like a chilly fall day in Salem.

Adam parked the car on the right side of the boulevard between Cervantes Boulevard and Avila Street beside a row of fancy townhomes, which enjoyed an unobstructed, breathtaking view of the marina and bay.

"Here we are," he proclaimed, pulling the key from the ignition.

"Where?" I asked curiously, staring enviously at the carefree sightseers lounging on the marina's green.

Adam coughed once and cocked his head toward the ivory stucco mini mansion with a black wrought iron gate standing majestically behind me. "Home."

"No way! Are you serious?"

He nodded and smiled, happy that I was happy. He lifted the house key and dropped it into my palm. I rushed up the handful of steps to the front door, burst through it and up a flight of stairs that led into a massive living room with floor-to-ceiling windows overlooking San Francisco Bay. Beneath the living room was a one-car garage to protect my baby, the Viper. An enormous white kitchen with stainless steel appliances and black granite countertops led to a cramped deck covered in a rainbow of ceramic potted plants and trellised vines offering complete privacy from the neighbors behind my house.

"There are three bedrooms upstairs," Adam began as we made our way back into the empty living room. "We took the liberty of unpacking your rooms. We assumed you would want to decorate the rest, so we didn't bring additional furnishings." He paused to glance at my speechless gape. "I hope you don't mind," he added contritely, misinterpreting my silence.

"Not at all," I rushed to explain. "I just can't believe this is mine. Are you really serious?"

"It's all yours," he laughed.

"Thank you so much!" I burst and without thinking gave him a quick peck on the cheek in my exuberance.

Unsure of how to react, he looked away and scratched the back of his neck nervously. "Um, well, you're welcome."

He coughed to clear his throat and center his business-like thoughts.

"As you know, the Bellatori will keep an eye on you. And don't forget while you're here, you have work to do," he warned. "Listen to your heart, and you'll know when you're on the right path."

I nodded at the reality check.

Adam smiled and his ultra-pale face glowed brilliantly.

"Try to have fun too, and, Angel, I *will* be back to check on you."

His eyes cautioned me, one last reminder of the job at hand. Then Adam faded into thin air, his magnetic, radiantly shining energy dissolving into nothingness.

In my dream-like state, I floated over to the window and stared in awe at the beauty of the world outside my window. The house key prickled in my clutch. Dangling it from my fingertips I noticed the key chain—a pair of silver angel wings, which glistened like diamonds as a ray of sunlight illuminated it.

Chapter 5 – Intuition Practice

Preoccupied with getting settled into the house, August slipped by in the blink of an eye.

"Wanna go to the outlets," I asked Kelly. "I need new shirts and pants for fall."

"Sure," she answered easily. Kelly loved shopping. "Where?"

"Petaluma," I replied. "It's about an hour north."

Top down and music blaring, the first forty minutes of the ride was smooth, straight, and pretty much mindless until I saw an exit for Diablo Avenue. A strange instinct took over all sense of reason as I swerved from the passing lane across two other lanes of traffic to make the exit in time.

Terrified, Kelly gawked at me with one hand gripping onto the car's door handle and the other clutching her car seat.

My heart nearly beat out of my chest in exhilarated excitement. The maneuver was easy with my Viper even if completely irresponsible and reckless to my rational mind. With no idea where I was or where I was going, I followed my impulse and followed Diablo Ave. to its end.

Speechless, Kelly waited for me to explain myself. Unfortunately, I had no logical explanation, so I jumped out of the car and told her to wait inside.

The dead end backed to a forested hillside. I wound around the oaks, pines, and redwoods until I lost my way. No longer feeling a pull toward any direction, I glanced around the trees until I found my X-marks-the-spot.

The exposed roots of a massive redwood provided a perch for a dusty red wine bottle. Not knowing where it'd been, I pinched it disgustedly between two fingers.

The white label featured a silver and gold border of suns, moons, and stars with the winery's name boldly marked in the middle: Aeternus Bellatori. I smiled at my discovery. Glancing in the bottle, it was half full. Wondering what to do with my prize, I examined the outside of the bottle and the base of the tree to see if I missed a note or directions. Without any more details, I figured the message was fairly clear. I could view my situation as half-full or half-empty. The choice and perspective was up to me.

Yeah, that day was Kelly's first major exposure to my supernatural side. She lectured me for the rest of the trip on the importance of driving safely and the hazards of picking up garbage in the woods. Having found a few amazing sales on sweaters and jeans made it a little easier to stomach her nagging.

Thankfully, San Francisco's chilly summer weather with lots of fog put my new, warmer clothes to good use immediately. As an added bonus, the long sleeves conveniently hid my vampire tattoo, which had been itching an awful lot lately.

Kelly began classes at UCSF for a degree in nursing. She had an enviable ability for staying calm and collected during mishaps, ranging from scraped knees to broken bones. Helping people was her life-long passion. Nursing was a perfect fit.

Since most of my nights were spent pouring over occult and new age research, I met Kelly every day for lunch at the campus for some quality friend time.

"So, what do you think about this weekend?" she asked again.

"What about it?" I asked distracted by a handsome, messy blonde haired college co-ed, who was sitting on a nearby picnic table and laughing at something his four guy friends were debating heatedly.

Kelly huffed furiously. "Hellooooooo, Angel! Are you listening?"

"Sorry," I said, refocusing my attention on her.

"I said why don't we check out Fisherman's Wharf this weekend? We've been here for a month and a half and haven't done any touristy stuff yet."

"Sure," I agreed easily. "It's a date." I smiled, hoping she'd forgive my inattentiveness.

"'K," she smiled half-heartedly and bit into her spinach veggie wrap.

My gaze shifted back to the muscularly lean

blonde commanding the attention of his friends. My interest wasn't based so much on his cute looks. I envied their untroubled laughter. That's what college life should've been like for me and Kelly too. Instead I dragged her along on my selfish journey, and now she had nobody but me to rely on in this strange but beautiful city.

Late Friday afternoon we made our way to Fisherman's Wharf and Pier 39 along the bay. This was the center of everything touristy in town. The numerous cheesy shops, which could charge whatever they wanted because tourists would pay anything for their products or services, outnumbered the more unique holes-in-the-wall that were hard to find. Still, it was fun to visit. Living dangerously, we ate freshly steamed crab from a street vendor and grabbed a couple rolls of sourdough bread from Boudin's to complete our San Francisco experience.

After a visit with the smelly sea lions camped out in the pier's west marina and a ride on the carousel, we started our trek west to Ghirardelli Square for an ice cream sundae from the world-renowned chocolatier.

Jamaican steel drum percussionists and robot dancing street entertainers painted in metallic silver and gold amused us along the way. Although we tried to dodge the men aggressively handing out flyers advertising rides and restaurants a few feet away from each other, one managed to get a bright orange ad into my hands.

There wasn't a trash can in sight forcing me to hold onto it longer than necessary. Sighing in frustration, I glanced at the ad.

Endlessly

"Ridiculous!" I muttered. "Why give out flyers for something like this to tourists?"

Kelly stared at her orange flyer. "What's wrong with the Blue and Gold fleet? They give boat tours of the bay."

I looked at her paper and, true enough, it offered a two-for-one boat ride. Shoving my message from the Bellatori in my pocket, I tried to hide my surprise.

"Oh yeah, forgot about that," I mumbled stupidly. "Let's get to Ghirardelli's before it gets too late."

Or too dark, I wanted to say, looking around nervously. I knew the Bellatori would be dropping hints for me, but what if Aeterna Flamma intervened? I wouldn't know the difference. Would the Bellatori realize what was happening before the vampires got me?

Up before sunrise the next morning, I stared at the 20" x 26" blank sketching paper in front of me on the bare hardwood living room floor. Sitting in the center of five vanilla pillar candles, the dark night sky offered no natural light through our curtain-less living room window. Hiding in the dark connected me with my inner turmoil. Plus, I didn't want strangers outside seeing me in the black satin PJs that CJ got for me last year.

Sprawled all around me were my pencil sketches of Zach, CJ, Sam, Cynan, Matt, Mark, vampires, werewolves, and the scarier moments from last summer—Hadrianus as a semi-human vampire animal; falling into my lion protector's lair; and swimming through the blindingly-black River Styx. But the most haunting images were the ones of Rick— dressed as a vampire for his movie shoot; kissing my neck before I collapsed in Endymion Manor; and lying helplessly on the ground after Hadrianus' attack. CJ's invisible embrace encircled me tightly in response to the feelings of terror shaking me.

I closed my eyes and opened my mind pointing the charcoal pencil on the blank sheet. My hand moved across it, drawing, shading, detailing. Allowing my hand to lead instead of my mind brought a sense of healing relief to my all-too-real nightmares.

"Angel?" a voice whispered behind me.

Covering the surprised gasp with my hand, I spun around to see Kelly staring at me curiously.

"Sorry, didn't mean to frighten you, but I came down for a glass of water and wanted to make sure you were ok," she said sincerely.

"I'm fine," I replied curtly, irritated by the interruption, as I glanced at her.

Kelly paced backwards a few feet, her eyes clearly scared of something.

"What?" I asked on edge.

"*Are* you ok?" she breathed. "Your eyes are…um, glowing."

She stepped further away.

I closed my eyes and turned back to my papers

breathing to calm myself. Apparently my powers were ready to use in case of an attack, but what if they would've unleashed their strength at Kelly? Was it only a matter of time before they exploded at someone?

"Kell, I think you're still half asleep," I lied, focusing on the paper in front of me and wishing my eyes back to normal. Hopefully my gift of turning wishful thinking into reality was still available.

She rubbed her eyes and stepped toward me cautiously. Avoiding my gaze, she knelt down and sifted through my drawings. Her fingers lingered on the ones of Zach, but she steered clear of asking about them. I peeked to gauge her reaction to the rest and saw her eyebrows rise in interest at the supernatural images.

"Is this why you scream at night?" she asked, pointing to the one of Hadrianus attacking CJ.

I couldn't find my voice and squeaked, "I scream?"

She nodded slowly. "Every night."

A shiver shot through my frame while Kelly continued to stare at the drawings. This new development was interesting and bothersome. My mom hadn't mentioned this back at home. Why was it starting now?

Her quick giggle caught me off guard. "Since when are you into Rick Kingston? I thought you hated celebrities."

And here's where my situation got

complicated. Kelly knew nothing about Rick's true identity as my vampire stalker. To the world he was Rick Kingston, popular British actor who'd gone missing last summer. I was one of the few who knew the truth.

"It's all the tabloids running stories about his disappearance. They must be getting to me," I fibbed flippantly.

"Why don't you just call him?" she asked, pointing to this morning's sketch.

"Rick?" I asked, horrified that she may have seen a clue in one of my other pictures.

She nudged me playfully. "I think you're the one half asleep," she laughed. "*Dave*," she clarified.

"Davey?" I stared at the picture in front of me wondering why she saw Davey. It was clearly a close-up of Rick's eyes. I couldn't trust myself anymore. Perhaps I was thinking of Rick, but drew Davey unconsciously since I missed him.

Kelly hopped to her feet and bounced lightly on the oak hardwood floor to our black futon, the only piece of furniture in the otherwise bare living room and kitchen area. She retrieved my new purple cell phone and tossed it to my shocked hands.

"Kell, it's like four in the morning," I hesitated.

"Yeah, here. Last I heard, he was somewhere in Asia. Just call," she urged forcefully.

I dialed his number and waited nervously until voicemail picked up. Relieved, I hung up. "He made it crystal clear he doesn't want to talk to me again and I told him I'd leave him alone."

"It just doesn't sound like him though," she argued. "I'll get him to change his mind."

"Don't hold your breath," I mumbled sarcastically, staring at Rick's gorgeous, yet impish eyes on the paper in front of me.

"Well, since you're up so early, do you have anything planned for today?" Kelly asked, yawning and stretching across the futon.

"There's a book store across town I want to check out." Not wanting to endanger her any more than I already had, I didn't want to invite Kelly along.

"Oh, wish I could go," she replied jealously, not realizing what type of bookstore I had in mind. "I've got a paper due Monday."

"That's ok. I'll catch up with you for dinner."

I thanked God under my breath for this easy escape.

After a nap and late breakfast, I sped the Viper along the fog-covered marina and up Van Ness toward Satan's Spot. Parking along the steep hills of the city scared me, probably more than encountering Hadrianus. One tremor along the San Andreas Fault and the cars would topple like dominoes. In fact, many of the sidewalks had steps built into them to ease the burn on your quads when walking from point A to B.

Expecting the store to be tucked into the darkest corner of a dangerous city block with dodgy looking people and drug dealers ducking in and out of shadows, I was pleasantly surprised that the store's black stucco exterior was the only dark spot on a bright, clean street lined with clothing and jewelry boutiques, book stores, and a couple of Indian and Vietnamese restaurants.

Not sure of what to expect, I dressed in my Gothiest clothes—a black lacy top, dark jeans with silver studded jewels on the pockets, black leather boots, and a black leather choker with a silver buckle. After adding thick lines of black eyeliner, dark purple eye shadow and ebony mascara along with deep ruby lipstick, I felt more like a woman of the night than a Goth girl. Still, hopefully my stereotypical interpretation would be accepted by the others inside. I paused just beyond the store's borders, my heart thumping loudly in nervous anticipation.

I got the message from the Bellatori to come here. Now what? I didn't know what they wanted me to find and I sure didn't want to spend more time in the bookshop than was necessary.

Taking a breath of encouragement, I slipped into the store, hoping my entrance remained unnoticed.

"Hello. May I help you find something?" a deep voice asked from behind me.

Damn. "Uh, just looking," I blurted, turning to face the voice's owner.

"Well, if you change your mind, you know where to find me," the handsome stranger replied kindly.

Speechless, I nodded silently trying to remember where I left my tongue. He turned back to a red bookcase against the black wall by the register where he was organizing several rows of books. I hid behind a bookcase, but my eyes peered around the corner to follow his every move.

His short, straight, dark brown hair and deep, dark black-brown eyes were complemented perfectly by his mocha-colored skin. His good looks and generally pleasant demeanor stood in stark contrast to the store's evil name. The black walls and matching gauze curtains were only outdone by the silver skull and cross-bone chandeliers with red tapers, menacingly gazing gargoyles, and upside down pentacles gracing every open space. The display window and the front corner held numerous daggers, vials of unmentionable fluids, incense, crystals, candles of various heights, shapes, and scents, dark spell books, and apparel for those who wandered the night.

Caught up in my own thoughts, I fell against the bookcase as another store patron knocked into me.

"I'm so sorry," he spurted genuinely, grabbing my elbow to steady me.

Furious, I turned to complain about his lack of eyesight and coordination but caught my tongue.

"Hey, do I know you?" the friendly blonde from UCSF asked.

Oh, no, no, no, I thought desperately. I looked horrific in my fake getup. I was in no mood or position to meet anyone today, but I couldn't pretend I didn't recognize him.

"UCSF?" I offered barely audibly, hoping he wouldn't remember.

"That's it!" he pointed at me in a quick staccato.

Of course he'd remember.

"Looking for a little adventure outside of school?" he laughed lightly.

"Uh," I hesitated, pulling on my lacy sleeve nervously. "Actually, I'm taking a break from school."

I felt embarrassed admitting this. It sounded like I was a quitter. I hated not being able to explain myself to others. His curious look begged for clarification.

"I visit my friend who goes to school there. I think I saw you near one of the pizza places."

"Yeah, that's right. Wow, you, um, look different," his blue eyes popped open when he remembered the connection.

"Well, I can't go out like this every day," I smiled, knowing I looked totally hideous and unlike me.

Time to divert his attention. "You're a bit far from campus yourself. I didn't realize that Satan's books offered any helpful knowledge about medicine and healing."

His hearty laugh echoed in the empty store.

"Yeah the store's got a great name, but it's misleading. It's more like a refuge for New Agers than a hot spot for devil worshippers. I'm studying medical anthropology right now so I'm looking for info on alternative therapies. Today's quest is for earth's energies and their impact on human health."

He shook the book in his hand slightly to show off his find.

"Wow, that's quite a topic," I said impressed. Based on the way he carried on with his friends, I somewhat expected him to be a mindless jock, not a seriously studious student.

"Actually, where are the New Age books?" I felt a draw and thought that just might be why the Bellatori sent me here.

He pointed over his shoulder. "Back section, right corner. It's huge. You can find almost anything there—feng shui, homeopathy, after-life stuff, regression therapy—it's endless. Check it out. It's all cool."

He glanced at his watch and did a double take. "Shit. I'm late. It was nice meeting you…uh…what's your name?"

"Angel. Nice meeting you too…"

"Justin." He reached for my hand and shook it quickly, vigorously. "Catch ya later."

And with that he swept past me dropping a twenty beside the register and rushing through the door.

The knots in my stomach loosened up a bit. Relieved, my body relaxed. I suddenly realized that my energy was completely tied to Justin while he spoke to me. Now that the connection was broken, it fluttered about me, loose and confused.

I was going to have to find an outlet for a major energy release soon. If it was so strong that it attached itself to others without me knowing, I didn't have control over it and that wouldn't end well for me or anyone else.

Sauntering to the back of the store, my fingertips dragged along the books' spines until one nearly glued itself to my hand. Simply entitled "Ley Lines," I shrugged and pulled it from the shelf.

I continued around the store allowing the books to pick me and ended up with "The Vampire Book," "Secrets & Prophecies," and "Magic & Witchcraft."

"Vampires, huh?" the handsome bookstore clerk asked, making awkward small talk. His dark brown eyes looked up at me bashfully. "My name's Diego."

"Hi," I cooed like an idiot. "I'm Angel."

As he rung up each of the books, his even breaths hypnotized me and I could swear I heard each beat of his heart.

Without warning my energy jumped beyond my grasp. It wrapped around Diego.

NO! I shouted to myself concentrating on peeling away the stringy, cobweb like grip from my innocent victim.

"Forty three fifteen," Diego said evenly, apparently unaffected or not noticing that I just nearly wrenched the life from his body.

I swallowed hard and bit my lip to keep from screaming and handed over my debit card.

Once the card and books were securely occupying the rabid energy in my hands, I said 'thanks' to Diego's bright smile and rushed from the store.

The Viper's engine mimicked my internal drive for unstoppable speed. Turning down Geary, the car weaved through traffic far more recklessly than I'd ever allow when I felt normal. As the tight streets and car congestion gave way to wider pavement, the smothering tension began to ease. Veering left onto the Great Highway, it was smooth—and fast—sailing till Ocean Beach. The Viper screeched to a halt in the nearly empty parking lot. Grabbing my bag of books, I leapt from the car and ran across the vacant stretch of gritty sand to the freezing Pacific's edge.

Tossing the books behind me, I reached toward the foggy sky feeling the electrically charged atmosphere tingling in my fingertips.

"Aaaaaah!" I screamed in frustration, throwing my arms in front of me, closing my eyes to concentrate on letting the energy go.

Anger filled my thoughts. Anger at CJ being so far away. Anger at getting into my current situation. Anger at the Bellatori and their educational treasure hunt.

Miles from shore a massive column of water shot from the ocean and disappeared into the misty sea air. I glanced around hoping no one noticed.

A honey-gold Labrador fetching a ball nearby whined and grunted fearfully before running back to its owner at the far end of the beach. Thankfully, the dreary, cold day discouraged all but two beach goers, and they were preoccupied with their pets.

Drained yet liberated, I dropped to the sand and wondered where the energy came from. The amount of power I had during last year's fight still astounded me.

I couldn't believe I was capable of generating it in the first place. Then again, Sam always said I just needed to believe in myself. It was a convenient enough explanation though I still shuddered at the memory of jumping from Endymion Manor's second story window and fighting the half man, half vampire, Hadrianus. How I managed to escape permanent damage was a miracle.

The memory of watching Hadrianus' black eyes burn and melt into the red-gold flames of the fire, which helped kill him, made me queasy.

Needing a distraction, I pulled the books into my lap. The wind flipped through "Magic & Witchcraft" until my hands jumped onto page 192. Shoved into the seam was a tiny, folded note written on a blood-red card.

Curious but no longer surprised by the Bellatori's strange way of communicating, I opened the message.

"The Suicide Club – Bring a Friend"

I reread each word wondering if there was a hidden meaning behind it. Maybe it was a joke. Maybe the first letter of each word stood for an acronym that meant something else. Or maybe it was just what it said.

"The Suicide Club"

Suicidal tendencies were a thing of my not-so-distant past. Could I survive the Bellatori's first major challenge? What would be asked of me? Would it push me back to the brink? Was my life to be put on the line again? Already?

"CJ, I can't do it," I worried fearfully, feeling tears well up in my eyes. His hands brushed the length of my arms before enveloping me completely. "What should I do?"

What should I do? The thought echoed until a more powerful thought made it disappear entirely.

I had no choice.

Chapter 6 – Procrastination

"Hey, Angel!" Diego greeted enthusiastically.

Satan's Spot became a regular hangout over the past two weeks. It was more like a library to me than a bookstore. Feeling my way around the shop, I let the books find me and took note of the topics that interested me most.

"This came in today and I thought you might like it," Diego said cheerfully, holding a box in his hand.

I pulled off the gold-brown lid and nestled inside was a Feng Shui set of candles.

"Cool!" I exclaimed, "How much do I owe you?"

"Don't worry about it. It's on me," he said quickly, his cheeks flushed with shy embarrassment.

All of a sudden, a knot twisted in my stomach. Did Diego like me? I wasn't ready for a relationship and I didn't want to hurt Diego's feelings. Still, I knew that CJ was gone and I should move on with my life, but the sick and warped attachment to Rick wasn't far from my mind either. I couldn't bring another guy into my emotional mess. Juggling two memories was bad enough; there was no way I'd be able to handle a live and fully available man too.

Deep breath.

"Thanks," I said simply and sweetly, pretending not to notice his possible interest.

"I'll keep it up front for you, k?" he added with a charming smile.

Avoiding any other uncomfortable moments, I rushed to the occult section and sifted through the vampire books. CJ's story from last year had been playing on a loop lately in my thoughts.

'Vampires? Everyone knows they're not real,' I said.

'Well that depends on your definition of a vampire.'

'Do they run around sucking people's blood?'

'Depends on which ones you're talking about.'

'There's more than one kind?!' I screamed horrified.

CJ nodded serenely.

Diego appeared out of nowhere beside me. "Why are you so interested in vampires? It doesn't seem to be your type of thing."

"What is 'my thing'?" I asked sarcastically.

"I don't know. New Age, maybe. Just not the dark stuff."

"That's 'cause you don't know me well enough," I retorted, as my eyes kept scanning the titles along the bookcase.

He paused and then leaned against the shelf to look me straight in the eye. "I'd like to though."

Damn it!

I took a deep breath. "I've really enjoyed talking to you over the past few weeks. Can't we just leave it at that? I'm not looking for a relationship right now, Diego."

"Whoa, who said anything about a relationship?" he said affronted. "I'm just sayin' a cup of coffee and a talk would be nice."

I nodded, feeling stupid for jumping to conclusions and for being rude. "Ok, sometime soon then."

He flashed a dazzling, winner's smile. "Vampires though? Seriously?"

I sighed, stalling while I figured out a way to explain my weird obsession. "Did you ever wonder what life would be like if they really existed?"

"Everyone knows they're not real," he scoffed. "Night crawlers with fangs, come on," he added sardonically.

"Yeah, but what if they were?"

"The blood-sucking ones are Hollywood fiction based on misinformation and diseased corpses."

"Could there be other kinds though? Ones that might be real?"

"Well," he paused hesitantly, "history *is* filled with vampire myths—evil things—spirits maybe—that wanted to take something from the living. The incubus, succubus, vrykolakas, hirudo, Camazotz, Kalika—the list is endless. Even real-life people have been considered vamps. Take Erzsébet Báthory, the Transylvanian countess who drank and bathed in the blood of those she murdered, or, of course, Vlad Tepes, the most famous of all."

He pointed to a section of books about the "real" vampires.

I nodded. None of this was what I needed. I knew the real vampires' story. They were the descendants of the fallen angel Gaap. Their tale hadn't made it into mainstream media, intentionally I'm sure.

Diego's black eyes studied my disappointed expression.

"There is another kind of vampire," he offered uncertainly.

My eyes popped open.

"I don't like to mention it because people would think I'm crazy." He walked into the next aisle and returned with a book called, "Psychic Vampires."

My hope deflated. Despite the fact that I knew real vampires didn't have fangs, my imagination conjured a picture of a shark-toothed Rick wearing gold hoop Gypsy earrings and a Swami Turban in gold lamé.

Laughter burst through my lips before I could squelch it.

Diego blushed. "I knew I shouldn't've said anything. Forget it."

He took the book and stepped back to replace it in the other aisle.

"No, wait," I managed to say between fits of laughter. "I'll take it. Seems interesting."

Though I had no intention of reading it, I wanted to make him feel better somehow.

His face brightened up again and I couldn't help but smile. Diego was such a pleasant person to be around.

Kelly, on the other hand, had grown rather cranky over the course of the past few weeks as her courses were piling on work and pressing deadlines. She was running late again for our Tuesday lunch, so I sat against the bark of a massive oak and closed my eyes as the sun peaked through the dense cloud cover occasionally.

Immediately, guilt jumped to mind. I'd been avoiding The Suicide Club. The intense feeling of irresponsibility was pushing me to the point of puking. Clearly, the Bellatori were sending a message.

The task was certainly a problem, and thankfully, since I released my energy at the beach not too long ago, it was the only problem for now. Hopefully, I bottled the energy issue sufficiently and wouldn't have any more unwanted outbursts.

"Sweet dreams?" a pleasant voice asked.

I gasped and shot upright.

"Oh, it's just you," I muttered relieved and sank back to my napping position, closing my eyes again.

"Sorry, expecting Prince Charming?" Justin asked, dropping beside me.

More like I'm expecting the Prince of Darkness, I thought morosely and pushed Rick and my masochistic need for life-averse adventure to the back of my thoughts again.

"So, what are we up to today?" he asked in his typical cheerful attitude.

"Just waiting to have lunch with Kelly. You?"

"Waiting for the guys. Heading down to the marina to play football."

"Oh, hey, can you give me a ride home then?" I squinted in his direction to see his reply. As much as I loved my new car, parking in San Francisco was a nightmare, so I walked or used the bus whenever possible. But today, I was hoping to avoid another tedious bus ride.

He nodded and reached into his backpack to grab a bottle of water.

Justin was easy to like. Diego may have been handsome and mysterious, but Justin was an instant, steadfast friend. Ever since our first official meeting, I'd seen him nearly every day here at campus or at the bookstore.

"Ready, Angel," Kelly said bitterly. For some reason she didn't like Justin. I couldn't understand why. It's not like he ever gave her reason not to like him.

Endlessly

"Hey Kelly," Justin offered nicely. He, on the other hand, always made an effort to be nice despite her unpleasantness.

"Mmmm," she nodded without taking her eyes off me.

"Dude, where were you?" Gabe, one of Justin's friends, bellowed behind Kelly.

"Where else?" Ray answered sarcastically before smiling at me. "Hi, Angel."

"Hey guys," I greeted them as Mike and Uri walked up alongside the group. Justin's four friends varied in appearance from Mike's stocky frame and friendly face to Uri's lanky build and J.Crew appeal.

Thanks to their ripped muscles, Gabe and Ray had my vote for body builders of the year though their unkempt style could've used a major makeover. Regardless, the five of them were inseparable and very sociable with everyone.

"Hi Kelly," Uri said, moving closer to the very obvious object of his affection.

"Hi," Kelly stammered, liking him equally as much.

"Let's go," Mike pushed, kicking Justin's legs to get him off the ground.

Justin stood and helped me to my feet. "Angel's coming with."

"Awesome, brah, she's on my team," Mike goaded eagerly, bumping his fist against Ray's.

"Not today. Just need a ride," I tempered their

enthusiasm.

"Aren't you staying with me for lunch?" Kelly asked, her tone both irritated and deflated.

"Sorry, Kell. You were late and I've got stuff to do."

"Yeah, not having a job or school must keep you super busy," she bit sarcastically.

In a flash my energy leapt at her. Concentrating, I stopped breathing as I pried each sticky, invisible tentacle-like string of energy from her.

"I *am* busy," I argued weakly focusing on not killing my best friend.

She gave me a dirty look of disbelief.

"Listen, I get you're angry. We haven't spent any quality time together lately. Why don't we see a movie tonight?"

Furious rage slowly melted from her face. "I'll be home at 5."

The guys started walking across the tiny tree lined court toward the street.

"I'll catch up with you later," Uri told Justin. "Want company for lunch, Kelly? I'm starving."

She nodded, ogling at Uri's enchanting face framed with warm red-brown hair and olive-green eyes.

"Hope you don't mind, but I invited Uri along tonight," Kelly said later that afternoon as she walked into the living room where I was meditating on The Suicide Club.

My date with the internet all afternoon yielded few facts about it other than it was an organization intent on finding extreme adventures in hidden San Francisco treasures. Getting arrested was a very real possibility, but at least I wasn't too scared about the "suicide" part anymore, which was just a bad-ass moniker.

"Ok," I muttered from my comfy place on the futon. A slight breeze from the bay swept through the room.

"I'm exhausted," she said, falling onto the seat by my feet. "All day I've got tons of energy, but when I get home to you I'm wiped out."

"Kell, you study all day. Of course it'll wear you out." I looked at my friend and another wave of guilt washed over me. I sat up to face her.

"I'm sorry I haven't been much of a friend lately. Remember, I told you before we moved out that I had to learn about some…stuff," I swallowed, worried about saying too much. "Anyway, it's been keeping me really busy. Between that and the nightmares keeping me up most nights, I've been tired. I promise to spend more time with you."

"Don't worry about making it up to me. Let's just have fun tonight." She gave me a quick hug.

"So, do you want to hear what Uri said?" And then she was off like bullet from a gun rattling off every word, every breath, and every movement Uri made at lunch today.

She was falling in love. I was happy for her…and selfishly unhappy for me.

CJ.

I smiled and nodded at all the right places while Kelly spoke, but my mind was with CJ. I missed him. As Zach, he took me to concerts, serenaded me, and wrote poetry for me. We spent hours walking in the park and just talking about life. Sure he had drawbacks, just like every teenage guy does. Despite it all, he was a part of me, which I never wanted to let go.

As my super-human, angelic protector CJ, his electric touch tingled on my skin and vibrated through every fiber of my muscles. Our souls connected instantly in a humanly impossible way. Human or immortal spirit…I didn't care. I just wished he was with me now.

"Hey, you ok?" Kelly stopped as a tear crawled down my cheek.

"It's nothing. Sorry," I muttered, swiping the tear away. "You were saying Uri wants to take you out to dinner Friday?"

She nodded but her skeptical eyes studied mine. "You're thinking about Zach, aren't you?"

I didn't move a muscle. Her perceptivity caught me off guard.

"I'm sorry, Angel. I wasn't thinking…"

"Don't apologize," I interrupted. "You deserve to be happy. I'm just being selfish…"

"Angel," she interrupted my thought, "he's gone. It's ok for you to be selfish. I have no idea what you've been through. I should be more sensitive…"

"No!" I exclaimed as I sat up and grabbed her hands. "I want you to tell me these things. I want you to be happy and head-over-heels in love with someone. You deserve it! Enjoy every second of it. Don't worry about me. Seriously."

"You sure?"

I nodded and she spent the next hour and a half talking about Uri's hair, mannerisms, and chivalry. I was truly happy for her and enjoyed reliving the feeling of first love vicariously through their experience.

The evening's slasher movie was predictable and uneventful. Thankfully, Justin showed up to keep me company while Uri and Kelly snuggled and shared popcorn. Justin provided hilarious subtitles and turned the horror flick into a comedy for my benefit. It made the night bearable.

As I lay down on my bed alone later that night, CJ crept into my thoughts and a newly found layer of remorse was added to the guilt-ridden Bellatori and Kelly levels already festering there. I knew he'd be ok with me moving on considering he was dead, but *I* wasn't ready. It still felt like I'd be cheating on him. I twirled his gold wedding band around my ring finger. CJ's last memento was literally a gift from our past; it was the 500-year-old ring he gave me on our wedding day at the chapel in Mwnt along the Welsh coastline.

His soft, invisible embrace enveloped me and lulled me to sleep.

In an effort to be more conscious of my friendship with Kelly, I made roasted chicken glazed with orange, lemon, and lime and jasmine infused rice for dinner the next night.

As I finished the arrangement of sweet peas and passionflowers, the sound of her footsteps resonated up the stairs and through the living room promptly at five.

"Hey, Kelly, hope your hungry 'cause…" I lost my train of thought as I watched Adam take a seat at the kitchen bar.

"Not expecting me, I see," he said smugly.

"No," I replied quietly while dread pulled me into the dark depths of procrastination and irresponsibility.

"You know why I'm here," he said without wasting any time.

"The Suicide Club? Are you serious? How is that gonna teach me anything except scare the crap out of me or get me locked up?" I asked sarcastically.

"You know we won't risk your safety."

"You're freakin' nuts," I responded snidely. "And remind me why you can't just tell me the lessons?"

He sighed in frustration. "Because you won't learn if we hand the information to you. You need to learn to trust your gut feelings and those around you."

"I think this is all—"

"Mmm, is that chicken?" Kelly shouted from the front door. Her steps rushed upstairs.

Adam gave me a warning glare as if to say, 'this is all nice, but you know you have a job to do.'

"Oh, sorry, Angel, I didn't realize you were having someone over," Kelly apologized hurriedly, her eyes downcast in embarrassment.

"I didn't either," I sneered. "Kelly, this is my, um, friend, Adam. Adam, Kelly."

They exchanged awkward pleasantries.

"Adam was just heading out, so—" I tried to lay a hint for him but to no avail since he interrupted.

"Actually, I'm starving for a good home-cooked meal." He smiled at me indignantly.

"Don't be rude, Angel," Kelly chastised.

"Fine," I huffed and prepared our plates.

Adam and Kelly became fast friends as I stared in silent, incredulous fury. He asked her endless questions about her classes, periodically casting a dark look toward me to emphasize Kelly's studiousness and my lack thereof. Thankfully, Kelly didn't get much of a chance to ask him anything. All she found out was that he worked for a bank. *Heavenly Bank of Hellish Torture*, I wanted to add but bit my tongue.

While I cleared the plates, Adam piped up. "So, Angel, weren't you saying something about going on an adventure soon? Maybe Kelly would like to go with you."

I shot him the look of death, and it took every ounce of my will to keep my web of energy from killing him on the spot.

"That's not really Kelly's thing," I shrugged him off.

Kelly raised an eyebrow fully aware that something unspoken was percolating beneath our words.

"Kell, I thought maybe we could drive north next weekend. Hit up some beaches or something," I rushed to offer an alternative.

Unseen by Kelly, Adam scowled at me.

Kelly nodded, but her eyes begged for an explanation.

Ignoring her, I jumped at the chance to kick Adam out. "Adam, I need to do some research tonight. How 'bout I drive you home?" I offered a little too kindly.

He sweetly wished Kelly a goodnight. Her unspoken rapt reaction to his angelic beauty and alluring holy personality was undeniable. I must've been growing immune to the angels' glory. Their gorgeous glow no longer captivated me especially since I knew they were using me to win their battle—a battle in which I wanted no part.

I escorted Adam to the front porch, closing the door behind me to block out the sound of clattering dishes and utensils as Kelly began to clean up.

"This is your last warning, Angel. Otherwise the Concilii Patri will intervene. And trust me, neither of us wants that. You know where to go; just get it over with." His neon blue eyes glared at me to make sure I understood his threat's severity.

Turning toward the dark, starlit bay, I shook my head in annoyance before glowering at him. "Message received."

He smiled. "Trust me. It's better this way." And with that he vanished.

I jumped into the Viper and sped away not knowing where I was headed. Somehow I ended up at Satan's Spot just as Diego was closing shop.

"Mind if I have a quick look around?" I blurted desperately. I just didn't want to go home yet and I didn't want to be alone either.

"Sure," he said. "You ok?"

"Yeah, I'll be fine," I muttered angrily.

I rushed to the 'Dark Arts' section. Naturally, no books were popping out for me in this area. So, I searched on my own, since the Bellatori clearly didn't want me in here to get any ideas I could use against them. Unfortunately, I couldn't find any books on angel banishment or harming heavenly entities, which irritate the living daylights out of you. I grunted in disappointment.

A growing headache pounded its rhythm in time with my heartbeats. With each staccato my vision turned red and the words "Suicide Club" appeared in my thoughts.

Diego stepped beside me. "You don't look good." He paused brushing the hair from my eyes and laying the back of his hand against my forehead. "Let's get out of here. Taqueria La Cumbre's still open. You need food or a drink. Something," he urged with real concern.

His offer didn't sound bad and I wanted a distraction from the terrifying task at hand.

"Ok. In a minute," I replied, turning back to the books and hoping to find a new message saying the Bellatori changed their minds.

Like a magnet, my hand automatically reached for a book and ripped it from the shelf. Its spine stated, "Black Magic for the Powerless." Page 255 opened in my hands with a huge red note tucked in its seam.

"The Suicide Club – NOW!"

How much did I hate my guardian angels right now? I crumbled the note in my palm, slammed the book shut and shoved it back onto the shelf.

"Problems tonight?" Diego asked.

"Yeah." A sharp pain shot through my brain. A response from Adam or the Bellatori perhaps? "Um, ever heard of The Suicide Club?"

He shook his head totally confused.

"Wanna go on a date?"

Chapter 7 – The Suicide Club

The mini date for late night burritos with Diego kept my thoughts preoccupied for at least one night, but Wednesday arrived far too quickly. Thinking about this day, I couldn't eat or sleep. The anticipation alone was ready to kill me.

After sunset, Diego and I arrived at the Palace of Fine Arts where four other suicidal idiots were blindfolded along with us and delivered via an unmarked white van to the secret destination. For security purposes, no one was allowed to know where we were going because we were trespassing.

As our blindfolds were removed, pitch-black darkness enveloped us. We turned on the flashlights we were given to reveal a dark, damp, and frigid cavern. I wrapped my arms around me in a wasted effort to warm up and wished I had worn a winter coat instead of my black hoodie and jeans.

"This is one of the hundreds of underground caves that've been utilized for centuries by Native Americans, the Mexican army, and the U.S. government. It lies beneath San Francisco," explained our group's stout, white-haired leader who was a relic of Haight-Ashbury's heyday. "It's been used for lots of reasons, from sacred rituals to arsenal storage facilities during the world wars and cold war.

"There're lots of tunnels, escape passages, and hidden rooms throughout the area. Use your flashlights and feel free to explore. Don't venture too far. We need to be outta here before sunrise and we won't have time to find ya if ya get lost."

With a few yelps of excitement from the college frat guys joining us, we hurried in different directions. Diego and I walked off on our own to the end of the long gray cement tunnel covered in graffiti and came to a T in the path.

"Where to, fearless one?" he laughed, his face glowing with carefree happiness.

"Hmmm, left." Simultaneously, we turned our flashlights down the corridor and caught a rat scamper across the wet path about twenty feet in front of us.

"That doesn't bother you?" he asked calmly yet

curiously as water droplets dripped from the ceiling all around us and echoed in the empty tunnel.

"Nope." After battling werewolves, a rat seemed more like a cuddly, stuffed toy.

Diego chuckled. "You're definitely not like other girls, are you?"

"Nope," I replied curtly. The seemingly shifting shadows had my undivided attention. I had to focus. Besides, I didn't think Diego would care to know just how different I was from other girls.

My guts twisted in a strange, unsettled way. Then, as if my heart was attached to a hook, I was pulled through a massive spider web and against one of the dirt-caked walls. Diego stepped behind me and placed his hand on my elbow.

"You wanna turn back?" Disappointment was apparent in his tone.

"No. Just need a second to breathe." Evidently, the Bellatori were going to guide me tonight.

Thanks to Diego's company, fear wasn't the first thing gnawing at my thoughts. He looked so handsome in his open, black canvas jacket, light jeans, and blue and purple pinstripe dress shirt. He was dressed for a date at a nice restaurant. Lucky for him, I thought mockingly, I was treating him to a night of spelunking. Poor guy. He didn't know what he was getting into with me.

With the flashlight firmly implanted in my right hand, my free fingers dragged along the filthy, cold walls for hundreds of yards. The crooked passageway bent and coiled like a snake all the while angling slightly, leading deeper underground. The scamper of rodents echoed around every corner.

Then without warning, my left arm fell into a chasm. I jumped back, hitting Diego. He flicked his flashlight toward the wall, but there was nothing unusual about it.

Feeling stupid, I muttered, "Must've just tripped over my feet again."

"Mmmm-hmmm," he agreed not totally buying my explanation.

Apprehensive and on edge, energy tingled in my palms. I stepped to the wall, hands outstretched. Feeling my way from the grimy top to the slimy bottom, it felt solid. I pushed against it. Nothing. I knew I wasn't crazy. I didn't imagine my hand disappearing into a wall.

"Come on. Let's see what else we can find. I wanna look for one of the ritual rooms," Diego suggested, tugging on my sleeve.

"Ok," I replied without moving my gaze from the massive stones. I leaned my left hand against it convinced there was something hiding in plain sight.

With an enormous shove from behind, I hurtled through the cave wall's veil.

My screams echoed through the winding tunnel as I slid along its wet path. Tossing, turning, and banging into the unforgiving, jagged rocks lining its sides, the infinite ride had no end and no grips upon which I could brace myself.

The beam from my flashlight danced wildly

along the black walls, blinding me as they reflected off of glimmers in the dark stone. My butt caught on a bump and launched me into the air dropping me feet first several yards down into a meat locker of a cave. The ride's jostling rendered the now dead flashlight useless. A warm trickle of blood dripped from my palms and along my face. I was sure my left ankle was sprained and my butt was sore from knocking into the rocks.

"Angel! Angel!" Diego's shouts sounded faintly from a great distance.

"Help!" I screamed at the top of my lungs. The words faded into a weak echo.

My breath warmed the air around me.

Déjà vu.

But last time the dark room in the Welsh bookstore's basement was much smaller and CJ saved me. Seeing as he was holding onto me right now, I had no savior tonight.

Dripping and streaming water resonated from far away. Blind and helpless, dread caught up to my false bravado. Where was the Bellatori? Why weren't they coming?

And, hey, did Diego actually push me? Was he with the Bellatori? Or was he with Aeterna Flamma?

Dread turned to terror.

Something heavy splashed through the water not far from me.

"Stop!" I shouted at it without any authority whatsoever since my voice trembled.

Diego's dim hollers reverberated unintelligibly in the background.

The splashes multiplied and drew closer.

Anger, anger, anger…where was my anger? Perhaps I *should've* spent the past year practicing.

Since I couldn't rely on myself, I shook the flashlight as I limped backwards. "Damn it, you stupid thing. Turn on!" I reached into my pocket looking for a weapon. The cell phone wouldn't help me, but the house key might. It was a stretch to think I could do serious damage with it, but I could maim an attacker with a strike to the eye.

Suddenly the flashlight burst a beam of light into the vast stone cave. I spun around searching for the sound's source.

A howl pierced the silence.

The light shook as my grasp loosened on it. Creeping toward me were the golden-green eyes of a small arctic snow fox. The very same fox from one of my nightmares last summer. Still as fluffy white and cute as I remembered it to be, only now I was wiser. There was no way I'd chase it knowing it would lead me to Aeterna Flamma.

I stabbed the key into my thigh to make sure I was wide awake.

Major pain! And it was sure to leave a mark in the morning.

Was my nightmare coming true?

The animal seemed to smile at me

omnisciently, but it didn't beg me to follow it this time. It inched closer and closer and then sprung.

I crossed my arms to block it, but it vanished into me, not through me. It felt like I had a twin wriggling inside of me for a minute.

Distracted, I didn't notice the flashlight losing power again. As I glanced up, the beam's soft, gold, fading glow illuminated hundreds of deathly still red and silver eyes—the very real red and silver eyes of the vampires and werewolves who were hunting me. The ones that grabbed my undivided attention however, were the pair of vivid crimson orbs floating toward me. They stopped about five feet away.

And there he stood—the living embodiment of my nightmares and my daydreams' obsession.

Rick.

His dark brown loose curls and movie star good looks remained immortalized in his pale five-thousand-year-old vampire body. Cocking one eyebrow seductively, he reached for me, simultaneously commanding and begging me to accept his hand.

With my heart beating its way out of my body, I reached for him. My heart skipped a beat in ecstatic joy as my fingers brushed lightly against his frozen palm.

CJ's invisible arms tightened around me and shook me back to reality.

My hand recoiled. I almost willingly gave myself to Rick. What was I thinking?!

My mouth tried to scream, but the sound caught in my throat. Gripping the key chain with all my might, I closed my eyes and mumbled, "Adam!"

As I opened my eyes warily, Rick's gaze dropped sadly just as Adam stepped through him.

"What did you see?" Adam asked calmly.

Spinning around in all directions, I tried to find the all-too-real apparitions, which were apparently just figments of my crazy imagination. Everyone was gone except for Adam, my invisible dead boyfriend, and the sound of dripping water in the distance.

"Angel, what was it?" he asked again more urgently this time.

"Um, they were here. Waiting for me," I sputtered flustered.

"Did you recognize any of them?" he pressed.

"Rick," I said simply. Was he really here or was my wishful thinking getting carried away?

"How close was he standing to you?"

"What?" I asked confused. "What difference does that make?"

"How close?" he pushed again.

"I don't know. Within touching distance. Five feet, give or take a little. Why?"

"That's too close," he mumbled to himself.

"What do you mean?"

"We need to increase your learning curve, because they're getting closer to capturing you."

"How do you know that I'm not just being delusional?"

"There's a very powerful ley line that runs under this cave. It acts as a conduit between worlds and affects psychic premonitions. Stonehenge lies on one. Endymion Manor on another.

"The stronger the earth's energy is in a particular area, the easier it is to communicate between this plane and the spiritual one. Essentially, you're more in tune with your psychic awareness."

"What the hell are you talking about?" I demanded belligerently. As I muttered this, last year's premonition of vampires swirling around me at Manorbier Castle replayed in my memory. They were close and they did capture me soon after.

"You and Rick share a connection in that you're leading the Bellatori's efforts, he Aeterna Flamma's. The connection could only reveal its strength in an area where the energy from one world to the next is separated by a thin veil. His proximity in your vision shows that their side has nearly completely recuperated from last year's loss. As soon as they're ready, they're coming for you."

I nodded not feeling any better. The dread in the pit of my stomach began to flip in nauseous circles.

"By the way, it took you long enough to figure out the key's purpose."

Confused, I turned to face him.

"It's a key not only to your house, but to my world as well. Kind of like a car to get you from one dimension to the next."

"That would've been good to know when you gave it to me," I sneered. "So, what now?"

"Continue with your lessons and stop procrastinating," he warned.

"Fine." And with that I hurtled through a colorful, whirling vortex, which dropped me back beside Diego.

"Come on. Let's see what else we can find. I wanna look for one of the ritual rooms," Diego suggested, tugging on my sleeve.

Apparently Adam rewound time or I just completely lost my mind and imagined the whole thing.

"O..kay," I replied slowly, moving my gaze from the wall cautiously to the path ahead. My flashlight was in perfect working order and my body was no longer sore or bleeding.

Finding nothing at the end of the corridor, we headed back to the group. My mind vaguely registered the voices of the frat guys around us.

"That shit was hella awesome!"

"We're definitely getting the house award."

"House award? Think bigger. We're gonna sweep the whole Greek Race!"

The guys hollered in excitement and fist bumped each other.

My thoughts were completely preoccupied by Rick, Adam and the hundreds of red and silver eyes not to mention the white fox which was inside of me somewhere.

Diego's hand brushed mine lightly. Jumpy, I pulled away. No one had touched me in forever. It felt awkward and uncomfortable.

He intentionally reached for my hand again and held it loosely in his grasp. Tickly tingles of infatuation rushed through my arm.

"Did you have fun tonight?" he asked casually.

"Could've been a little more exciting," I remarked ironically.

"If you're looking for an adventure, I've got something for you," he said, interpreting my comment literally. "Wanna meet some *real* vampires?"

Chapter 8 – Three's a Crowd

I kept most of the prior night's events from Justin, but I knew he'd want to hear the other details. He and his friends knew every part of the city and were always up for an adventure. The Suicide Club would surely peak their interest.

"I can't believe you didn't ask us to go with you!" he barked angrily after I finished recounting the night's events, minus the part with the vampires and Adam. "Mike and Gabe love that kind of crap. Next time?"

"There won't be a next time," I said, concentrating on the row of past life regression books at Satan's Spot.

"Why? Was it too scary?" he laughed.

I didn't answer.

His tone turned serious. "Maybe you should've asked *me* to go with you instead of that guy," he nodded toward Diego, who was reading a cult magazine behind the counter. "I could protect you."

For a second I really wished he could protect me. Unfortunately, no one, who was alive anyway, could keep me safe from my enemies.

"I'm kinda new to the whole dating scene, Justin. Diego happened to be there when I decided to go, so I asked him."

"Do you like him?" he asked curiously, stepping in front of me and leaning his back against the books I wanted to read.

"He's cute," I offered simply and truthfully. I snuck a glance at him and his tall, dark, and handsome good looks were nearly irresistible. My heart fluttered as I remembered him holding my hand.

"Then what am I?" Justin pushed.

"What do you mean?" I asked confused, still focused on Diego.

"I think I need to change my approach."

My eyebrows furrowed in bewilderment.

Justin continued. "Subtlety doesn't work with you, does it?"

Still perplexed, I answered cautiously, "I don't like to play games. What you see is what you get and I expect the same in return."

He took a breath and shifted his gaze to the books behind me. "I like you, Angel. I wish you would've picked me."

"Oh," was all I could say. I stared at Justin wondering why I hadn't noticed his interest in me. "Oh," I repeated in a whisper as I suddenly saw him in a new light.

He seemed so much like a brother I hadn't even considered him as anything else even though I did think he was handsome—definitely handsome. Justin was lean yet muscular, tall but not too tall. His spiky blonde hair and blue eyes were angelic though his impish demeanor said otherwise.

I glanced at Diego and he suddenly felt ordinary—still cute—but ordinary compared to Justin.

This sudden love triangle was too reminiscent of the Zach-Davey debacle, which ended up complicating my relationship with Zach and costing me my best friend in Davey. For a split second I wondered which was worse: losing someone to death or to their rejection and abandonment of you. Both sucked.

My heart sank.

At the thought of Zach, his superhuman alter-ego and my true love, CJ, appeared in my thoughts.

I couldn't betray him with Justin or Diego.

A selfish tear slipped from my lashes. I wanted the impossible and was hurting people by stringing them along while I figured out my relationship mess.

Justin handed a tissue to me and placed his hand lightly on my back. "I didn't think telling you I liked you would make you cry," he chuckled.

"It's not you," I whispered. "It's…"

Diego stepped behind me. "Angel, what's wrong?" he glared at Justin and turned me to face him. "Are you ok?" he asked tenderly.

I nodded quickly and wiped my eyes with the tissue.

He tried to gauge my reaction but gave up, not wanting to upset me anymore. "Are we still on for tomorrow night?"

Justin shifted his weight uneasily behind me.

I nodded.

"Good, I'll pick you up at nine." Diego smiled brilliantly, leaned in, and gave me a quick peck on the cheek.

I closed my eyes, wishing he didn't stake his claim on me in front of Justin.

The front door slammed shut and I knew Justin was gone. An all-too-familiar feeling of guilt twisted my stomach.

"I've gotta run. Justin's taking me home," I said but wondered if he stranded me here.

Diego's smile faded into a scowl. Clearly, the Justin-Diego juggle was about to fall out of balance.

"I'll see you tomorrow." I smiled reassuringly and waved a quick goodbye as I rushed through the front door.

I looked up and down the street wondering

which direction Justin might have taken.

"Ready to go?" his somber voice asked behind me. He was leaning against the building, waiting.

Why did relationships have to be so complicated? I didn't want to hurt anyone but ended up alienating everyone in the process of figuring my life out.

The ride home was painfully silent. And the next day, Justin didn't show up at UCSF though his friends were there. Uri wouldn't have missed a day there anyway. He and Kelly were staring into each others' googly-eyes over their untouched lunches at a picnic table hidden beneath the shade of a large oak.

Night couldn't come fast enough. I paced back and forth in front of the empty living room's bay window, gripping the marcasite cross pendant from Mark as it dangled from my neck. My energy pulsed nervously throughout my body. I could feel it building in eager anticipation of tonight's date and Diego's promise of meeting "real vampires."

Who were they? Were they part of the Bellatori Dei or Aeterna Flamma? Or were they a splintered off group who also wanted a piece of me? I'd find out soon enough.

I glanced down at my black satin long-sleeved top, denim mini-skirt, black opaque tights and black leather knee high boots. Was this appropriate attire for this evening?

"You know, a 'Thank You' would've been nice," Kelly quipped nastily as she flew up the stairs and into the kitchen past me.

"What?" I shouted defensively.

"Are you serious," she yelled angrily, slamming the fridge door and twirling the top off of a bottle of Snapple iced tea.

My feet stopped their automatic, mindless steps and I gazed at the crimson walls of our living room.

"You painted?" I asked in disbelief.

"Humph," Kelly grunted. "I did that weeks ago. Look behind you."

The wall surrounding our sleek, contemporary white limestone fireplace was covered in black-framed pictures. My pictures.

I ran to the wall and gazed in amazement at each drawing, sketch, and photograph.

"Oh my God, Kell!" I whispered in awestruck breathlessness. "Thank you!"

Amidst the black and white living nightmares of battling angels and a gorgeous vampire was a collage of pictures featuring Kelly, Davey, and my family. In the center was a picture of Zach and me belting out our favorite song at Junior Prom. My memories of the way CJ looked had begun to fade away, and since I didn't have any pictures of him, the ones of Zach were extra special.

Kelly walked up behind me sipping her bottled tea.

"When?"

"A few days ago," she muttered. "What's going on, Angel? You keep getting more and more distracted. You're worrying me."

"Just thinking about a lot of things, I guess. I'm sorry. This really is so cool." I squeezed her in a big hug.

"Well, we might not have furniture, but I figured we could decorate the walls. Your pictures are great," she hesitated, "a little scary maybe, but great. I feel like they're alive somehow."

A nervous giggle escaped my lips. *Dear God, I hope not,* I thought fearfully. They were bad enough locked up in my head as memories.

"Oooh, it's getting late. Uri's gonna be here any second. I've gotta get ready," Kelly blurted, running toward the stairs.

She stopped abruptly at the bottom of the first step and turned back to me. "Angel, I don't have a good feeling about tonight."

"Why not? Uri's a nice guy," I replied still captivated by the gift from my best friend, who deserved to be treated better by me. My fingers lingered on Zach's cheek behind the glass of the photo frame.

"Not me. You," Kelly clarified. "Promise you'll be careful."

A surge of terror constricted my throat. Glancing at Kelly, I nodded.

She nodded in response and rushed upstairs.

Distracted, I seemingly floated to the window again and stared at the nearly full moon rising over the bay. What was I getting myself into?

The Bellatori would save me if I got in over my head, wouldn't they? I didn't have anything to fear. My fingers tingled in anxious anticipation. Somehow, I had to figure out how to keep my energy in check. I was overdue for a trip to Ocean Beach.

Now that Kelly planted the seed of doubt in my thoughts, I began to second-guess my motives and the fact that I knew nothing about where we were going or what we'd be doing tonight.

Before I could call Diego to cancel, the doorbell rang.

Diego's brown eyes sparkled in the clear, starry, and cold late September night.

"Good evening," he smiled sweetly, lifting my hand to his lips.

Deep breath. I tried to calm the anxiety rushing through me.

"Hi," I mouthed breathlessly, pathetically. "Hi," I repeated louder, feeling my cheeks burning in embarrassment.

Diego's responding grin matched the nearly full moon reflecting on the midnight black surf of San Francisco Bay behind him. A dark red collared shirt complemented his handsome looks. A casual black sports jacket and boot cut jeans mimicked his relaxed demeanor.

"Ready to meet some vampires?" he asked eagerly with an arched eyebrow.

His white Ford Focus sped along 19th Avenue and away from the bay in record time. All the traffic lights were green as Diego wound his way through the dark green foliage and shrubbery of Golden Gate Park. *Could that be a sign?* Did I have the go ahead from the Bellatori for tonight? Or was it a sign from CJ that he was ok with my date?

"Haight Street?" I asked as we made an unexpected turn into the Haight-Ashbury neighborhood.

"Just a few blocks down from here," he smiled easily.

We were almost there. The nervous anxiety suddenly exploded into excitement in my chest as my heart began to pound happily. *Why* was I *happy*? Fearful, tense, worried—yes. But happy?

The car stopped beside Buena Vista Park. I let myself out and walked over to Diego, who reached for my hand and held it lightly.

I felt nothing. And it was nice. Not having to worry about hurting someone because we shared some unearthly, energetic, electrical connection was a relief.

We walked a couple blocks south on Lyon Street to a Victorian house with a delicate white lace trim. The area was rather dark as dimly lit parks with dense forests bordered both ends of Lyon.

In his excitement Diego nearly skipped up the ten steps to the front door, pulling me along the way. Though it was dark outside, the home looked beautiful and clean—certainly the last place anyone would suspect as a vampire hangout. It reminded me of my grandma's place.

Diego rapped on the door twice. The door

creaked open on its own. Creepy, but expected. Last summer taught me not to be frightened by weirdness. Anticipation eased into guarded curiosity.

We stepped through the threshold into a vast dark room with black walls. The room's hardwood floor was also painted black.

As Diego shut the front door, the mirrored wall behind it reflected and multiplied the only light in the room. A cluster of five black iron chandeliers hung from the 12 foot ceilings over the middle of the room. The luminaires held five candles, one each of red, green, yellow, blue, and black.

Adjusting to the darkness, my eyes dropped to the empty room's floor. As the candlelight flickered off of it, the faint stain of a blood red circle shined off of the floor's perimeter. I stepped into the center of the circle and stared around the floor unable to make out any other markings. The walls were also void of any decorations. My gaze shifted to the chandeliers overhead, which were arranged in the five points of a star.

Circle.

Star.

Pentagram?

The space didn't have the positive energy of Sam, Cynan, and Morgan's Wiccan home. Actually, the space didn't have the negative static charge of Endymion Manor either. Nothing about this place felt otherworldly. Where the hell was I?

Diego stared at me from outside of the circle.

His face was void of emotion. For once, I felt confused and slightly insecure. Usually I could read other people based on their demeanor or energy. Something was blocking my intuition or, perhaps, I'd given myself too much psychic credit in the past. Maybe I was just ordinary, wishing I had some sort of ability like my friends from Wales.

The faint sound of rustling material grabbed my attention. Immediately, my head turned toward the noise. As Diego moved to face the sound as well, I realized my reaction was a tad too fast and abnormal for a normal person. Training and intuition betrayed my ease. Something was wrong.

Two black shadows melted from the darkness on the opposite side of the room. Dressed in black satin hooded capes, the petite figures raised their identical heads toward us.

"You're late," the twins hissed in unison. They were beautiful—not angelically beautiful—but certainly model like. Their dark, smooth skin was complemented by silky cinnamon and black curls and jet black eyes.

"We're here now, aren't we?" Diego replied antagonistically.

"Come," the girls ordered angrily.

"Ready?" Diego asked me, a smile curling his lips. I gripped his cold, clammy hand tightly and nodded.

We marched behind the girls' elegant, floating figures through a labyrinth of unlit rooms and down a flight of steps into a tiny room. Unlike the ominous room upstairs, this felt like a cozy living room. White couches lined the two longer white walls. The brightness of the white washed oak floor reflected cheerfully off of five rectangular floor-to-ceiling mirrors around the room.

"Wait here," the girls ordered simultaneously before disappearing through a doorway, which led into a pitch black space.

Diego and I sat on opposite couches. I leaned forward, taking in every minuscule detail around us.

"Are you ok?" he asked concerned.

"Yeah," I lied nonchalantly. My thoughts focused on the Bellatori and called out to Adam knowing if I concentrated hard enough, he'd be able to listen. *'Keep an eye on me,'* I ordered, picturing the location of the house and path to the basement in case they needed to find me.

Dressed in tight fitting black blouses and floor length black skirts, two girls with silky shoulder length brown hair entered from the black room carrying trays.

Keeping their eyes downcast, they didn't meet my gaze or Diego's. They reminded me more of abused slaves than the pretty, young women they were.

After they slipped quietly back to the other room, Diego and I looked at the glass trays they left behind on the square white coffee table between us. Two glasses of water and an array of black grapes were arranged neatly.

Diego handed a glass of water to me, which I accepted mindlessly.

"How do you know them?" I wondered aloud,

breaking the silence.

"We met at Satan's Spot a few years ago," he replied casually, popping a couple of grapes into his mouth.

"Do you hang out often?"

"Sometimes," he responded, washing the grapes down with a splash of water.

"What's going on? Where are they? Why haven't they come out yet? What are we waiting for? Who are they?" I blurted finally, unable to make sense of the situation.

Diego smiled. "They need to prepare for the ritual. Being an outsider, you're not allowed to see what they're doing. They'll get us when they're ready. Ok?" he asked, tossing a grape to me. "Trust me. It's worth the wait." He winked.

"Ritual?" I asked skeptically. I'd witnessed vampire rituals. Unfortunately, I'd always been the guest of honor. CJ saved me then. Who was going to save me now?

"Preparations," Diego clarified.

I smirked and nodded, wishing the show would just start. Waiting was always the worst part of any situation. It gave me too much time to fantasize about what would or would not happen. I took a gulp of water.

Silence rang in my ears as the white room's lights faded to black and my brain shut down.

Chapter 9 – Wannabe

Deep chanting stirred me from groggy unconsciousness. As my eyes rolled around trying to find a focus on the crimson walls, panic set in.

Gurney straps constricted my arms and legs to a bed covered in black satin sheets.

Son of a bitch! Not again! I swore to myself. I did not want a repeat of last summer's forest encounter with the Aeterna Flamma vampires. Yet, I willingly and idiotically walked into this trap. And why?

The Bellatori's lessons? My twisted need for adventure? Curiosity?

Eight black-cloaked figures closed in around me, still chanting.

Hot wax dripped from a black chandelier directly over me. Each splatter burned into my paper-thin blouse, easily scalding my skin.

The twins who welcomed us appeared between the four men on either side of my arms. As the young women pushed their way through, the candlelight danced like hell's fire off of their naked arms and tight, long flowing black satin gowns. Hanging from a black leather strap at the nape of each of their necks, a single, silver upside down pentagram dangled delicately.

The girls' eyes locked on each other as they raised their palms over their heads and clasped each other's hands over my body.

Curiosity kept me from moving. What were they going to do?

The girls' hands reached for my waist and slid up my side toward my chest.

"Hey!" I yelled, my defensive energy jumping into hyper-awareness.

Ignoring my outburst, their cold fingers swept my hair away from my neck. Each girl bared her fangs and bit into either side of my throat.

"Owwwww!" I yelled, as they grinned with my blood dripping from their teeth and lips.

They turned to the cloaked vampires beside them and kissed them passionately, sharing my blood.

As each man received his share, he grumbled in hedonistic pleasure.

"Initiate!" barked a voice from the dark shadows beyond my feet.

"Lord?" a voice behind my head responded, dropping his hood.

"Diego?" I breathed his name in anger at this unforgivable betrayal.

"Beautiful dinner," 'Lord' said to him in approval while stepping forward between the two-cloaked men at the end of the offering altar, upon which I lay.

'Lord' wore a goat's head over his own and stood shirtless against the soles of my boots. The heat from his body was palpable through my thick leather soles.

"Let us begin," he ordered and the twins stepped alongside me again to un-strap my legs. Their hands slid up my skirt.

"ENOUGH!" I roared, grabbing everyone's attention. Staring into the blank dark stares of every person present in the room, my situation became crystal clear.

And then, I laughed. Hysterically. I couldn't stop.

The empty gazes of my captors turned in confusion toward each other.

They were no more vampires than I was.

Closing my eyes, I called on the night's full moon and channeled its energy as the 'Lord' knelt onto the edge of the bed between my feet and slid his hands along the inside of my calves.

Opening my eyes, the invisible strings of energy, which I had constricted for so long, unfurled furiously and wrapped around each cloaked 'vampire,' squeezing them so tightly I could literally feel their energy being sucked into my body. Once they were drained, the tentacles whipped them free tossing them like ragdolls against the walls where they collapsed to the floor.

The gurney straps snapped open with the slightest pressure from my over-energized arms. Staring at me in unmistakable horror, the twins shook in fear against opposite walls. I sat up and let my energy grab both. They struggled against my pull by reaching futilely for the wall. As they reached the bedside, my hands gripped their necks and lifted them off the ground.

"You like blood, don't you?" I asked sarcastically and dug my nails into their necks. Their helpless screams were a satisfying retribution for what they had done to me. As their blood began to stream along their bodies, its smell ignited a flash of putrid images in my thoughts.

Memories of their past "rituals" played before my eyes. The screams of innocent children, the rapes of men and women, the literal blood baths, murders, dismemberment, and cannibalism twisted my stomach. Feeling vomit creeping up my throat, the girls dropped from my grip and the horrific images disappeared.

I shook my head trying desperately to gain control. A creaking door caught my focused attention in a microsecond.

STOP, my inner voice screamed and the figure remained paralyzed mid-step.

I jumped from the black satin sheets as my thoughts yanked the coward to me.

Standing at about six feet, he easily towered almost a foot taller than me. My energy fed off of his tangible fear as he shivered in terrified anticipation.

Still wearing the expressionless goat head mask, the 'Lord's' half-naked body no longer exuded the leader-like confidence of only moments ago.

I snickered.

The surge of power I had over this asshole was exhilarating.

I ran my finger up his torso to his neck and walked behind him tracing a line around his trembling frame.

"Why are you scared?" I purred seductively,

powerfully. "Isn't this what you wanted?" I whispered, digging my fingers into his neck and drawing blood as my nails scratched a path along his tiny, pasty white pecs. The sound of trickling made me halt for a moment as I realized he lost control of himself.

But that wasn't going to keep me from giving him exactly what he deserved. Pulling the mask from his head revealed a scraggly, dirty-blonde haired scum bag whimpering in fear.

"This is for the others," I said, shuddering as I saw the ghosts of his prior victims in my mind's eye. Drawing on all of the energy I could muster and concentrating on the target, my boots made contact with his unmentionables and sent him flying across the room and through the wall.

"Bastard," I muttered, staring after him in disgust.

Cries echoed from the corner of the room. I stepped over one of the unconscious twins, hopped over the sprawled out body of one of the other devil worshippers and stopped before the cowering figure.

"Please, please," he begged, staring at me with penitent eyes.

"Initiate?" I scowled at Diego. "You were about to kill me to become part of this group! It's easy to beg for mercy when you're on the other side, isn't it?" My energy raised him to his feet.

"Please, Angel, I didn't know," he lied blatantly, tears streaming down his face.

I scoffed. "You worthless piece of shit. You'll

never do this to anyone again," I threatened through clenched teeth that ached to bite him, to kill him.

Stop, I commanded myself and suddenly saw through the red haze of hatred blocking all sense of reason from my thoughts.

I stepped forward purposefully and punched Diego square in the face. He collapsed not so much from the strength of my hit, but from fear, I think.

Breathing to calm myself, ripples of energy rolled off of my body sending shockwaves against the remaining walls causing them to shake as if an earthquake was rumbling underfoot.

Try as I might to stop it, the anger still racing through me wouldn't allow the electrical current running through me to stop. The more I thought about it, the worse it got.

My courageous front wavered as I wondered how I'd get out of this mess. The ransacked room began to spin around me as fear replaced bravery. I lost control and fell to the floor.

CJ's invisible arms caught me and steadied me upright.

"Angel, you must get out of here," his inaudible voice said through my thoughts. "Pull yourself together."

He flashed a picture of the moon into my mind and I knew instantly what he meant.

I was Artemis, Goddess of the Moon and Hunt. The hunting part was obvious as I looked at the unconscious bodies lying around the room. In the past, the moon brought me both power and understanding. I still didn't fit my definition of what a goddess was supposed to be, but I embraced CJ's version. All people have talents. I just happened to be more aware of mine than others were of theirs.

Closing my eyes, I pictured a little moon grow in bright intensity right in front of me. It pushed away all of the negativity vibrating in me and began to steady me.

I made a wish—one I knew would come true if I believed it strongly enough—to wipe the memory of this evening clean from everyone inside of this hellhole. Karma would find them. Of that, I was 100% positive. I didn't need to exact any more revenge.

What I did need was to get out of there before the negative energy consumed me.

I ran upstairs and rushed through the front door. As I burst onto the front porch, the moon's knowing gaze met my face and filled me with energy, knowledge, and satisfaction in what I had just done.

Proud and relieved though I was, fear caught up with me. Vomit rose in my throat. The chill of the frigid San Francisco night froze me to the bone but didn't relieve the feeling. Running as fast as my high-heeled boots would allow, I sprinted up the street to Buena Vista Park and into the woods covering the hillside.

Unearthly groans echoed from the aromatic eucalyptus and redwood trees nearby. Surrounded by blackness and unable to contain the rush of emotions causing a storm inside of me, I doubled over in excruciating pain and threw up until the only things left were my guts, which, I was pretty sure, were about to come up too.

The ghostly moans and responding animal howls grew in both urgency and proximity. I didn't know if they were good or bad, but they were annoying the hell out of me, so I didn't care in the moment.

Channeling the full moon for the millionth time tonight, I bellowed, "Shut up!" And the woods silenced instantly. I reluctantly had to admit that this goddess thing had its benefits.

Using the trees as climbing gear, I hiked and pulled my way through thorny bushes and scratching twigs to the park's summit. There, a little clearing overlooked the preserved oasis amidst the concrete jungle. The city's bright lights and the bay in the distance glowed in the full moon's white blue midnight light.

Sick energy churned in my empty stomach, but this wasn't just energy. It wasn't even my out-of-control energy. It wasn't mine, period. When I sucked the energy from the so-called vampires, I absorbed their negative energy into mine and now it was looking for an escape.

Involuntarily, my arms threw themselves toward the sky, releasing a black stream of painful lightning screeching from my hands. Another seizure twisted my body and sent a dead black river from my eyes into the woods below.

"Hey, lady, what ya doin'?" a homeless woman barked from her park bench bed hidden beneath the trees at the clearing's perimeter.

I turned to respond, but as I opened my mouth the last jolt of negative energy burst from my gape knocking the woman out cold before shrieking off into the distance.

"Shit," I swore under my breath, running over to her.

I placed my hand on her head and sent healing, positive energy into her. Once she looked like she was sleeping peacefully, I situated her body on the makeshift bed and walked back to the clearing.

The smell of burning wood and decaying leaves hung in the frigid air. Indian summer San Francisco nights were like winter days in Salem. Shivering in the cold and wishing I had remembered to wear a coat, I shoved my hands into my pockets and my knuckles scraped against the house key.

Adam! Where the hell was he anyway?

"Adam!" I shouted, gripping the key chain's silver angel wings. "Adam, I need you!"

His body took shape from the leafy bushes in the background. "You called?" he asked with a sarcastic grin, walking over to me.

I couldn't decide what to do—ask questions or rip his head off. CJ's hands gripped my arms tightly to control the energy rippling through them. Apparently, I wasn't going to be allowed to kill Adam tonight.

"Where the hell were you?" I hissed. "Weren't you keeping an eye on me?"

"We were," he said simply, staring at me as if I just asked the stupidest question in the world.

"You were," I repeated, about to lose my

temper. "When exactly was the Bellatori going to intervene? I assumed that blood-letting, ritual sacrifice and attempted murder would constitute needing help."

"Always so dramatic." Adam rolled his eyes.

"Roll them again and I'll rip them out," I threatened in complete seriousness as my arms of lightning ensnared him.

"Calm down," he ordered and swiped one arm in front of his body cutting my tentacle-like ties to him. "Walk with me."

He led me to a playground where four swings swayed back and forth as if ghosts were at play in the empty night.

I dropped into one of the swings while Adam leaned against one of the structure's poles.

"There was no need for us to intercede, Angel."

"Humph," I grunted. "I beg to differ."

"You're just saying that because you were scared, but who did you face tonight?"

"Satanists," I shuddered. "Your point?"

"Precisely. They were human and no match for you. You just needed to be reminded of your abilities. Besides, they needed to be punished for their past actions. Although, you might want to consider using your energy instead of your fingers."

At the memory of 'their past actions' and 'my fingers' ripping into their necks, my stomach lurched. "Please don't remind me," I begged.

Adam nodded and continued. "Remember, you

can defend and heal yourself. Nice move on goat guy, by the way," he chuckled.

Despite my stubborn insistence on remaining angry, I cracked a smile.

"The Bellatori won't intervene unless it's absolutely necessary. They would have saved you if it had gotten any worse," Adam continued. "These challenges will give you the experiences you need to face the future. Tonight served as a reminder of who you are and what you can do, but even this wouldn't be enough to keep you safe from Aeterna Flamma's vampires and werewolves, and certainly not Anchises."

At the sound of Rick's real name and true identity as Hadrianus' son, my energy leapt in excitement.

Adam's eyes narrowed in concern. "Angel," he warned.

"I know. I'm dealing with it. Ok? Drop it," I muttered, turning to face the forest.

"Are you feeling better now?" he asked, referring to my calm demeanor.

I nodded, still avoiding his eyes.

"May I escort you home?" he offered sweetly, extending his hand.

I accepted his help to stand up from the swing. "Thanks, but I need some air. I think I'll walk for a little and grab a cab. You *will* keep an eye on me, won't you," I wanted to confirm.

"Always," he smiled with a wink and vanished into the blue-black night.

Now that I'd purged the dark energy, a surge of my own pulsed in my fingers. Similar to the charge I felt before last year's battle, a powerful yet peaceful energy radiated through my body then. The big difference now was that I lacked confidence. In Endymion Village my friends surrounded and supported me. Here, I was alone. Our combined efforts and strength helped us take down Hadrianus and stop Aeterna Flamma. Now without my team, I had to face everything by myself. It's easy to hide behind others and rely on them to survive. It's quite another to stand up for yourself when no one else will help you.

Peeking through the foggy cloud cover, the moon's cool gaze lit my path along a narrow wooden staircase built into the park's hillside. I hopped off the last step and back into the cityscape.

Haight Street was an easy walk just around the corner from the park's perimeter. An easy path it may have been, but the lonely road echoed with sounds from busier sections of the city reminding me just how alone I was in the moment.

Head facing forward confidently to mask any fear, my long strides hurried toward Stanyan. The night air was as refreshing as it was growing eerily uncomfortable. I had forgotten about the sketchier areas around the Haight-Ashbury district.

Energy tingled in my fingertips. I knew I could save myself and any other victims I encountered in the dark night. But I wasn't Batman, nor did I want to be. I couldn't be the town's night watchman, saving everyone who needed help. So, where did I fit? What was I supposed to do? Was my job restricted to the battles or was I expected to do more? Did I want to do more?

A dark BMW sped by me changing lanes without a signal in order to turn onto Stanyan. It screeched to a halt, grinding the gears in the process. Flying in reverse, it fishtailed backwards along the street before slamming on the breaks right beside me.

Chapter 10 – Not So Normal

"Hey!" the driver shouted from his open window.

The dim neighborhood lights and dead street didn't exactly feel welcoming or secure. Like a drum increasing its pounding beat, my heart began to race in time with my rushing footsteps.

The car kept pace.

I wasn't about to tempt fate a second time tonight. I sprinted past Amoeba Music to the nearest refuge. At the end of the block, the golden arches of McDonald's beckoned me like a midnight Mecca for the lost and faithless.

"Hey!" the driver shouted again keeping pace with me.

What could they possibly want? I just wanted to grab a McD's coffee, call a cab, and get home to the comfort of my bed.

I refused to turn to face the sound of a car

window rolling down. The restaurant was only 50 feet away. My feet flew toward the protection of its golden, welcoming lights.

"Yo, Angel!" another voice shouted from the car.

I spun around to see Justin hanging halfway out of the car's back window and Ray trying to keep control of the car and not lose his friend in the process.

"Justin?!" I sighed in relief and then the tears started.

"Angel?" Worry replaced his mischievous grin instantly. Barely waiting for Ray to stop the car, he burst through the door and rushed to my side.

Grabbing both my arms he looked me up and down and exclaimed, "Holy hell! What happened to you?"

I stood there shaking my head. There weren't words to explain what happened tonight. Even if I wanted to, I couldn't tell Justin or anyone else. The only people who would understand were thousands of miles away, and I had to be wary of both sides' eavesdroppers and hackers in my e-mails, phone calls, and text messages as it was.

Justin was a friendly face—just the friendly face I needed right now. My tears melted into hysterics and Justin wrapped me in a huge hug, the safety of which felt like the familiarity of an old, worn blanket.

"Shhhh, you're ok now. I won't let anything happen to you," he whispered into my hair.

I was vaguely aware that the rest of his posse had parked the car and were now crowded around us in the empty parking lot.

The guys shuffled me into the restaurant and led me to a corner booth. Curious stares from the employees followed us. Their expressions clearly painted their thoughts across their faces. *Why is she with them? Are they going to hurt her? Why is she crying? What did they do to her? Maybe we should call the cops.*

Ignoring their endless speculation, I focused on the steaming large coffee with three creamers and two raw sugar packets sitting loosely between my palms. My head dropped to the table out of sheer exhaustion and frustration. What could I tell the guys?

A warm tingly sensation radiated through my hands. Turning my head to the side, I peeked to find Ray and Gabe resting their massive palms on top of mine. Their expressions were filled with worry.

As my energy stepped aside, it allowed theirs to creep up my arms and their positivity healed the parts of me that felt broken and worn. I sat up allowing them to share their gift—whether or not they realized what they were actually doing. I just stared at their hands.

Ray's smooth, dark brown grip and Gabe's caramel skin contrasted my ghost white, frigid hands. Though we looked different, we were the same. I wasn't the religious type anymore, but I could see God in them—in their goodness, in their daily playfulness. God was evident in this simple act of kindness. When I was at my lowest 'God, this-can't-get-any-worse' moment, my friends let me know I was not alone, no matter how much I felt like a freak.

Justin, who had been sitting beside me and

staring the whole time, leaned back and placed his left arm onto the booth behind me. "What happened?" he asked directly.

"Why are ya alone in Haight-Ashbury…at night?" added Mike very seriously.

"Are you hurt?" Ray asked kindly.

Gabe exchanged a glance with Justin before repeating the first question slowly, "What happened?"

I looked at the guys wondering what I could reveal without revealing too much, but something about them seemed out of place. "Where's Uri?"

"With Kelly," Gabe responded, still waiting for me to answer their questions.

"Angel?" Justin encouraged.

"My date ended badly," I answered as truthfully as possible.

"Diego?" Justin clarified.

I nodded and sighed, leaning back in the booth and into Justin's arm.

"Diego?!" Justin roared, lurching forward.

"Calm down," I shushed him. The employees behind the counter were staring again. "It's been handled."

"Handled?!" Justin shouted.

"But are you all right?" Mike pushed.

"Yeah," I replied, and I was ok now that the guys were with me. I felt safe with them.

Replaying the night's events on fast-forward

through my memory, I turned to the window and stared at the empty street. I scoffed at the thought, but windows scared me—not so much the windows themselves, but the things that mysteriously appeared on their other side to terrify me last year in Wales. The blonde, cloaked vampire who stalked me all of last summer first appeared to me behind glass. Thankfully, he turned out to be one of my protectors. Still, I wondered where he was today. Actually, I wondered where all of my protectors were at the moment. I really could've used their help tonight.

My focus shifted slowly from the street to my reflection. I gasped.

Justin's hand dropped from the seat to my shoulder.

"Oh…My…God!" I shrieked, staring dumbstruck at the disheveled girl looking back at me.

Various shades of hardened candle wax dotted my black blouse and its arms were ripped to shreds thanks to my hike in the park. Dirt, leaves and a twig or two decorated my Einstein coif and what once resembled a date-night outfit. But the worst was the mascara streaming down my cheeks and drawing attention to the bleeding bite marks on both sides of my neck. My hands jumped up to cover the wounds.

"Let me out," I squealed to Justin, wanting to escape the lights which would reveal just how much trouble I'd been in.

Worried and baffled, he jumped up and I ran out of the front doors to the darkest part of the parking lot behind the building. I leaned against the back wall. My body crumpled to the ground just as the guys reached me.

"Brah, she's wiggin out," Mike commented to Justin.

Ray squatted beside me. "Let us take you to the hospital," he offered calmly.

"No! No hospital," I shouted vehemently. I needed to get home. Adam's reminder that I could heal myself was worth trying.

"That's going to get infected," Gabe added knowledgeably; his face contorted in disgust.

I hadn't thought about that problem. What if the twins had some sort of disease they passed on to me?

If I was anyone else but me, I would've run to the nearest hospital for tests and treatment. But I did have some healing abilities; I patched up Sam and Mark when the werewolves attacked them last summer. I had to try fixing myself to avoid the hospital staff's inquisition.

"No, I'll be ok. Just take me home, please," I commanded.

The guys clearly did not agree with me, but they turned to Justin waiting for his decision.

"Fine." His voice burned with furious disagreement.

Mike and Justin sandwiched me in the backseat of the sedan and sped north on 19th Avenue toward the marina.

"What exactly were all of you doing out in the middle of the night?" I asked, realizing it was just as weird for them to be in the seedy area as it was for me.

"Da Hui!" Mike exclaimed, laughing at my perplexed expression and ignorance at surfer lingo.

"A group of his friends have a surfer club nearby," Gabe explained.

"You went clubbing?" I asked confused, staring at Ray not being able to picture him dancing.

"It's not that type of club," Ray said, smiling in the rearview mirror, seeming to read my mind.

Ray, Mike, and Gabe started reliving the moments from their much happier night—laughing and carrying on like normal college students.

I glanced at Justin. Staring at the outside world, the window reflected a murderous scowl. Although I knew he always had my best interest at heart, the look on his face was intense and chilling. He was not happy, that much was abundantly clear.

I slid back into my seat, closed my eyes, and wished the night would end.

𝔠𝔥𝔞𝔭𝔱𝔢𝔯 11 - 𝔥𝔲𝔪𝔞𝔫

Believe. That's what Sam's gift to me said. The sun's dawning pink-orange rays peeked through my navy curtains highlighting the plaque hanging over my bed. The pale blue plaque with fancy, black and silver lettering simply stated, "Believe."

The biggest lesson I learned last summer was that I needed to believe in myself. Sam's year-old present served as a constant reminder.

The problem was that I didn't really believe in who I was. But after last night, how could I deny it? I just didn't want to be *that* person—a goddess incarnate. I scoffed.

Rolling onto my side on my fluffy light blue and white bed, I wished I could just crawl under a rock and disappear. I envied the normal people jogging, playing, and laughing on the marina's field below my window during the day. Every second of their carefree, happy existence felt like the stab of a hundred daggers of misery. I wanted to be ordinary. I wanted to be simple. I wanted to be a nobody.

My eyes danced around the room and landed on a picture that Zach had drawn for me in History class. 'Twinkle' it said in dark purple with yellow-gold stars all around it. It was a reminder of my normal days.

Worse than wanting to be a nobody now was that I could picture my life the way it should've been. Zach and I would still be dating and attending a prestigious college somewhere. My family would be happy and intact with my dad very much alive and well. Life's average worries—friends, school, job, money—would be our only concerns.

Anger bubbled in my gut. I hated the Bellatori. *HATE YOU WITH A PASSION*, I thought vehemently hoping their intrusive eyes and ears would get the message.

Regardless of the manipulative angels, why couldn't I just fit in and blend in with the masses? Instead, the pressure of responsibility weighed on my shoulders like a ton of boulders. I really wanted to know what situation I got myself into five thousand years ago to cause the angel-vampire conflict currently revolving around my reincarnated existence. Clearly this was my path, whether I wanted it or not. I was paying for whatever I did all those millennia ago.

Sigh. A week's worth of exhaustion was leading to unmotivated laziness. I glanced at the clock: 6:00 a.m. Time to get up.

Jogging for two hours every morning was the only thing that kept my body's energy from freaking out every time my mind wandered to the memories of last week's encounter. Just to be sure, I voluntarily went to the hospital for blood work. In case I overestimated my healing abilities of what turned out to be surface scratches, I wanted to make sure I was disease free. The results were due any day now. A bone-chilling shudder ran down my spine at the possibility of having been infected with a serious illness because of my stupidity. Of course, had the Bellatori shown up, it wouldn't have gotten that far in the first place.

A black stream of electricity shot from my fingers and gouged a two-inch hole in the sidewalk. *Great*, I thought sarcastically. Thankfully no one was around. Although, now I had to add cement patching to my growing list of repair supplies from the local hardware store. My room was also dotted with little black holes when my uncontrolled energy leaked.

I gulped the frigid morning breeze as I turned back to lock the front door behind me. Zach's playlists ran on a loop on my iPod, keeping my thoughts sufficiently distracted from the weightier issues. However, thanks to the recent events I had all but forgotten about Aeterna Flamma and the fact that it was only a matter of time before they found me. Whatever that future held, I wasn't sure. I just knew it would be highly unpleasant and painful, both physically and emotionally, if they attacked my friends and me.

It was an uncharacteristically clear morning on the bay. The deep blue sky was giving way to the sun's golden warmth. By 8 o'clock the buses hurried noisily through the city neighborhoods and I was sufficiently drenched in sweat. As I turned the corner from Scott Street onto Marina Boulevard, I was ready for a break.

I jogged across the street from my house to the Golden Gate Recreation Area's lush grassy field and stood at its perimeter. The early morning's frigid sun danced off of the cargo ships passing under the Golden Gate Bridge into the deep navy bay while the seagulls' air ballet twisted and twirled overhead.

The scene was picturesque and yet I didn't feel its beauty, unlike my adventure with CJ to the Pembrokeshire coastline in Wales. That day every single aspect of my senses appreciated the white-grey cliffs dotted with purple-pink heather, which were contrasted by the dark blue waters of the Celtic Sea.

Closing my eyes, I inhaled slowly, deeply.

Without so much as the warning of the slightest sound, I was brutally yanked from this sweet reverie by the impact of a speeding pickup truck, which catapulted me through the air, sending me spinning dizzyingly across the field.

This is how I'm gonna die, I thought terrified.

My body crashed; it crashed hard. As I

scrambled to get up, I realized that my landing was softer than the grassy ground. Pushing myself up, my safety net started laughing.

"Justin?" I asked confused as he sat up next to me. Mike and Gabe high-fived each other, while Uri and Ray were doubled over in laughter at the field's edge.

"You freaking tackled me?" I asked in furious disbelief shoving his shoulder away from me. "What the hell is wrong with you?"

Justin choked his breathless laughs with a conspicuous cough as he adjusted his baseball cap and sweatshirt. "Sorry. I'm just excited that you've released yourself from seclusion. It's about damn time. I was beginning to think you were avoiding us."

Actually, I was—and not just the guys but everyone. I wanted to avoid anyone with a connection to the fateful night filled with memories that I so very badly wanted to purge from my thoughts.

Ray walked over to us and handed a large coffee to me. "We were going to barge into your place anyway. You saved Kelly from getting the scare of her life," he laughed.

"Yeah, and the guys from getting butchered," Uri added protectively on Kelly's behalf.

"Right," Gabe said sarcastically. "I'd like to see you take all of us."

"Chill," Mike ordered the argumentative three as he tossed a football at Gabe's head. "Come on, brah. Let's go!"

"Maybe Angel wants to play," Gabe invited me. "If she could survive a tackle like that, I want her on my team!" he laughed, hurrying to Mike.

Partnered in twos, they rushed into an entertaining version of football more closely resembling 'tackle anyone who has the ball.' Personally, I think it was just an excuse to release the testosterone-fueled aggression they felt toward each other.

"What've you been up to?" Justin asked nonchalantly, avoiding my eyes by staring at the bay. The ease of his words was a little too relaxed. He was burning with curiosity.

"Avoiding everyone," I admitted freely, pulling my knees into my chest and wrapping my arms around them.

"I knew it!" he exclaimed. "That's how you repay us after we saved your ass?"

"It's not you," I tried to clarify. "That night…well, it was embarrassing…"

"You're worried about what we think of you?" he interrupted.

"Uh, yeah," I responded derisively. "You obviously thought I was stupid."

"Because you were," he added simply.

"Gee, thanks." My tone was biting.

"Come on. Do *you* think what you did was smart?"

I didn't respond.

"Exactly," he added like an overly confident big brother. "We just wanted to make sure you survived."

"You guys really didn't need to call and text Kelly every ten minutes though. I'm fine," I replied bitterly, twirling the wedding ring mindlessly, furiously.

"You're gonna wear your finger away if you keep doing that," Justin observed coldly.

A smirk escaped my otherwise stern expression, but I didn't respond. Choosing not to start crying, I stared emptily at the cargo ships and sailboats floating effortlessly through the flat bay.

"You seem hollow," Justin pressed as a gust of wind smacked our faces.

My eyebrows furrowed defensively.

"You go places, hang out with people, do things, but you're not passionate about anything. At least not that I've seen," he paused pensively before turning to face me, his dark brown-black eyes burning intensely. "Something's missing from you. I just can't figure out what."

As if a light bulb lit up in my head, Justin pinpointed what I'd blindly been searching for all along. It wasn't in my lessons from the Bellatori. I couldn't find it in my drawings. My friends didn't cure it.

I *was* hollow. And empty. Nearly soulless— without the evil implications.

What was missing?

The only thing I couldn't have.

Love.

No amount of distractions could hide me from the pain, which was as much a part of me as the scar on my forearm. At the thought, the edges of my unwanted vampire tattoo tingled.

Still, somehow Justin's discovery of it felt good. I didn't have to pretend to be happy anymore, to be someone I didn't want to be anymore.

"Hollow, huh?" I scoffed and gave in. "I see beauty," I said looking at the Golden Gate Bridge and the glistening deep blue bay, "but I don't feel it. I know friendship, but I don't fully appreciate it. The world is kind of meaningless right now."

"But why?" his concerned gaze drifted to the gold band encircling the third finger of my left hand.

I didn't answer. I couldn't. My eyes tried to focus on the bay, though my clouded vision made it rather difficult.

"You want breakfast?" Justin asked, changing the subject.

I nodded, rubbing my eyes with the back of my hand quickly. He helped me to my feet and I took a quick gulp of coffee in an attempt to gain composure. He hooked my arm and dragged me back to my place.

Justin stared through our bay window the entire time I took a shower and got dressed. He was as enamored with the view as me.

I fried a few eggs with green peppers, bacon, and cheese, figuring a treat was well-deserved after running over 14 miles during the past week.

Justin and I sat in the bay window eating in silence. I scarfed everything without nearly so much as a breath between bites. Justin's fork played absentmindedly with the eggs, building mountains and valleys.

"Are you ok?" I asked, suddenly wondering if I missed something.

"Just debating something," he said, but didn't look up at me as 100% of his attention remained on twirling his fork through the breakfast.

"What?" I pressed, both curious and worried.

"Considering what you just went through and," he glanced at my ring, "I don't want you to think this to be inappropriate, but," he paused, clearly fighting with his conscience—or courage—internally, "you need to get out more," he blurted.

Taken aback by his order, my left eyebrow arched instinctively in surprised disbelief.

"Justin," I started.

"The Diego thing may not have turned out the way you expected," he rushed to explain, "but that doesn't mean you can't have fun with friends you trust. Whatever happened in your past is, well, past. That shouldn't keep you from moving on—safely—and living, right?" His piercing stare echoed the conviction of his words.

I sighed and turned my gaze toward the window. If only it was that easy.

The sound of the mail slot clanging interrupted our pensive silence.

Jumping up, I rushed downstairs to grab the mail. I flipped through the junk and, there it was in the very last envelope. My test results.

Like a zombie, I wandered back to my window seat debating if I was brave enough to read the results, which could seriously impact my future and those around me.

"What is it?" Justin asked.

"I went to the hospital for bloodwork."

Justin's head popped up to stare at me with one eyebrow arched.

"Yes, it was because you were so insistent. The idea of catching something from—that night," I paused, trying to remember how much I had told Justin, "scared me, so I went."

I breathed to calm myself and my static charge. Surely, Justin wouldn't appreciate a smoking, black hole gouged through him.

"Here. Open it," I shoved it into his hand.

He took the bright white business envelope gently and ripped the seam.

He shook his head.

"What? How bad is it?" I asked anxiously.

"Go out with me," he begged, changing the subject.

"The letter?" I reminded, avoiding his question.

"You're clean! Let's celebrate," he smiled brilliantly. "Come out with me," he asked again sweetly. "Please."

Hesitantly, I nodded, "Ok."

The gleam in his grin was blinding. Maybe I gave him too much hope by accepting his invitation. I wasn't ready for another boyfriend when I still needed my invisible one to keep the nightmares away. However, a night out with friends was certainly doable.

Thanks to the guys' connections, Kelly and I got into the club even though we were underage. Kelly didn't like to break rules; her unease with the situation was painfully obvious until Uri dragged her to the dance floor.

Justin, Mike, Gabe, and Ray took turns making fun of my uptight, awkward white girl moves, but I didn't care. Dancing provided a welcome release. The later it got, the faster we moved. The hazy club atmosphere and pulsating body-reverberating beats generated a positive energy, which grew with the bass line of every song.

Warm electricity throbbed throughout my body pushing the concerns and depression of late completely out of my system.

"Want a drink?" Justin leaned in and shouted in my ear.

I nodded. Placing his hand on my back ever so lightly, he guided me to the bar.

"What'll ya have?" the statuesque, spiky

haired, androgynous bartender with countless facial piercings asked.

"Pepsi."

"That's it?" Justin asked me like I was crazy.

"Uh-huh." Just because I got into the club didn't mean I had to drink too. Besides, I wanted to remember every part of tonight. It was the first time in a long time that I felt alive.

"You know, they won't card you. You can get something," Justin urged, whispering in my ear.

"That's ok."

He sighed and turned to the woman. "Anderson Summer Solstice, bottled."

She nodded and reached into the mini fridge behind the counter.

"Having fun?" Justin asked. I read his lips since the music drowned out his voice.

"Yeah!" I shouted.

"Feeling better?"

I nodded, taking a sip of my soda and watching Kelly and Uri sway slowly to a romantic melody on center of the dance floor.

He took a few gulps of his beer and ran his hands along its sides, swiping away the condensation.

I adjusted my black tank top with the crystal accents forming a smiley face with a halo. An instant flashback to last summer reminded me of Rick's flirtatious comment about my being an angel or devil in disguise. I smirked at the memory.

"Are you ok?" Justin worried.

"As good as I'll ever be," I muttered, taking another sip.

"Listen. I was wondering if you want to get out of here?" Justin blurted.

"And go where? I can't leave Kelly here."

"No. I mean, I think you should get out of the city for awhile," he continued.

"Again, *and go where?* I just moved here."

"I don't mean permanently, but a vacation might do you some good." He gulped half his beer while I pondered.

"I don't know where I'd go and I don't want to go alone," I thought aloud.

"That's where I come into the picture," he smirked.

"What do you mean?" I squinted, worried about where his plan was heading.

"I have a research project in South America starting in a week. Why don't you come with me and Gabe? It'll get you away from whatever's bothering you here. Besides, a change of scenery might be refreshing."

He had a point and I trusted these guys.

I waited for the flip flops of anxiety to attack my stomach at the thought of exploring the unknown, but nothing happened. In fact, I felt exhilarated.

"Um, I can't believe I'm saying this, but yeah.

Ok," I answered with hesitant excitement.

Justin's brilliant smile beamed.

"What are you researching all the way down there?" I asked.

"Earth's energy and its effect on life," he took another swig of beer.

"You see, most people are jaded by science. My goal is to get to know the areas and indigenous people who are removed from our prejudices and compare it to what we know through scientific fact. Not to mention, it's a great way for us to learn in the field instead of a boring classroom for a month," he added like a typical college student.

"Sounds like fun," I added.

A month away from the doom-and-gloom surrounding me in San Francisco was worth it. Maybe it would kick the depressed funk I let myself fall into with the recent Diego debacle.

"There are so many legends down there," he continued. "It's a chance for us to find out for ourselves if there's any truth to the stories."

"How do you think the legends are tied to earth's energies? That's a bit of a stretch, don't you think?" I asked, wondering if he was as crazy as me. Then again, I knew a thing or two about mythic tales and mine were all true.

"The ancient Inca believed the Sun God to be their primary deity. Their spiritual connection was so strong that they worked for years on amazing structures devoted to him," he explained enthusiastically, turning to face me. "The interesting thing is that, whether they knew it or not, Machu Picchu and the Temple of the Sun in Cuzco lie directly over ley lines—areas where natural energy is concentrated. This may explain the psychic powers and visions that ancient priests and rulers had. They may have been able to tap into earth's energy and use it to their advantage over the general public who was unaware of it."

"But that's nothing new," I countered. "Different cultures and religions have explored the use of energy. Why would the Incan experience in particular be of so much interest?"

He stared me square in the eye and leaned in as if telling me the best-kept secret in the entire world.

"Because the person who finds the Sun God's energy at a precise point on earth's main ley line will be unstoppable."

Chapter 12 – Closing the Loop

The sunrise's orange-pink glow filtered through the blinds and curtains illuminating the pitch darkness surrounding me as I lay on my back.

Eyes wide open, I didn't sleep for a second since Kelly and I got home a few hours ago.

'Because the person who finds the Sun God's energy at a precise point on the main ley line will be unstoppable.'

Justin's words played on an unending loop in my thoughts. He had gone on to tell me how a World

War II conspiracy theory speculated that Hitler's death was staged in Germany, and he actually escaped to the now dilapidated Gran Hotel Viena in Argentina where numerous prominent Nazis had come to seek refuge and plastic surgery from being caught and sentenced for their war crimes.

It was no secret that the Nazis stole riches and were after world domination. What better place to go than South America on a hunt for ancient treasure? Or, more specifically, could they have headed to Cuzco where an alleged Incan treasure lay hidden for hundreds of years? But what if they weren't after physical treasure? What if the Nazis knew about the ley lines and the Incan myths? What if they were after the one thing that had eluded modern mankind? What if the Bellatori meant for me to pinpoint the Sun God's energy? Is that why they were ok with me going on this expedition?

Moreover, if I found the Sun God's energy, I would become unstoppable, and, as a result, so would they. I was just a pawn in their game against Aeterna Flamma, after all.

For as powerful as I felt at the chance of finding the prize, my stomach sank in disgust knowing I was a means to an end for the Bellatori. As quickly as the Bellatori entered my thoughts, I distracted myself by staring at the photos lining my dresser just in case they caught my rebellious stream of consciousness.

The static smiles of friends and family stared back at me blankly. My eyes caught a matching set.

Dad.

He was my confidant through exuberant highs

and every self-castigating low. The second anniversary of his death passed on August 11—my birthday. The pain of losing him still burned as much as the day he died.

Dad, I wish you were here with me. You'd know what I should do. I'm lost without you, I thought.

"You'll always be my little girl," a voice whispered in my mind.

Great. Now I was hearing voices too. Too much wishful thinking about missing my family and friends was slowly driving me insane. I guess it was only a matter of time before I plummeted off the cliff of sanity anyway.

Three soft raps on the bedroom door stopped me in mid-judgment of my slipping grasp on reality.

"Yeah?" I asked, rolling onto my back to stretch.

Kelly peered around the door, afraid to come inside.

"I was just wondering if you wanted to go to church with me…with us," she corrected bashfully. "Uri and I are going. He's going to be here in twenty minutes and I thought you might want to come with us to the early mass."

Saved by the bell, Kelly's cell beeped and interrupted my need to come up with an excuse not to go.

She pulled her phone out of her pant's pocket. "Oh!" she exclaimed, surprised.

"Uri?" I wondered aloud, thinking gleefully that he may have backed out on her too.

"No. I thought it was Uri. It's…nevermind," she said sheepishly.

"What's going on?" my suspicions aroused. For a second I thought it might be my mom checking up on me, but I called her vigilantly for at least a few seconds every day since the move.

She dropped her head as if ashamed. "It's Dave," she mumbled.

"What?" I asked in disbelief.

She hadn't spoken about him since the night we decided to move to California. I assumed he stopped talking to her as well.

"What does he want?" I pressed.

Kelly turned to face the window so I couldn't see her reaction. The morning sunshine highlighted her short blonde curls in a warm orange hue.

"He's checking on you," she whispered as if he could hear us, though he was probably in Timbuktu for all we knew.

My heart skipped a beat. Could he have forgiven me finally? Though he had said some unforgivable things to me lately, there was something about him. I wanted him in my life no matter what. I wanted to help him move on from the pain I inflicted unintentionally.

"Why does he care?" I asked gruffly, hoping she wouldn't hear the excited relief underlying the statement.

"He cares a great deal," she defended him instantly. "He always has, Angel. He'll kill me if he finds out that I told you, but I'm sick of being stuck in the middle."

"He still doesn't want to talk to me?" I asked. Hope deflated.

"No. He's still upset, but he's concerned about you, which is why you need to come to church with us," she brought the conversation full circle and craftily avoided any other questions about my absent best friend.

"Not a chance," I replied and jumped out of bed reaching for my soft lavender robe on the back of the bedroom door. "But say a prayer for my soul, will ya," I winked at her grimace before rushing down the hallway for a long, hot shower to wash away the building tension and ruminate my soul's punishment in the afterlife. It couldn't be that bad. After all, I reincarnated every hundred years or so.

A hundred years of purgatory—if it existed—on the other side followed by roughly twenty years of hell here. It was a give and take situation; both good and bad elements. On the other side, I'd be with my dad and CJ, but I'd be subjected to whatever punishment awaited me. Here I lived in constant fear that Aeterna Flamma's legions were in hot pursuit and that I'd royally screw up my mission causing the whole of humanity to suffer. So really, neither option seemed terribly appealing.

I breathed the steam and let the water run down my back.

Justin and Gabe spent the morning with me

doing our least favorite thing in the world—shopping! The least I could do for Kelly before I left for South America was furnish the apartment. Couches, bookcases, end tables, mirrors, area rugs, pillows, blankets, stainless steel pots and pans, plants, candles, luminaires, and $10,000 later, the guys shoved our purchases into a truck Gabe borrowed from a friend.

As if nothing weighed more than a feather, Justin and Gabe unloaded the truck effortlessly and assembled the furniture by nightfall. I focused on arranging the 12-inch by 12-inch square mirrors intermittently between my framed sketches around the fireplace. In order to create an endless room effect, I added rows of mirrors to the opposite wall which reflected the view in the other mirrors as well as the countless cream colored taper and pillar candles lining the bookcases and fireplace mantle.

The entire room was transformed into a rather comfortable little oasis. Black, cubist couches contrasted the deep red walls perfectly and the white, fuzzy shag area rug added a bright pop to the room. Potted plants—some real, some fake—were tucked into each corner. The burst of green life added a subtle, positive energy radiating through the room. Rich vanilla perfumed the air as the candles began to melt.

"Sucks that you don't get to enjoy this for long, huh?" Justin asked, plopping onto the couch next to me.

He leaned back and placed his arm on the top of the couch behind me. Sitting cross-legged on my new plush seat, I'd forgotten how comfy real furniture felt. Absentmindedly, I massaged the tense knots in my neck and shoulders. I was too tired and too lazy to move over and reply to Justin's comment, though now that my home was homey I agreed with him.

"Can you believe we'll be in Peru this time next week?" Gabe added while grabbing a bottle of Perrier from the fridge, sauntering back to us, and dropping onto the couch facing the massive picture window overlooking the setting sun beyond the Golden Gate Bridge.

"Oh my God, how am I gonna pack lightly?" I complained, wishing I could've enjoyed the room's serenity for a few minutes longer.

"Bring clothes to layer. It'll be freezing in the mountains, but warm in the cities," Gabe offered.

"You have a passport, don't you?" Justin asked concerned.

I nodded just as a knock at the front door interrupted our conversation. Skipping down the stairs, I threw open the front door and did not expect to see who was standing there.

"What do you want?" I asked cautiously.

Justin and Gabe's footsteps echoed on the hardwood floor as they walked to the top of the steps to see what was happening.

Adam's glance shifted infinitesimally to catch the guys' curious presence.

"Can't I wish you safe travels?" he asked sweetly. Too sweetly.

My eyes appraised him suspiciously as I pulled the door closed behind me to avoid Justin and Gabe's earshot.

"Fine," he muttered, dropping the pretense. "There's one last task before you leave."

I waited, worried.

"Satan's Spot," he said simply as if it would be nothing more than a trip to the grocery store.

"Are you out of your freakin' mind?!" I shouted. "Why would I go back to see…him?" I swallowed hard, avoiding the bile creeping up my throat at the thought of Diego and his club of murderers.

"You must. You'll know why once you're there," he added in his smooth, even voice.

"Adam!" Kelly exclaimed, bouncing up the stairs to the porch with Uri and Mike on her heels. "Are you staying for dinner?"

Adam looked at me and smirked. Of course to irritate me, he'd like nothing more than to stay. The daggers shooting from my eyes warned him against any such notion.

He coughed conspicuously. "I best be on my way. Lovely to see you again, Kelly."

He smiled angelically and Kelly's knees buckled. Uri caught her by the elbow steadying her. He and Mike exchanged a quick nod with Adam, pushed past us, and followed Kelly upstairs.

Not two seconds later, Kelly's ear-piercing shriek echoed through the house followed by her flying down the stairs. She threw her arms around me. I didn't break my stare down with Adam.

"Thank you!" Kelly screeched. "It's gorgeous!"

she hugged me again, ran back upstairs and squealed in delight.

Adam smirked. Motioning toward the stairs, he said, "Take one of your friends with you. You'll be fine."

His eyes were sincere. Then again, he was an angel. He could convince me to do anything.

"Fine," I murmured. I was about to ask *'When?'* but he beat me to it.

"Before Peru," he added as he backed down the landing, turned, hopped down the front steps and disappeared into the crowds walking along the marina.

Pushing Adam to the back of my mind, I focused on the party starting in our living room. The warm glow of candles, lights, and friendship filled our little space blocking the cool gaze of the moon and dark night just outside our window. We laughed. We ate pizza. We told stories. We played cards. Well, the guys tried to teach poker to us and gave up after ten minutes because Uri threw a punch at Mike for an uncouth comment he made about the way Kelly looked tonight, and Mike fell off of the end of the couch from the force. For a split second the room fell silent wondering if a fight was going to break out, but we burst into roaring laughter.

Eventually, we fell asleep scattered around the living room in the early morning hours. As the dawning sun streamed through the window to wake me, I realized something happily. For the first time in over two years, I felt like the old Angel—the one who didn't know what losing a parent or boyfriend felt like; the one who wasn't a goddess with the power to wish the Bellatori to victory; the one to whom vampires and werewolves were just the stuff of vivid imaginations and nightmares. No depression. No sorrow. No worries. No awkwardness. And above all, no weird supernatural stuff.

Of course, that sense of elation couldn't last though I desperately grasped onto the memory as Justin and I drove in my Viper to Satan's Spot that afternoon. Justin was furious that I was even going to set a toe in there knowing Diego had harmed me in some way, but he—and Mike—came along for the ride just in case.

What would I say to Diego? Could I keep my bursts of angry energy from killing him? Could I keep my own hands from killing him? With these thoughts plaguing my mind, we walked in silence hesitantly yet purposefully along the bright block of colorful storefronts and through the black front door where my nightmare in this city began.

At the sound of the tinkling bell hanging from the front door, Diego, wearing his typical all black get up and silver chains, spun around from behind the cash register to face us. A startled look of confusion and assessment painted the dark features of the face I once admired.

"Hi," he said hesitantly. "Uh, welcome to Satan's Spot. How can I help you?" he recited robotically.

In an instant, my head tilted to the left in confusion and my eyebrows furrowed.

"Diego, it's me," I said, exchanging bewildered glances with Justin and Mike.

"Do I know you?" he asked curiously. "I'm sorry. I've been having momentary lapses of amnesia lately, so if we met over the last couple of months, I'm sorry, but I don't remember."

Diego's gaze slowly shifted to Justin. "Oh, hey! Justin, right?" he smiled hopefully.

"Yeah," Justin responded curtly. "Let me get this straight. You remember me, but not her? You don't remember anything about her?" he asked pointing at me.

"Sorry," Diego shrugged apologetically. "I woke up in a hospital a couple weeks ago with no memory and all my friends were in jail. Um, do you need help looking around?" he asked me awkwardly.

"No, we're fine," I replied unsure of what was happening.

Justin followed me to the book section on alternative energies as my mind raced to figure out the puzzle of what the Bellatori did to Diego. Mike, clearly uncomfortable with the store and its contents, hung close by the entrance staring at Diego like he was part of a circus sideshow.

"*That* was *weird*…really weird," Justin commented. I could feel his probing glare burning at the back of my head. "Wonder what happened to him?" he pushed, clearly wanting me to answer.

"I don't know!" I shouted in a whisper.

"Don't get pissy with me. I'm just askin'," he retorted though it was obvious he thought I knew more.

Trying to keep my hands busy, I plucked random books from the shelves, flipped through them without absorbing anything, and shoved them back in place.

"What are you looking for?" Justin asked.

"I don't know," I replied honestly, squeezing the twelfth book carelessly in a space not meant for it.

Reaching for another, Justin placed his hand over my wrist.

"Angel, calm down," he ordered and I did, momentarily. "Breathe," he commanded and I did.

"What's going on?" he whispered. "Why did you want to come back here? Do you know what happened to him?"

"No," I defended myself, pulling the book I was reaching for off its black perch. Turning to face Justin, I leaned against the bookcase and began flipping through the book. Tucked midway through the pages was a piece of red paper. Tilting the book so Justin couldn't see the note, I opened it.

See what happens when you believe in yourself. Wishes do come true.

"Huh," I gasped and nearly choked on the air. Justin arched an eyebrow, looking at me like I lost it.

I peered around him and the bookcase he was leaning against to glimpse at Diego, who was reading "Metal Music" magazine behind the counter.

Although I tried to purge every memory from that horrible night, I suddenly remembered one integral detail.

Endlessly

I made a wish—one I knew would come true if I believed it strongly enough—to wipe the memories clean of this event from everyone.

"Oh my God!" I exclaimed in a hushed whisper.

"What?" Justin asked urgently.

"I did it!" I blinked in disbelief.

"Did what exactly?" he asked not following my train of thought. Then again, he couldn't know.

"Nothing," I smirked smugly, turning to face the bookcase so Justin couldn't see me. But I had done it.

Until now, every wish I made since the summer in Wales was nothing more than a hope—something I wanted and was genuinely surprised when it happened because I didn't really believe in my abilities. Diego was proof that I could make anything happen, if I believed it strongly enough. I never had to doubt myself again.

I did it without Sam's prompting, without CJ's support, and without the Bellatori's guidance. My energy, my power, and my wishes could work together to do whatever I needed them to do as long as I believed in myself.

Powerful energy pulsated in my palms and fingers. It danced in wild ecstasy at the revelation. I never wanted to be the damsel in distress again, and, now, I knew I didn't have to be. I just needed to know I had the strength within me. I finally, truly understood the meaning behind Sam's lesson, "Believe in yourself."

Slipping the note between my fingers, I shoved it into my pocket unnoticed as I placed the book back on the shelf where a black slip of paper I hadn't noticed before was sticking out between a couple of books.

While Justin busied himself by glaring at Diego, I opened the note. The impeccable white calligraphy issued a warning:

Many have sought the power. No one has ever found it...AND survived.

My heart stopped. What was I getting into? The Bellatori would protect me, wouldn't they? Then again, they were all about experiential learning, so maybe not.

"I'm ready to go," I said to Justin and walked toward the front door. I had to get out of Satan's Spot before the Bellatori revealed any other notes to me.

"Come again," Diego said obliviously from his seat on the back counter as we opened the front door.

"Goodbye," I replied, knowing I would never set foot in there again.

We stopped near Union Square for a bite to eat at an amazing Asian fusion restaurant. While Mike devoured his meal and Justin played with his, I contemplated the Bellatori's notes in distracted silence.

My wishes were powerful. My energy could devastate. What would happen if I found the Sun God's energy and was able to channel it? Would I be able to keep Justin and Gabe safe from me? Better yet, what would the Bellatori do with me or expect me to do once I became the unstoppable force they so desperately desired? Could I survive whatever was coming?

Moments ago I'd never felt so powerful and confident in my life. Suddenly, I felt like a minnow lost in a pool of sharks.

Chapter 13 – Mystery Meets Myth

Chills radiated along the length of my arms and legs. The closer our taxi got to Qoricancha, aka the Temple of the Sun, in Cuzco, Peru, the worse the butterflies tossed and turned in my stomach. The sound of my heart's stiff and hesitant beats pounded in my ears. Children's laughter, the tingling of bicycle bells, and street merchants negotiating with tourists melted into loud background noise though they were squeezing no more than a few feet past our car.

Shaking my head to get the noise out and focus on the hurricane building momentum in my guts, I covered my ears with my hands, closed my eyes, and leaned forward to block everything out.

"Problems?" Gabe asked.

I shook my head, though it was useless trying to hide it. "Just feeling weird."

"You're not gonna throw up are you?" he worried, and rightfully so since I was sandwiched between him and Justin in the back seat.

"No," I muttered and dropped my head between my knees. Both guys shifted away from me and closer to the doors.

"Qoricancha y Catedral de Santo Domingo," the driver announced as the car rolled to a stop along the brick paved walking paths criss-crossing the plaza toward the nearly five-hundred-year-old structures.

Justin hopped out of the car and shoved money into the driver's expectant hand through the front window. As I slid across the seat and stumbled out of the car, he caught my arm and helped me from my claustrophobic prison. The guys slung their backpacks over their shoulders and began recapping the day's agenda. I staggered along behind them, struggling to keep up.

"Angel, maybe you should go back to the hotel," Justin suggested. "You're not looking too hot."

"Thanks," I mumbled sarcastically. "Just go. I'll follow you."

His eyes narrowed in speculative concern but eventually shrugged giving into me. They started for the Cathedral of Santo Domingo. My legs walked behind them reluctantly, while my thoughts struggled to make sense of the unsettled feeling of me not wanting to be here at all. I'd been so excited about visiting Cuzco and the Temple of the Sun in particular. Now that I was here, part of me wished I was somewhere else.

However, the hesitance wasn't entirely in my head. An array of emotions battled inside me.

Fear. Pride. Joy. Power. More fear. War. It didn't feel supernatural. It seemed like I was picking up on the emotions of the people who had lived and died in the area over the millennia. There was more to this place than I realized.

Or maybe it was jet lag. Or maybe I was crazy. I don't know. I stopped trying to figure out the constant flow of thoughts and feelings running in and out of my head. The problem lay more in the fact that I was unable to truly see or appreciate the historic surroundings. I would've had the same amount of interest and awareness had I been sitting alone at a bus stop.

Justin and Gabe entered through the church's main door and waited for me to catch up.

I lifted my foot to cross the threshold when something stopped me mid-step. My foot couldn't touch down past the door. In fact, it felt like I'd run into an invisible glass wall. Using my hands to push my way inside, I banged into the unseen obstacle and knocked myself backward landing on my butt.

Justin and Gabe stood inside in astonished silence and exchanged skeptical glances.

Trying to ignore the stares and glares of other tourists, I jumped to my feet with only my ego bruised in total humiliation.

"Guess I'll just wait outside," I mumbled, avoiding the guys' questioning eyes.

Justin shook his head. "You sure?" he asked only out of courtesy as he inched a few steps further inside.

I nodded and hurried from the scene of my

latest idiocy. A couple times I glanced back wondering what would bar me from entering a church. It's not like I was evil. Maybe Kelly was right. Maybe I should've gone to church more often. Maybe God was pissed at me and wasn't letting me inside.

Oh please, a voice inside my head muttered in exasperation. I couldn't tell if it was CJ, the Bellatori, or my conscience, but I agreed with it, so I let it go.

Still reeling from my unsettled feelings and the odd encounter, I meandered aimlessly along the street toward the back of the church. Stopping alongside a rusty metal railing, I stared at the green, grassy expanse reaching from the church's smooth yet massive brownish-grey foundation stones across an empty field scattered with Incan ruins. Trapped between Spanish-style buildings with white washed façades and faded red clay roof tiles, the visible remnants of the end of one civilization were quite literally used as building blocks for another.

Lost in thought over the conquered Incas, I wondered about the similarities between their situation and that of humanity's today. Wealth and power meant nothing to Aeterna Flamma. If they set out to destroy you, nothing would stop them. Governments and soldiers were nothing more than games and plastic action figures. They stood no chance against fallen angels, vampires, and werewolves.

Suddenly my thoughts flooded with a vision of a black hurricane spinning around me through which multiple red and silver eyes glowed searching hungrily for me.

I swallowed. Swallowed hard. Focusing on individual blades of grass in the field, I forced my mind to sing the first song that popped into my head. Unfortunately for Aeterna Flamma, the song was "Ring Around the Rosie." Horrible choice it may have been, but it gave me a good distraction.

That was close. Too close. I couldn't have Aeterna Flamma find me here, when I was so far away from the Bellatori's protection. I had to keep them blocked out of my head at all costs.

The cheerful, clear blue sky and warm sun did nothing to pacify my fears. Deep breaths. My feet started walking again. With no specific destination in mind, they followed a brick path until I found the entrance into the grassy remnant of what once was the Temple of the Sun.

The field was empty. I probably shouldn't have been walking there, but I wanted to. For a second, I felt I was where I needed to be. Then, confusion set in again. Dragging my fingers across the seams between the ancient building blocks, which once made up a temple wall, I wandered aimlessly along the perimeter of the once holy site.

As I reached the steps leading from the lower level to the first terrace, a vise tightened around my waist drawing me back to the field.

"CJ?" I asked under my breath, completely baffled. The invisible energy pulling me back was frigid and the complete opposite of CJ's warm embraces.

Suddenly CJ's strong grip encircled my arms tugging me forward, but the freezing, evil feeling won the battle spinning me around, forcing me to walk in a diagonal path across the soft vivid green field.

CJ's presence fluttered around me but was no match for the force directing my every move.

My feet turned 90° abruptly to the right followed almost immediately by a 45° turn to the left. Stepping along the invisible path for about 30 paces, my feet came to an abrupt stop, did a quick side step as if avoiding something, and swiveled me around 180°.

As I continued along this bizarre route, the bustling sounds and sights of the modern world melted into a fuzzy grey vision. The massive walls of a long corridor comprised entirely of gold popped up out of the ground.

"Wow," I breathed in wide-eyed disbelief while I picked up the pace and started walking on my own, motivated by sheer amazement.

Countless gold bricks lined the hallway's floor each featuring an emboss of a sun with a myriad of overlapping wavy rays reaching from its center. The reality of the ruins faded away entirely into this surreal, dream-like world with its statically charged atmosphere and hazy, dream-like appearance.

The warm sun gleamed through narrow rectangular windows reflecting blindingly off of the shiny metallic walls illuminating the otherwise empty space. The hall was no more than five feet wide—I could easily touch both sides simultaneously—but it stretched seemingly infinitely overhead.

Heartbeats echoed strongly in my chest and I realized I was out of breath because I was nearly sprinting down the corridor. An uneasy feeling crept up along my spine. Forgotten yet familiar, it was identical to the fear that chased me through the labyrinth of tunnels beneath Wales last summer.

Though I tried to look back, the all-too-real vision pulled me forward.

A glimmer of sunlight shone brilliantly through the last window slit at the end of the hallway and illuminated a black hooded figure holding my hand and leading me. I lifted my hand and realized that the see-through hand being held wasn't actually mine though it felt like it was attached to me.

The figure turned to face me and lifted his hand to his lips motioning for me to be quiet.

The real me gasped as his eyes flashed crimson.

Like a million puzzle pieces rearranging themselves around me, the vision unhinged, speeding like tiny particles in a tornado, and matched together again. It revealed a new view. I was standing outside in front of thousands of people.

An endless sea of indigenous people—the Inca—were kneeling for as far as I could see. Each person wore a simple woven tunic held together with a bright yellow, red, and orange sash. Men, women, and children bowed on command and touched their heads to the ground remaining prostrate while someone spoke in a language I didn't understand.

Standing on an elevated platform in front of all the people, I searched the blurry vision for the voice's owner. A man, who I assumed to be the chief, delivered an impassioned speech to the perfectly still crowd. In contrast to his people, the chief's bright red-brown woven clothing and gold shoulder pads, gold chains, rings, bracelets and earrings clearly set him apart from the commoners. With purple and red paint marking their faces and armed with wooden spears some with gold or silver star shapes attached to them, the eyes of his soldiers glared stoically and dutifully at me as hundreds stood guard on either side of the people, who still faced the ground.

Pressure on my hand made me realize I wasn't alone in front of the massive crowd. Glancing down, my hand was being held safely and steadfastly by a strong, big grip. It calmed the fear and hesitation growing in my trembling body. Following the path from the hand to the forearm to the shoulder, I strained to see the face of my lone friend in this strange land, but the blazing sun directly overhead obscured his details. A glimpse of a kind smile was all I caught. He squeezed my hand again in reassurance and I turned to face the masses.

Clad in yellow sleeveless tunics tied with red sashes, a dozen or so young women with hip length jet black hair and smooth sun-kissed skin processed before us. Each held a basket of maize in an offering.

Something didn't feel right. Why were they treating us like royalty? We didn't belong here, yet they welcomed us openly. Part of me wondered if their reaction was out of acceptance or fear. The unsettled feeling in my stomach spread throughout my body instantly. Shaking uncontrollably, I swallowed hard trying to regain composure. I couldn't appear weak in front of these people. They expected more of me. What exactly or why? Of that I wasn't sure.

But I was weak. As the mid-day sun reached its apex overhead, I felt like I was going to sink into the ground. My limbs, my bones couldn't hold me any longer.

Leaning against my lone acquaintance, I

searched the crowd for the familiar face of the man who got me into this mess.

Kneeling and curled to the ground with his head down behind the row of statuesque maidens, the black cloaked figure raised his eyes momentarily to meet my pleading gaze.

Sensing my pain in a way that only he could, he jumped to his feet allowing the hood to fall to his shoulders.

Rick.

While he didn't look like Rick, his energy and presence were undeniable. I recognized his eyes instantly.

"Rick?" I yelled in twisted excitement. I should've been terrified, but I wasn't. He was the only person I knew here and I needed him even if he'd end up killing me any way.

An earth shattering boom of thunder and a flash of lightning in the distance erased the glorious warmth of the sun as grey-black clouds heavy with rain raced across the clear blue sky. The man by my side yanked me behind him in an act of protection.

Glancing around his broad shoulders in growing terror, I searched the crowd, but Rick was gone.

Hundreds of white angels plummeted from the sky encircling me and my partner. However, we weren't alone. Out of nowhere, Rick appeared beside me and pulled me into his side.

The pandemonium of screaming people rushing

from the Temple of the Sun faded into white noise as I became solely preoccupied by the horrifying scene immediately around me.

Two angels wrenched me from Rick's grip.

Rick's eyes flashed in vivid crimson as he roared and lunged at the angel holding my left arm. He ripped the golden head from its divine white perch streaking its pure, glowing white naked torso with black-red blood. The angel fell forward as five others pounced on Rick.

For a second he disappeared beneath a blanket of fluttering white feathers. Beyond them, the field was scattered with angels in hand-to-hand combat with the Incan soldiers. To my horror, hundreds of black werewolves—enormous half-human, half-wolf like creatures—encircled the battlefield. With one lone howl echoing in the distance and signaling their advance, they pounced into the fight laying bloody siege to the glorious white glow of the heavenly hosts.

A bone chilling growl of pain roared through the cover of feathers in front of me followed by a burst of black as Rick jumped up from the center of the attacking huddle. His cape's hood slipped backward revealing the almost sheer, ultra pale skin tone of his neck, which shone brilliantly against the golden brown curls of his tousled hair.

My mesmerized speechlessness turned to terror as he spun around to look at me. Thick rivers of black blood seeped from scratches and gouges in his ears, mouth, and neck.

In one seamless motion he pulled a sword from his cloak and swiped it around the circle of angels imprisoning him. In quick succession, the heads toppled like dominoes.

Stunned at the instantaneous turn of events and incapacitated, the headless, winged seraphs fell at Rick's feet.

Heaving in exhilaration and breathlessness, Rick glanced up in ferocious determination. His angry, crimson eyes burned into me. I should've been scared, but I was relieved.

Rick leapt over the almost dead angels whose arms searched blindly for their bodies' heads.

Without a word, Rick swept me into his arms beneath his cloak and muttered a strange rhyme in a language I didn't understand. All I knew was that as long as I was in his embrace, I was safe. Wrapping my arms around him and squeezing myself against his frozen body, I clutched him with all my might and tucked my head into his shoulder to avoid the death surrounding us.

The living nightmare of heaven's unleashed hell began to fade into a blur as we were sucked into a hurricane-like tunnel of wind.

Suddenly, two scorching hands grasped my arms and pulled my body back through the tunnel into the Incan temple.

Blindingly white, a swarm of angels fell upon Rick and trapped his arms behind him though he struggled against their inhuman strength.

"No!" I yelled in frightened alarm, though I wasn't sure what scared me more: Rick's capture, the half-dead angels at my feet, or lack of concern for my own safety.

Frozen in shock, an angel easily ensnared my other friend—the one who had held my hand to keep me grounded. His eyes met mine briefly, desperate but resigned, as another angel plunged a sword through his chest. Gasping for his last breaths, he collapsed to the ground. A stream of bright red blood began to pool around his body, inching its way toward my feet.

Mesmerized and calmed by the ocean blue glow of the remaining dozen angels' eyes as they approached me, I was completely unaware they had laid me on the platform until two of them pinned my arms and legs to it.

Rick's eyes darted around our surroundings seeking an escape.

Lifting a silver dagger high into a gleam of sunlight, the instrument of death delivered mine quickly and relatively painlessly.

My heart stuttered to a stop.

Leaving my side, the angels released Rick from his prison and vanished.

Rick dropped to his knees beside me and grabbed my limp hand. The fight in his eyes fought to focus on me and not the blood flowing freely from my chest. He shook in vampiric convulsions as the smell of blood overcame him.

"No!" he snarled, gaining his composure. "All the plans…not again," he muttered in agonized disappointment.

Plans? What plans? For whom? What was supposed to happen? Curiosity flooded my dying thoughts.

Feeling light as my soul slowly let go of my body, I pulled back into it one last time and stared into Rick's red eyes.

"Anchises?" I whispered, recognizing his true identity. In that minuscule micro second my mind was clear. I felt a smile spread across my face as my soul was wrenched from my body.

I embraced death.

Chapter 14 – Sanity Check

Everything felt heavy, like a ton of bricks were pushing on my arms and legs. Even shifting my head from side-to-side took the mighty strength of a god—strength that I didn't have.

Fluttering in a vain attempt to open, my eyelids blinked and my eyes rolled around trying to focus on a fixed object in the spinning room.

"Angel?" an anxious voice asked.

"Where am I?" I struggled to ask, giving up trying to pry my eyes open. At least I could hear.

"The hospital," the voice replied.

A rush of questions popped into my head, but I focused on the one I could actually ask. "Why?"

"You had a seizure," the voice explained calmly. Too calmly. A cold touch gently pressed against my right hand. "A few tourists managed to keep you from cracking your head open on the stone platform in the ruins and brought you here."

"Justin?" I asked as my mind started catching up with reality.

"Yeah?" he replied.

"Oh, ok," I sighed in relief. I trusted Justin to keep me safe. He had to, right? He and Gabe were the only people I knew in Peru. "How long?"

"It's been three days. The doctors thought it best to keep you in a coma until they could finish their tests to make sure you were ok."

"Am I?"

"They can't find any reason for what happened and you have no medical history of anything that could've led to it."

"History?" *Oh no.* "They called my mom?" I worried.

"Yeah," he replied simply. "I found her number on your cell."

"Is she ok?"

"She's fine. We talked her down from the proverbial ledge." I could hear a smile in his words. "I promised to call her with updates twice a day."

"I'm sorry."

"'Bout what?" he asked confused.

"Your research!" I felt like such a schmuck. My stupid experiences were keeping the guys from completing their schoolwork.

"Forget about it," he offered quietly, though a pregnant pause filled the void for a few moments.

"Listen," he started. "After the doctors clear you, we think it's best that you fly home..."

"No!" I interrupted.

I was on the verge of something here and wasn't about to abandon my own search for the Sun God's power and, more simply, finding myself. The vision was a clue to my past and, though my body felt like a truck had hit it, I was confident my presence here would give me the knowledge I needed to fight Aeterna Flamma.

"Angel, we can't take care of you. We're not doctors and we're not about to leave you alone in the hospital while we finish our last two weeks in the mountains."

"I wanna go," I argued like a belligerent four-year-old.

"Gabe is already making arrangements for you to fly back. Your mom will meet you at the connecting flight in Dallas and she'll take you back to San Francisco. Kelly, Uri, and Mike have scheduled round-the-clock nursing to keep an eye on you until your condition stabilizes."

"No!" I growled furiously, forcing my eyes open to glare at Justin who lurched back and away from me.

The bright fluorescent lights and stark white walls blinded me and I had to back down.

"I want to stay," I pressed ardently before

softening to the reality that everyone just wanted me to be safe. "I *need* to stay," I begged quietly, closing my eyes and laying back on the soft pillow.

"Why?" Justin asked. "This sight-seeing adventure is over for you. You haven't been norm…well," he thought of a more positive word choice, "since we arrived. It's just not worth risking your health and safety over a vacation."

"I have to," I muttered, wishing I could look in his eyes to convince him. Lacking the use of my eyes I felt shut off to the outside world, which truly scared me. Rick and Aeterna Flamma could be standing in the room for all I knew.

I had to tell Justin something, but what and how much?

I opened my eyes ever so slightly. "What do you think about psychics?"

"What?" he asked completely perplexed. "What kind of pain meds are they giving you?" he stood up to check my IV drip.

"Seriously," I urged. "What do you think about psychics?"

He settled back in his seat beside my bed. "They're bogus. What the hell does that have to do with you being here?"

"Bogus?" Any hope of getting him to understand my situation dissipated.

"It's easy to read people and assume things about them. They speak so generally, their crap can be applied to anyone. There's no hard scientific evidence proving they're real or right." He paused. "Again, what's this got to do with you?"

"Regardless of what you think, I'm psychic." It was the easiest way to explain my eccentricities.

"Like fortune telling and talking to dead people?" By the skeptical tone of his voice, he clearly thought I was crazy.

"No," I clarified defensively. "More like feeling things about places and people and seeing the past."

"I didn't realize there was more than one type," he mocked.

"There are," I fumed.

"Who cares?" he argued. "What does that have to do with you staying here?"

"Everything!" I yelled. "It explains why I've felt like I was going to throw up since we got here; why I couldn't step inside the damn church; and why a vision of me dying caused me to nearly die again. I'm not really sick. It's the stupid psychic crap in my head."

Justin sighed. "Did you ever consider that you're just losing your mind? Maybe some time in a psychiatric ward will do you good."

"Or maybe I'm right and the rest of the world is insane," I sneered, realizing too late that this sounded absolutely ridiculous. "Please, Justin. I have to stay. I'm here for a reason. Whatever lies between the Temple of the Sun and Machu Picchu is something I need to find. I have to find it. My life depends on it."

Justin's breath caught. *Major oops!* I shouldn't have said the last part.

"Your *life* depends on it?" he repeated in disbelief. "Are you trying to find the Incan treasure? Is that why you're here? That, at least, would make sense."

"Justin," I said softly trying to pacify him, "you go to a physical school. You can touch it and sit in it and you have teachers to explain things to you. As weird as this sounds, my school is the world. It's nothing like yours, but we're both learning. I can't leave Peru until I figure out why I'm here and why I need to be here. Please, please," I begged genuinely, "let me stay."

He took a deep breath and stared out of the window trying to make up his mind. "If one more thing happens—anything that even remotely puts you in jeopardy—you're outta here. Got that?" he threatened.

My mom was not happy. For that matter, neither was Kelly. Both of them were worried and couldn't understand why I'd want to risk staying in a country so far from home.

Smiling smugly to myself, Justin shook his head in exasperated worry, but he gave up arguing with me about the decision. He and Gabe needed to catch up on missed schoolwork and I was intent on helping, not hindering, them any more than I already had.

The next leg of the trip took me out of my comfort zone as we prepared to hike to Machu Picchu. The guys wanted to study the forests in search of untouched ruins that might give them a better glimpse into the composition of the area's geology and energy.

Since our arrival, my own energy felt entirely depleted. Endless cups of coffee and soda jump-started me every couple of hours throughout the day. Unfortunately, I was relatively worthless otherwise.

Our first stop was at a campsite near Cusichaca. Located just beyond a small patch of ancient ruins marking the beginning of the Inca Trail, it sat nestled between the rushing Urubamba River and the massive snow-capped peaks of the Andes. The main building, where hikers gathered before making their way into the mountains, was a simple one level home with a coral stucco exterior and a matching ten foot wall surrounding the perimeter. The wall seemed out of place in such a remote location. Then again, maybe it was to keep out the wildlife.

Nearby, the roaring river cut through the Urubamba Valley filled with dry brown-green grassy hillsides and dotted with meager, straw-thatched roof huts. Chickens ran free in the village's main—and only—street while a herd of Alpaca grazed on the rolling hills behind the homes.

San Francisco, this was not. Loving its simplicity, I smiled to myself. Justin had been right. It was good to get away from the city and, more importantly, my reality.

The next morning Gabe and Justin interviewed the locals working at this rest station, and I decided to take advantage of their preoccupation by going for a morning walk along the edge of the meandering river. Its loud rush and the teeming white bubbles hiding what lay beneath hypnotized me to everything in the outside world. I was lost to my thoughts of this life and the past.

"Pretty isn't it?" an unexpected voice asked.

Startled, I jumped backward and lost my footing as the soil and gravel along the embankment gave way. My hands clung desperately to the sharp grey rocks jutting out of the compacted dark red dirt while my feet scraped against the steep river wall struggling to find their footing a few yards above the speeding waterway.

The stranger grabbed my forearm and pulled me back to safety.

"Sorry, I didn't mean to scare you," she offered kindly.

Gathering my composure, I turned to face my hero.

Shoulder-length black hair framed her petite, frail, and very pretty dark tanned features. Deep black eyes seemed to wisely and instantly assess everything about me.

"Uh, don't worry about it. I didn't hear you walk over," I muttered quickly. "And, yes, it's beautiful," I said, turning to face its simple and powerful splendor.

"I come here every morning," she began, also facing the river, "to be reminded of my place in the world. It's humbling."

'to be reminded of my place in the world.'

She perfectly captured what I'd been feeling. We're each important and yet seemingly insignificant all at once.

"Very true," I nodded.

"Hi," she smiled, "My name is Tica."

I happily returned her contagious smile. "I'm Angel," I said, shaking her hand. "Are you visiting Machu Picchu too?"

She grinned. "No. I work here."

"Doing what?" I blurted before realizing this sounded incredibly rude.

"I'm a doctor."

"Doctor?" I asked confused. She looked no more than 21 and at less than five feet tall, I would've guessed even younger.

"Yes. I received my degree in America and came back to help my people," she said proudly.

My gaze shifted from my newfound friend to the poor, rundown camp-motel of sorts in the distance behind her.

"It may not be a glorious hospital, but I know I'm making a difference here. The locals and visitors count on me."

I nodded and smiled in response to her beaming grin. Everything about her exuded sheer happiness.

"I came to make sure you're feeling well. Your friends mentioned your recent condition in Qoricancha," she said politely in a light Latino accent.

"Oh, I'm fine," I replied curtly. I hated being doted on or worried about.

"Would you like a cup of coffee?" she offered sweetly.

"Sure," I shrugged. It was 7 a.m., and I only downed three cups so far. My heart was racing a million miles per minute, but my body couldn't seem to wake up.

Tica and I enjoyed a light conversation about local life as she guided me back to camp where Justin and Gabe were packing up the last of their gear.

"Got some great information, Angel," Justin said surprisingly cheerfully. "We may have found a fairly good lead."

Gabe scoffed. "Yeah, a *lead* that *may* cross paths with chupacabras."

"Chupa-what?" I asked.

Tica shuddered. "Chupacabra. It's a hairless, wolf-like creature that drinks the blood of animals. Many think they are myth and think the locals are crazy."

She looked around to make sure no one was looking and whispered, "The villagers see the creatures steal their animals at night. They find what's left of the bodies there." She pointed toward the serene hillsides behind the village.

"If people have seen them, why is their existence in doubt?" I asked matter-of-factly.

"Science hasn't proven they exist and who is more likely to be believed—an uneducated farmer or a Harvard scholar?" Tica asked bitterly.

"What are they?"

"No one knows," she shrugged. "They seem to be both wild dog and vampire bat. They have the body of a wolf, red eyes, fangs, and claws. Some people say they have wings."

Red eyes? Sounded like another breed of vampires to me. Maybe this is what CJ referred to when he explained that there was more than one kind of vampire. He mentioned the Aeterna Flamma vampires were nothing compared to the others. If this was true, how would the three of us survive against even one of them? What did I get Justin and Gabe into?

"Doc, you forgot the best part," Gabe interjected before turning to me. "They're six to eight feet tall and drain their victims' blood completely," he winked playfully at me.

I smirked. "Very funny, Gabe."

"I'm serious," he said, shoving his notepad and pen into the front pocket of his hiking backpack.

I turned to Tica for verification. She nodded.

"Great," I muttered sarcastically. "Anything else we should be worried about before we head out…alone…into the mountains?"

"Pumas, bats, condors, about twenty venomous snakes…" she answered honestly.

"Thanks," Justin interrupted. "She's already afraid of spiders. Don't need to scare her anymore."

"Spiders?" I worried as a grossed-out chill ran through my body.

Taking a cue from the guys, who tossed their camping gear over their shoulders, I reached both arms through the straps of my survival pack and adjusted it on my back.

"Beware," Tica began forebodingly. The room instantly transformed with a creepy feeling. "The mountains are the homes of the spirit gods. I'm sure they," she glanced at some of the locals clearing dining tables nearby, "spoke of other paths. Stay on the main hiking trail and stay together."

Chapter 15 – The Hunt

Before long the deafening rush of the river by the campsite faded into the background and we reached our hiking goal by sundown. The rocky terrain of the valley's floor gave way to a dense forest and brush. Focusing on Justin's back as he led the way, I tried to ignore every unfamiliar sound echoing around us and squeezed my eyes shut at the sweeping, split-second movement of shadows caught out of the corners of my eyes.

The guys cleared the camp area and had a roaring—yet safe—fire burning in no time at all. They also had a good laugh at my expense as the tent collapsed on top of me in my first of three attempts at setting it up. Granted, I refused to let them help me. I was determined to do it on my own. And, I'm proud to say, I did!

If nothing else, this trip helped me realize I was a city girl. I needed the amenities of civilization—a private bathroom instead of a grove of trees while being assaulted by a bevy of large unidentifiable insects; a soft bed and pillow instead of a sleeping bag sandwiched between two snoring guys; and running water. Oh, how I missed my shower! Never again will I take it for granted.

Day two consisted of off-the-beaten-path excursions. Thankfully, my nagging and the reminder of Tica's warning convinced the guys to touch base with the main trail periodically throughout the day. They constantly analyzed their Electromagnetic Field and Life Energy Field meters, took extensive notes on the plants and animals, and debated how the changes at different heights above sea level affected the energy and growth in the area.

Other than the fact that the area was growing colder the higher we climbed the mountainside, I was pretty oblivious to everything else other than trying to keep from getting attacked by bugs and snakes. Ravenous chupacabras haunted my thoughts. Imagining them to be a mutation of vampires, I figured they would be less terrifying than Hadrianus' human-vampire form covered in visible veins pulsating with black blood.

Deep breaths, I thought to myself as I began to hyperventilate at the thought of Rick and CJ's freakish immortal—though now dead—father carving the crescent moon into my forearm with his dagger-like fingernail.

With my thoughts sufficiently distracted by the creepy crawlies around us (real and imagined), we reached the end of day two in no time at all. And again, I wished for a bed of my own when Gabe rolled over and pinned me beneath his shoulder. Justin's reverberating snores kept me wide-awake most of the night. My only solace was in the consistent, albeit weird sounds emanating from my friends, which would surely scare the strangest creatures lurking in the night.

"God, you look like crap," Justin commented in the morning as I emerged from the tent at dawn to find the guys gulping coffee over a crackling blaze.

"No thanks to you," I muttered still half asleep and plopped beside him.

I pulled my pale blue fleece blanket with clouds tightly around my shoulders in a useless effort to keep out the early morning mist and freeze. Despite my thermal leggings layered with jeans, a long sleeved top, and winter wool sweater, I still felt about as warm had I been wearing a bikini on a ski slope.

"So, what do you think?" Gabe asked Justin, ignoring my intrusion as I yawned. "That's twice as much coverage as yesterday without giving us the chance to analyze the energy fields. They're growing around us, you know," he said to Justin, raising his eyebrows to convey his sincerity. "However, if we push too hard to get to the summit, we risk missing something."

Gabe glanced at me quickly before focusing a little too intently on his coffee.

"Are you sick of me?" I yawned again, negating the angry tone of my question.

"No," Gabe lied.

My glare had him backtracking.

"Come on, Angel. It's clear that you're still sick," he said, motioning to the campsite and frigid, foggy wooded landscape around us.

"I can deal with another two days. Let's just

go," I yawned again, but stood up to show them I meant it.

Gabe stared intently at Justin letting him make the final decision.

"We take our time, Gabe. There's too much at stake," Justin said seriously. "Can't fail this class dude," he added before smiling at me reluctantly.

Mid-day and mid-way through our hike, Gabe decided to go off on his own. "Not too far," he promised. For whatever reason, Justin stupidly agreed despite my pleas.

Justin and I sat on a fallen tree and decided to share a mixed bag of Inka Chips.

"Am I holding you guys back?" I asked honestly, staring at the speckles of seasoning lining the sweet potato chip.

"We're fine," Justin assured, taking a very small bite of a corn chip.

"What about Gabe?" I worried.

"What about him?" he asked, staring at the limited chip options inside the plastic bag.

"Come on," I whined. "You know he thinks I'm the biggest idiot ever!"

Justin turned to face me. "Angel, he has a goal in mind and knows what he wants to accomplish. It's not you. He's always like this when he has work to do. When you put your mind to something, you don't let anyone stop you either."

He had a point.

"Are you guys gonna fail because of me?" I thought aloud still staring at the reddish-orange chip, which was the only bright spot in the otherwise brown and green hues around us.

"No," Justin said emphatically.

I nodded, not believing him entirely. Sensing my unease, he wrapped his arm around me.

"Angel," he began.

I looked into his eyes waiting to hear his explanation.

And then something happened. Something completely unexpected, but something I should've seen coming.

He wasn't just Justin. He felt comfortable, like I'd known him forever. A small part of me leapt for joy. I hadn't felt this iota of true infatuation in a long time. It felt deeper than the Diego thing, certainly nothing like CJ, but it was a spark of something.

Feeling that same flicker, Justin looked at me, pulled back, and dropped his arm. He stared at a row of unusually large red ants marching a few feet in front of us.

"Angel," he started again, composing himself, "we invited you along. Yes, we're working, but you've been great so far. You've barely complained," he grinned. "And, this was supposed to be vacation for you," he reminded me, nudging my arm, "a vacation spent almost entirely in a hospital and wandering around the wilderness. It didn't quite turn out the way I planned."

"Why? What were you planning?" I raised my

eyebrows curiously.

"Don't get your hopes up," he laughed. "Nothing special. I just wanted to get you away from SF. You seemed so depressed."

"Really?" I thought I'd done a fairly good job lately of keeping my sad CJ-related feelings and those regarding Sam and the others locked away in my head. Then again, the fallout from the Diego situation and the Bellatori's "lessons" were taking a toll on me. My neck and shoulders were constantly cramping with knots.

"Come on. I want to make you happy, not force you to dwell on the past," Justin continued.

He stood and offered his hand to help me up. An icy blast of air raced through the trees. It was a good thing we were bundled up in layers. The wind chilled me to the bone and a shiver shot through my body.

"Aren't you cold?" I asked Justin.

"Nope. Toasty," he smiled, rubbing his gloved hands together.

I scowled.

"Are you really able to track energy lines here?" I asked as we began packing our gear again.

He nodded. "The problem is that we're trying to find the main ley line. All of the lines are straight, but lesser lines intersect with each other making it damn difficult to find the one we need. The energy fields are like massive grids."

"How does that tie into the alternative therapies you're studying?"

"Gabe and I hypothesize that certain plants grow along the main ley line, which can't be found elsewhere. Those may hold the secrets to finding the cure for diseases like cancer and AIDS. Think about it," he said, shoving my blanket into his backpack, "The witch doctors and shamans who've lived here for thousands of years healed local people with plants they found in the wilderness. They might not have known how special their finds truly were."

"Jay!" Gabe's terrified scream echoed through the trees.

We immediately turned toward the sound of breaking branches and rustling brush.

"Jay!" he screamed again only to be drowned out by the roar of a wild animal, one that was apparently in hot pursuit.

Gabe flew into view. As he stopped beside us, the swift footsteps following him halted as well.

"What is it?" Justin asked alarmed.

"Mountain…lion…" Gabe answered between gasps of breath.

With our backs touching each other's and our eyes providing a 360° view of the dense vegetation encircling us, we huddled together in a tight triangle.

Less than ten feet in front of me, a pale golden puma emerged from the bushes. Head low, shoulders hunched, she stalked us in a horizontal line looking for the best angle to attack.

My heart raced in terror.

Did I or did I not fight and win against the strongest beings alive—or dead as the case might be? The thought jumped into my mind. This was an animal and far easier to overcome than vampires or werewolves.

A false sense of confidence overrode rational thinking. I felt too weak to fight her off physically, but there was another way. I waited for the mountain lion to catch my eye and when she did, I made my move.

Standing tall to show her I was in charge, though she easily weighed as much as me, I stared intently into her eyes.

Not sure of what to think, I focused on calming her by telling her through our eye contact there was nothing to fear and that Gabe was sorry for being an idiot and wandering into her territory in the first place.

The mountain forest fell completely silent. My peripheral vision faded away so all my energy and attention centered on the animal's intelligent eyes.

After an eternal minute, she backed away and slipped silently into the dense cover of trees and bushes.

"Where is she?" Gabe worried frantically, searching the surroundings with his eyes and listening for the slightest sound.

"How'd ya get her to do that?" Justin assumed astutely, relaxing his vigilant stance.

Nervous she might pounce on us anyway, I kept my eyes on the area where she disappeared.

"I told her to," I mumbled, reaching for my backpack.

"You told her to?" Justin reiterated in disbelief.

"Survival 101," I said arrogantly, "make eye contact and show 'em who's boss."

"No offense, but who is going to believe you're their boss at five feet three inches," he mocked. "That was a huge cat."

"Just a cat," I replied nonchalantly.

I wasn't about to tell him that I had a heavy dose of help from my magical powers—so-to-speak. I'm sure it wasn't so much dumb luck as it was my connection as Artemis, the Goddess of the Moon *and* Hunt, to the animal that saved us. Either way, we were safe now.

Waiting for the cat to return, Gabe spun around brandishing a branch, fear plainly painted across his face and quivering body.

"She's not coming back," I said smugly, brushing past him to reach the trail.

Embarrassed, Gabe dropped the gnarled stick and straightened out of his defensive stance. Ignoring my remark, he mumbled, "Let's go," as he rushed ahead of Justin and me angrily.

The air was thin and freezing at our third encampment later that night. Though the massive and dense trees blocked the sky from sight, the moon's strong glow filtered through the leaves and branches lightly illuminating the three of us in a freakish blue-green hue.

Endlessly

With only my cheeks and nose exposed through my coat's hood, the wind's biting cold numbed my face as my shivering hand tried to shove a spoonful of canned barbecued baked beans into my frozen mouth.

The guys were in no better shape. After a couple of cups of coffee to warm us up, we climbed into the tent figuring our sleeping bags and huddled body warmth would keep us from dying of hypothermia.

Of course, not long after the guys' snoring had eased into a regular rhythm, I had to go to the bathroom. Climbing out from my spot quietly and gently, I unzipped the tent just enough to creep through the opening. Gabe grunted once and rolled over in response to the cold breeze, which blew inside and smacked his back.

Thankfully, I wore my boots and coat into bed, so I was fully dressed and as warm as I could possibly be. Not following any particular direction, I walked into the dark woods trying to find a little clearing that was far enough away from camp without being too far.

Afterwards, as I meandered through the brush and avoided knocking myself out in the tree trunks on my way back to camp, I realized that I felt alive. I felt more awake now than I did any day since we arrived.

Perhaps it wasn't so much 'alive' per se as it was that I had energy—energy that I suddenly wanted to use. With a quick about face from the tent, I made my way into the forest again looking for a clearing.

Of course, it being the wilderness, clearings weren't exactly commonplace. With my legs growing tired, I rested against the wide trunk of a huge tree to catch my breath.

Leaves rustled overhead. Not feeling a breeze, I glanced up wondering and worrying what kind of nocturnal animal would climb trees at night. The rustling stopped and I wrote it off to my overactive imagination.

Not a second later, the tree trunk shook violently and I plummeted through a blindingly dark doorway into blackness.

Chapter 16 – Rabbit Hole

Grasping desperately at the tree roots—or what I hoped were tree roots—and the rocky patches of soil surrounding me in the narrow tunnel beneath the tree, I managed to slow my fall enough to keep from breaking anything as I finally crashed onto my hands and knees.

Growling angrily, I stood, swept my disheveled hair out of my face, and stomped my foot like a petulant two-year-old.

"Are you kidding me?" I yelled out of sheer frustration into the empty blackness of my surroundings. "How many freakin' rabbit holes am I gonna fall through for you?" I grumbled at the Bellatori.

"Adam?" I asked aloud, waiting for him to show up before I realized my keychain was in my backpack inside the nice, warm tent.

"Great," I mumbled sarcastically.

The space was pitch black. I couldn't even see the tunnel which led me here.

"Now what?" I asked of no one.

Light. My wand would've been useful right about now. It provided a nice little beacon when CJ and I crashed into the ancient underground temple in Sam's backyard. Unfortunately, it was either lost somewhere in Scotland or Aeterna Flamma got their grubby fingers on it last summer when they kidnapped us.

I hadn't tried using my wish-making abilities in awhile and I was feeling potent tonight. Maybe I could get it to work.

"Give me light," I ordered pathetically not really believing myself.

Of course, nothing happened.

"Light, please?" I asked awkwardly.

Nothing.

Closing my eyes, I let the surroundings seep into my senses. Capturing the growing fear of the unknown and an anxiety which was beginning to squeeze my stomach in knots, the emotions overrode all normal, self-conscious thinking.

"Please," I begged, "Please God, Mother Moon, Creator, whoever is in charge up there, please let me see."

Biting my lip and clenching my fists nervously, the anxious energy began to escalate into a panic attack.

"I want to see. I need to see. Please, help me see," I begged again as my heart raced into a full scale sprint.

Raising my eyelids one at a time, all I saw was blackness.

"Fine," I said bitterly and dropped to the cold, dark floor.

Breathe—in one, two; out one, two.

Breathe—in one, two; out one, two.

Breathe—in one, two; out one, two.

Breathe—in one, two; out one, two.

Breathe—in one, two; out one, two.

Focusing on breathing always kept me grounded and allowed me to quiet my thoughts. As I contemplated how I'd get out of this latest predicament, my surroundings faded into view.

"Wow!" I whispered. "Thanks!" I exclaimed happily to the higher power.

There was no light source in the ten foot by fifteen foot cave, but the space was about as bright as a bedroom lit with a nightlight at midnight. Apparently my eyes were equipped with night vision, temporarily anyway.

Directly in front of me, there seemed to be another tunnel leading away from the room. I decided to investigate. It was better than staying in one spot waiting for help that may never come. Not to mention, I couldn't get out the way I dropped in.

A cold gust of wind shot through the black entryway.

Instantly, fear froze my feet in place. I

contemplated walking into the unknown versus climbing back up into the hole.

Another gush of frigid air smacked the back of my head as if someone was breathing on me. Even if I wanted them to, my feet refused to move. Another gust deliberately hit the same spot five seconds later. It couldn't have been a breeze because I was too far underground and, judging from the amount of wind, it was too big to come from a human.

Petrified, I sucked in a breath of courage and slowly turned to face my Peruvian cave companion.

There was nothing there. My hands reached out into the empty space, trying to grope for the breeze's source. All it found was cold space. Though I couldn't see another person, I could feel a presence. It felt like a body was standing next to me; the energy was palpable.

"Ok," I said to the nothingness. "I know someone is here with me. You don't happen to know how we can get out of here, do you? I mean, if you're not gonna show yourself to me, can you at least show me the way out?"

I waited a few moments and felt a strong, ice cold breeze rush past me and disappear through the back wall of the cave.

Stepping over to the location, I pushed on the wall and it opened into another tunnel.

The smell of the dank, dark space was akin to the aroma of redwoods, evergreens, and dry, dusty dirt along a hiking trail through Muir Woods outside of San Francisco.

Like a roller coaster tossing and turning while you keep your eyes closed hoping you're not going to die, I ran, jumped, slid down passages and leapt over chasms. Before too long, my path narrowed and I hit a dead end.

The air here was cold—a not-normal type of cold. My breath nearly froze as I exhaled.

"Now what?" I asked impatiently of whatever spirit was guiding me.

Things aren't always what they seem, the voice in my head whispered.

"Not what they seem, huh?" I repeated, running my hands along the walls. It all felt like hard, caked dirt to me.

I pushed. I shoved. I threw my body against one of the walls. Nothing worked. Taking a step back to look at the dirt walls creeping with tree roots, crawling black bugs, and worms, I brushed loose strands of hair from my face and huffed in frustration as I crossed my arms over my chest.

"You don't happen to have a key do you?" I grumbled.

With my hands on my hips, I turned around the room again wondering if I missed anything. Staring straight ahead, a movement in the wall caught my eye. Curious, I crept up to it.

Something long, thin and smooth pushed its way through the dirt.

"Snake!" I screamed.

The *snake* looped around itself and dug its way

back into the wall before becoming rigidly still. Fearing it might jump out at me, I stepped toward it very cautiously.

Not believing I was about to actually touch it, I extended my finger and poked it quickly. Nothing happened. Emboldened by this test, I stroked it lightly. Its texture resembled tree bark not smooth snake skin. Looking closer, the thing wasn't a snake at all. It was just a stem of a tree root.

"Here we go," I breathed as I reached my fingers through the natural door handle and pulled as hard I could.

A doorway inched open revealing the most spectacular sight I had ever seen. From my dirty underground precipice hidden inside the mountain wall, I stared across the valley far below at the nearly full moon illuminating the ruins of Machu Picchu perched majestically on the facing mountain top. The cool, lunar glow reflected an unearthly diamond-like sparkle in the decrepit, tumbling walls.

With a clear night sky and endless stars and galaxies lighting the navy-black heavens, the view made me forget all of my cares.

Though heights didn't normally freak me out, my palms began to sweat and my knees felt wobbly when I glanced past my toes into the Andean valley thousands of feet below. Stepping back into the tunnel, I sank to the floor and admired the beauty of the once powerful city's remnants in midnight's silence.

Imagining the walls rebuilding themselves, I visualized what the temples and homes once looked like. Such a glorious fortress was not only beautiful but a testament to human will. Who on earth with a clear mind would decide to drag building materials to the top peaks of the world and live there?

Crazy though they may have been, it was hard not to be grateful for their vision to live with the gods eight thousand feet above sea level.

In seeing the ruins my thoughts raced back to the Temple of the Sun in Cuzco. Either I had a vision of my past or I let Rick into my thoughts. If it was the former, I needed to be careful when I envisioned moments from long ago. Witnessing a past death nearly led to one in this life. If it was the latter, my situation was far more horrifying. Could Rick and his crew really kill me through my memories? Is this why CJ and Cynan taught me to protect my thoughts and block out Aeterna Flamma and the Bellatori?

The other puzzling component to the daydream was the man standing next to me on the podium facing the crowd. Though I didn't see his face and all I caught was a cloudy glimpse of his eyes, I had no doubt he was someone I knew now. But who?

He felt like a brother. But which of my brothers? Was it one of my blood brothers or one of my Bellatori protectors?

An image of my friends popped into my head. I missed them so much. Mark's pigheadedness. Matt's kindness. Sam's rash judgment. Cynan's thoughtfulness and warrior skills. Morgan's scary tendencies and wise advice. As different as we were, I needed them. They were my friends—the only friends with whom I could be completely honest. We were united by this supernatural war—a war brought on because of one man I loved and one I hated.

CJ was easy to figure out. The love between us overlooked our mistakes and shortcomings. Rick was complicated. His sole goal was to capture me for Aeterna Flamma, but he saved me from certain death at the hands of Hadrianus. And, more importantly, Rick didn't *feel* evil to me. Hadrianus' cold, heartless energy sent shivers down my spine even now. Rick lacked that cruelty. But why?

"Thinking of me again?" Rick's voice asked.

Gasping, I spun around but didn't see him.

"Show yourself!" I demanded.

"Close your eyes," he ordered calmly. His velvety voice echoed softly in my ears.

Reluctantly, I slid my eyelids shut and there he was leaning against the wall, sitting no more than five feet away from me.

Surprised, I lurched backwards into the wall and opened my eyes. He was gone. Closing my eyes, he was there again, waiting patiently, smiling seductively.

"Am I hallucinating?"

"No. You're seeing me in your mind's eye," he replied.

"Mind's eye?"

"Psychic awareness. I'm not here physically, but our connection is deep and real. Don't you speak to your dad this way?"

I sucked in a quick breath to stop the painful stream of thoughts. "I try not to think of him."

"Why not?" he asked surprised and truly concerned.

"Hurts too much, ok?" I snapped.

I was Daddy's little girl. He was my protector and my guide for seventeen years. When he was around, I had no reason to fear anything. Now that he was dead and gone, I had no idea where he was or how to reach him.

"What do you want?" I commanded, forcing myself to change subjects.

"Me? *You* were thinking about *me*," he retorted. He paused and curiously asked, "Why?" sounding a bit surprised.

I exhaled in exasperation. "Trying to figure you out."

He smirked. In the safety of the cave, the dark brown hair and pale skin of my vampire stalker appeared nearly sinister. But his clear, emerald eyes were kind and hypnotizing.

"Keep trying," he encouraged. "The more you think of me, the closer I get."

With a false sense of security in my secluded hideout high above the Andes Mountains, I wasn't entirely worried about Rick's threat.

I just stared at him absorbing every detail of his features. The monochromatic hue of his black shirt and pants was broken by a simple rectangular silver belt buckle. The top two buttons of his loose shirt hung open revealing a silver chain and pendant featuring none other than Artemis' moon symbol.

Endlessly

His brilliant smile brightened the room.

Avoiding the infatuated stutter of my heart, I gazed at the awe inspiring moonlit Machu Picchu.

"How long?"

"Until what?" he asked.

I glanced back at him arching my eyebrows. I didn't want him to play coy; he knew what I meant.

"It won't be long," he replied, shifting his eyes from me to the mountains. "We'll retrieve you soon. Keeping me from your thoughts won't keep us from finding you."

A shiver shot down my spine.

He grinned menacingly.

"Will there be another battle?" I asked weakly as my heart and courage slipped into my toes.

"As long as you are alive, it's a distinct possibility," he replied as he shoved his hands into his pockets.

And before I could think it through, I wished for it.

Why? Because it would reunite me with my friends. This hallucination of Rick warmed my heart. Though his intentions may not have been honorable, he belonged to that world of surreal insanity where I wished to be. Besides, I knew he wouldn't hurt me. I don't know how I knew that, I just did.

"Where are you right now?" I asked him.

"With the Bellatori."

That was comforting. The Bellatori imprisoned him after the last battle. As long as he was still there, his threats were nothing more than empty words trying to scare me. "You see, they may be able to manipulate us, but they can't control our thoughts…our choices."

He sighed.

"So, when are you coming back for me, Artemis?" his voice asked softly, but his eyes begged.

"Why should I? You got us into this mess!"

"I saved you," he reminded me politely.

"Yeah, right before you tried to kidnap me," I barked sarcastically.

"I'm not here to fight with you," he said softly. "I miss you and clearly you miss me too otherwise we wouldn't be having this conversation."

"Enough," I said definitively, shaking my head.

His lips curled into an evil smirk.

My heart skipped a beat. *Damn it!* Why couldn't I control myself?

"You know it's true," he grinned.

Our eyes locked. In that moment, the static electricity that painfully attacked us each time we touched reignited and bound us together like a tightly wound rope encircling me and my vampire.

Lost in his mesmerizing green gaze, he pulled me closer and closer and closer until my nose was only an inch from his.

I swallowed hard. This was so wrong on so many levels. Yet, I couldn't help myself.

Endlessly

Actually, in all honesty, I didn't want to help myself.

Rick snapped his head toward the moon as if in response to something I missed.

"You need to go now," he urged, breaking the spell he had over me.

My face fell in regret for not having better spent our time and conversation.

Reaching for my hand, he lifted it gently and kissed it, sending cold shockwaves of energy throughout my body.

"Mmmm. Dirt flavor," he quipped, scrunching his Greek-god-like nose and smiling mischievously.

"Shut up," I growled and yanked my hand away from his frigid grasp. Unfortunately, he was right. I needed to find running water soon. My fingernails were caked with dirt from my fall and I'm sure the rest of me looked a lot worse.

"Until we meet again," he grinned slyly and faded from my thoughts.

"Not likely," I shouted out loud bitterly, but I already missed him. Or, more accurately, I missed the ties to my supernatural reality.

"Why am I so messed up?" I growled into the cold night air as I stood up and brushed off my jacket.

The glorious sight of Machu Picchu was now tinged with a sense of depressed hopelessness. Like the fortress at the edge of the earth, I was lost and didn't quite fit in anywhere.

A howl pierced the night air.

My breath caught. That sound was a little too familiar and a little too close for comfort.

It wasn't just any howl. It was a howl that haunted my daydreams and nightmares alike. Shooting a painful charge of terror through my body, memories of my narrow escapes suffocated any ounce of rational thinking.

My head instantly turned toward the sound as a chorus of others responded. Glancing over the precipice, hundreds of speeding ruby red and silver eyes glowed throughout the mountain range beneath the ruins.

Chapter 17 – Midnight Moon

"Oh my God!" I gasped, suddenly realizing my safe haven was a prison without an escape. They were here. They were tracking me. They knew where I was.

"Stupid, stupid, stupid!" I grumbled at myself while I crawled quietly up through the tunnel and into the cavern that led to the labyrinth, which brought me here.

"Now what?"

I didn't have time to lose and I had no idea how to get out of here.

My thoughts flashed to a prayer I had said as a child long ago.

Angel of God, my guardian dear
To whom God's love commits me here

𝔈𝔫𝔡𝔩𝔢𝔰𝔰𝔩𝔶

Ever this day, be at my side
To light and guard, to rule and guide. Amen.

"Guardians, if you can hear me now. Help! Show me the way. Pleeeeeease!"

Very slowly and subtly, the anxiety and terror faded away. My mind quieted. My body relaxed.

I turned around to face one of the five tunnel openings and started walking towards it. The further I went, the surer I felt in my gut that it was the right way. I let go of the gnawing hesitance in my reason-filled thoughts and trusted my instincts.

Thanks to the dirt path, my footsteps' echo remained muted as I fled across the empty trail.

"Take me back to my friends, please," I asked my angels, though my survival instincts and their guidance were telling me to go the other way.

My feet hesitated for a second and then took a step through a wall and into another tunnel.

Unlike the others, this path was cramped and damp.

Drip. Drop. Drip. Drop.

Droplets of dirty water smacked my face and ricocheted off of my jacket as I squeezed my way along the footpath.

Stepping into an opening that was big enough to fit only me, I reached the very end of the tunnel, but it was still dark and I was still underground.

Scratching sounds echoed overhead.

Instinctually, I glanced up toward the source of the sound, only to have pieces of dirt and dust cascade over my face.

Muffling my coughs, I realized that my tunnel walkway came to an end, but the uphill climb was about to begin.

Foot-by-foot, I clawed my way upwards. My fingers dug into the hard soil, giving me just enough leverage to prop my legs against the tight walls around me. Digging, scraping, shimmying, my body followed my mind's thoughts. At present, the only thing that mattered was getting out of here so I could help Justin and Gabe.

Pulling myself through the last few feet of the tunnel, I lurched my body forward and fell through the tree trunk's doorway.

On the forest floor's cold hard ground, I lay, gasping to catch a breath of fresh air.

"Angel!" Justin's frantic voice carried on the freezing night wind.

"No!" I shouted under breath. He'd surely lead the vampires and werewolves to us straight away.

Somehow, my feet managed to stand up, though my body was having a tough time giving them the will to move forward. With my night vision still intact, I peered through the black forest and began running frantically toward the sound of Justin's screaming voice.

"Whoosh," my breath gushed as something tackled me.

"Get off of me!" I shouted and shoved the dark mass off of me with a burst of energy.

"Ow!" Justin shouted, lying on his back ten feet away from me and rubbing his chest.

"Justin?! Sorry, I thought you were something else," I muttered apologetically and crept over to him. Poor guy. An attack with my energy was enough to fend off a vampire or werewolf. I didn't know what it could do to a human.

Breathing in the moon's energy, I wished my hit wouldn't do any damage to him.

"Where have you been?" he said angrily and weakly, while I helped him sit up. "We've been looking all over for you."

"Um, I kind of got lost," I replied hesitantly. It wasn't entirely a lie.

A chorus of howls echoed in the Sacred Valley. They'd surely have my scent by now and, if they had mine, they had Gabe's and Justin's.

"We've gotta go," I ordered.

"Why? Are you gonna let a couple of animals scare you away? If a puma didn't frighten you, nothing will," he said confidently, bracing himself against a tree to stand.

"Yeah, well, these do," I said, whipping my head around to make sure they weren't nearby yet. Reaching for his arm, I tugged, urging him to move quickly.

"It's just a few wolves or coyotes or

something," he said candidly. Arching his back, he stretched his chest and back in an effort to loosen his muscles.

"Not exactly. More like chupacabras."

"Yeah, right," he scoffed.

"I'm serious and we *have* to go *now*," I ordered, dragging him back to camp. It was easy to find my way now that I could see in the black of night. The nightlight affect inside my eyes also picked up on hot and cold spots, making Gabe's sleeping body a beacon in the night.

"Adam! Adam!" I hissed on our way back to camp. If Rick could jump into my head without me calling him directly, Adam and the Bellatori had to be able hear me call them, but Adam didn't show up.

"Come on. Hurry up!" I yelled at Justin as he unzipped the tent irritatingly slowly.

A group of howls in unison called out eagerly and much closer than before.

Finally, Justin seemed to realize danger was a very real possibility and jumped on top of Gabe to wake him, while I rummaged through my backpack for my keychain.

Why is it that whenever you're in a hurry to find something, it's never in the place you remembered leaving it? Anyway, after opening the sixth pocket inside the pack, the angel wings shimmered.

I grabbed it and crouched in the corner of the tiny tent.

"Adam!" I shouted under my breath. "Where

are you?"

The guys started rolling up the sleeping bags and shoving our gear into their sacks.

"Angel, either help or get out of the way," Justin barked.

"I am helping," I replied caustically. *Trying to anyway.* Where was Adam?

"Meditating won't help us escape wolves," Gabe said as he finished securing his sleeping bag to his pack.

I jumped out of the dark tent and called for Adam again.

"We're coming. Run north," his disembodied voice whispered in my ear.

Justin tossed my backpack through the tent door as Gabe hurled my sleeping bag at my head. I secured the bags and tossed them onto my back just as they finished collapsing the tent.

While they were preoccupied, I extended my hands parallel to the bushes and sucked in as much energy as possible from them. Charging my body, I wished to protect my friends and hide our scent from the vampires and werewolves in close pursuit. I pictured a golden, impenetrable sphere encompassing us.

My head turned quickly toward a lone howl. The echo of breaking branches spliced the quiet, dead of night as a creature sped through the forest. One of them found us.

"Stay close," I shouted softly to Gabe as he took off in front of us due north.

"Keep up," he replied, quickening his pace.

Despite our bulky gloves, Justin grabbed my hand tightly and pulled me over, under, and through the dense cover of trees, bushes, and random branches, which smacked us, scratched us, and tugged on my loose hair.

With my energy field protecting the three us, I knew it would give us enough time to make it out of the vicinity of camp and deep enough into the wilderness to escape. I just hoped the vampires would assume we'd stick to the main hiking trail considering it was the middle of the night. Then again, they weren't stupid.

Believe in yourself, the voice in my head whispered. This wasn't the time to question whether I was losing it or not, so I followed its orders. I'd seen my energy save me before. It would help us get away here too. It had to.

Without stopping, we hiked until dawn and made it to Sanctuary Lodge, conveniently located beside the Machu Picchu ruins. Scraped up, bruised, and caked in dirt, we attracted lots of gawking stares as we made our way to the concierge who nearly threw us out. Gabe convinced them we had reservations and gave them an extra tip—or bribe—to let us in early so we could shower.

Hot water cascaded through my hair and along the length of my neck, spine and legs washing away both dirt and stress. Three days' worth of dusty dirt stained the shallow pool gathering at my feet.

Mmmm...dirt flavor, Rick had said when he kissed my hand. I smirked at the memory and then quickly focused on the grout in the tile to distract myself. The last thing I needed was Rick popping up out of nowhere in my shower with me. Although...

No! The voice in my head shouted.

"You're right," I muttered embarrassed, considering I didn't know who was communicating with me in the first place. Aside from that uncomfortable thought, hadn't my moment with Rick last night pretty much led Aeterna Flamma right to us? I couldn't be so careless.

A thought I hadn't considered before suddenly came to light. What if Rick was planting the thoughts of himself in my head? What if I was being manipulated to feel infatuation? If I gave into Rick, then that would certainly help Aeterna Flamma's cause. That had to be it. It was the only option that really made sense.

After a quick nap and lunch on our room's terrace overlooking the Andes, we walked along grassy lanes and stone paths snaking through the ruins under the warm midday sun.

"You've been yawning since we got here. Are you really that bored?" Justin asked.

"Not bored. Tired," I said through another yawn.

He tugged on my arm lightly and led me through the site pointing out areas of significance and pausing to show the spectacular views of the steep deep-green mountain facings that plunged into the

Urubamba river valley thousands of feet below. With a crystal clear blue sky overhead, the grey and tan colored stone walls of the ruins sparkled in the sun's glow. I smiled smugly to myself remembering my amazing discovery and view from the night before. The walls sparkled better in moonlight.

If I weren't so darn tired, I would've been deliriously ecstatic at this once-in-a-lifetime opportunity. I felt like a queen touring her magic castle on top of the world. A childish sentiment to be sure, but it's every girl's dream to have adventure, mystery, and romance. Well, it was my dream anyway.

"Jay, over here," Gabe shouted from the second level grassy tier behind us. Dragging my fingers along the stone walls, I ignored the tickling sensation it created in my palms as we walked upstairs. The energy of this sacred place was becoming difficult to ignore.

I propped myself against the wall and slid to the floor, sighing as my butt met the dirt-dusted stone floor. I was in desperate need of a gallon of coffee. Another yawn. Maybe a gallon of espresso instead.

"Right here. It's here!" Gabe shouted excitedly at Justin.

"Are you sure?" he asked astounded. "That was too easy. There's no way."

"Look," Gabe replied shoving his notebook filled with calculations into Justin's hands. "We followed this path. These were the ley lines along the way. If we extend them like this," he dashed several lines across his map with a pencil, "it runs right under here."

"Of course," Justin said, smacking the paper.

"It makes perfect sense."

"What does?" I asked ignorantly.

The enthusiasm on their faces was easy to read. They looked like they'd just discovered buried treasure.

"The medicinal plants we found along one of the ley lines coincide with the position of this particular monument. We just found the main energy line through Machu Picchu, which on a small scale should reveal the plants we need to gather for our studies on natural healing," Justin explained.

"On a large scale, we can estimate where the ley line may run through the rest of the world and compare other plants to those here. We've hit the proverbial jackpot," Gabe smiled.

"This sounds like a lifelong project, not a semester's worth of work," I interjected.

"It has been...errr, will be," Justin corrected as his smile beamed. "This is a researcher's dream."

"Think about the conductive mineralogy," Gabe said eagerly to Justin. "Granite, serpentine, rose and snow quartz, pyrite, and jadeite. Fire from the lava that once flowed here plus quartz—they're natural conductors. The earth energy trapped here is massive. It's no wonder they placed the Intihuatana stone there."

"The what?" I asked.

"This," Gabe pointed to the massive square stone in front of us with a carved stone sun dial set in the middle of it. "It was used to line up with the sun at the equinoxes and celebrated the balance in nature. It's unique because most ancient monuments aligned with the solstices for sun worship not the equinoxes."

"Whether the Incas knew it or not, they were harnessing earth's energies in conjunction with astronomical events. The combination could lead to amazing spiritual sensitivity and, with the use of the plants growing in the forest below, healing abilities for their shaman," Justin added. "To the regular people, it must've seemed like he knew magic."

"Interesting," I mumbled as my mind raced. I wondered what rocks were used in the Welsh caves dedicated to sun and moon worship. Apparently, the gems embedded in the ceilings weren't just for decorative purposes. They could've amplified the spiritual connection of each room and made me stronger or weaker.

"The Temple of the Sun," Justin muttered. "So obvious."

"I thought the Temple of the Sun was back in Cuzco?" I asked.

"The Sun God was an important figure to the people," Gabe explained. "There were lots of sites dedicated to him."

"And this is one of them?" I asked.

He nodded.

Suddenly, everything became clear. The path leading here was connected to the sun as was Machu Picchu itself not to mention the ley lines and the mineral composition of the entire place. No wonder I felt exhausted. The place was draining my energy. I shared a connection with the moon. The ancient memories and associations of the place were sending a direct message.

I did not belong here—at least not during the day.

Just past midnight, I pulled my coat over my flannel PJs and snuck out of the hotel unnoticed while the security guards were preoccupied with a card game.

With the full moon high overhead and my hand on my angel keychain just in case, energy danced in every cell of my being. I was wired. Ten cups of coffee didn't even come close to the natural high pulsing in my veins.

I closed my eyes and relished the brisk night air as the moonlight danced on my skin with a charge of electricity running up and down the length of my arms. Breathing deeply, light floral tones and the damp forest tinged the fresh night air.

Creeping quietly through the ancient corridors and up the stairs which held the secrets of millions of ancient footsteps, I climbed into the Temple of the Sun, stood behind the Intihuatana stone and raised my palms to the full moon. Its cold blue glow radiated into my fingers, down my arms and rushed through my body into my toes. Once the charge began to diminish, I opened my eyes to look at the moon in awe.

"Thank you," I whispered to the Creator.

Whatever higher power was watching over me, I felt an immediate and deep kinship with him or her in this spiritual moment.

Deep into the night, the stone walls released the sun's energy, which they had collected throughout the day. Cold to the touch, the only energy radiating from them was tied to the quartz—a familiar sensation and subtle vibration to which I'd grown accustomed thanks to my wand last summer.

Content, I propped my hands on the stone wall and gazed down into the empty ruins below. A sudden pang of loneliness echoed in my heart. Machu Picchu mimicked my loss not just in this lifetime but in all the others as well.

Reincarnation was meant to help me grow from one life to the next so that eventually I would have learned all of my lessons and no longer have to return here. If my lives were always cut short, I was facing an eternity of lifetimes and lessons. Would I never experience love and happiness or even joy in life's simple pleasures? Would the weight of the world always be on my shoulders?

"CJ," I whispered, my eyes dropping to the wedding band on my ring finger.

His warm yet invisible arms slowly encircled me from behind. I could almost feel his chest press against my back.

"This sucks," I exhaled honestly.

His hands rubbed my arms reassuringly, but it didn't help.

"This isn't what I want," I said sadly, feeling a tear about to drop from my eyelashes.

"I want you to be real, to be here, to be with me. Why is it that I always want the one thing I can't have?" I paused, taking a deep breath. "A real, human hug would be nice or holding hands or just going to the movies. You're just a memory," I sighed sadly.

His arms tightened around me again.

"It's just not fair. I love you and I don't want to hurt you but," I couldn't say it. I didn't want to let him go. He loved me when I didn't love myself. He sacrificed his life for me. He was everything I could ever want in a partner. He was my match. I didn't know any other man who could understand me the way he did.

I scoffed. What did I know though, right? I was *only* 19. The memories of many lifetimes aged me like no other. My soul was ancient. I knew what I wanted. It was the same thing I'd been fighting to attain for 5,000 years.

"I thought running away with Justin and Gabe would help…" I caught the cry in my throat before it escaped, "would help me heal. But the longer we're apart, the worse the pain gets. I miss you *so* much." I reached my hand up to touch the area on my arm where his energy lingered.

"Well, I miss you too," a voice behind me said.

CJ vanished as I spun around.

"What are you doing here?" I hissed at Justin for interrupting my moment and wiped my eyes quickly, embarrassed that he caught my private monologue.

"I couldn't sleep and when I checked your room and saw you were gone, I knew there was only one place you'd be," he said, stepping toward me as we turned to stare at the moon teetering above the mountain tops.

"How did you know?"

"The magnetism calls to us. It's magical, don't you think?" he asked, stepping beside me at the wall. "It's beautiful here. It doesn't feel like it's part of our world."

I nodded in agreement, leaning onto the stones in front of me. The moonlight cast a silver-blue glow on my ring capturing my attention and reminding my heart where its loyalties lay.

"Wanna talk about it?" Justin asked, staring at the piece of metal on my finger, handcuffing my heart to my past.

Sighing in defeat, what did I have to lose at this point? "I found the person I wanted to spend the rest of my life with only to lose him. Permanently," I figured that was worth adding to explain the true tragedy of my situation.

"How long ago?" Justin asked tenderly.

His face glowed with a pearlescent shimmer in the moon's cool light matching the blonde spikes of hair standing on top of his head. Oddly, the deep blue hue of his eyes appeared an almost sinister black in the darkness.

"A little over a year," I replied, avoiding his intense and worried gaze.

"At least you know it was real. Only true love's scars haunt with such lasting pain."

"Have you been in love?" I asked curiously. Justin always seemed like the life of the party. I didn't think to delve much deeper.

He nodded, sighed, and tilted his head to the side to stare at me. A wry smile spread across his face.

"What?" I asked, instantly self-conscious. Did I reveal too much? Did he think I was nuts? Well, that wouldn't be a first. Everyone thought I was crazy already.

"Nothing." He shook his head and chuckled. "A one sided love affair is not worth the time or agony. Your situation is worse than mine," he said, turning back to face the sharp mountain silhouettes of the Andes.

"Thanks for being so patient with me," I replied, feeling sorry for him. He obviously liked me. And after what I'd put him through, I still couldn't understand why. "I'm so not worth it, you know."

Focused intently, his eyes gazed at me sweetly, lovingly.

"You are," he said with such conviction, my unhappy heart stuttered to life. A light breeze blew between us.

Justin brushed a few stray strands of hair from my eyes and his hand lingered ever so lightly on the side of my head.

We stared at each other in silence for a few moments. Him because he wanted me to make the first move and me, well, because I wasn't ready.

Not yet.

Chapter 18 – Origins & the Secret

"Wow," was all I could say as I stared at the majesty of Angel Falls, the world's largest waterfall. Feeling like a tiny ant dwarfed by the three thousand plus feet of water cascading in front of me, there were no words to describe the sight or feeling of complete insignificance.

A week after Justin and Gabe discovered earth's main ley line in Machu Picchu, we followed one of the energy paths straight into Venezuela to the falls.

Justin stood beside me as we both stared in awe at the spectacle. "Pretty cool, huh?"

"Yeah," I muttered still taken with the sight.

Here and there, dim rays of sunlight struggled to shine through the foggy mist near the falls' basin and the patchy clouds hanging low overhead.

"Don't get lost in Devil's Canyon," Gabe winked at me motioning to the river area in and around the bottom of the waterfall. The rushing water was tainted red from the sandstone through which it flowed.

"I'm waiting right here," I said emphatically and sat on a boulder as Gabe wandered into the groves of trees.

We hiked for hours to reach this place and were miles from the nearest town. Devils or not, this dense and massive jungle was literally a no man's land.

Gabe spent the afternoon collecting samples and packing them in airtight containers. After making sure I was comfortable and leaving me with their gear for safekeeping, Justin joined him.

The roar of the crashing falls drowned out the sounds of chirping birds and other jungle creatures—for that, I was thankful. Immersed in nature and its awe-inspiring beauty served as the perfect reminder of my place in this world without regard to the supernatural crap chasing me. As much as I missed him, I blocked CJ from my thoughts, because they inevitably meandered to my confusion around Rick. And that would only lead Aeterna Flamma right to me here in Devil's Canyon. *How appropriate*, I thought snidely.

So, I focused intently on the hypnotizing cascade of the waterfall, the variety of plants in countless shades of green, and the disgustingly intriguing insects and creatures of the Venezuelan rainforest.

While the fascinating and fresh surroundings kept my eyes busy, I wondered about the sun god. The ley line harnessed or amplified the dominant, masculine energy—that much I understood. However, how could I—or anyone for that matter—use it for good or evil? How would we become unstoppable?

In the meantime while I pondered my task, the guys were searching for ley line offshoots—minor energy trails that connected other parts of the world to the main line. Our next stop would be in Sedona, Arizona, which was a renowned hot spot for supernatural energy.

Having a lot of me-time and being so far removed from civilization provided me with an unexpected opportunity. I wasn't afraid of being alone anymore. Aside from knowing the Bellatori were watching over me somehow, Justin and Gabe were decent company and all I needed.

The peace I'd discovered in myself and found in nature was helping me concentrate. Contentment created a barricade in my thoughts. Unless I wanted to let them in, I blocked the Bellatori and Aeterna Flamma simply by refusing them into my thoughts. Fear and lack of confidence made me vulnerable to them before. Now, I was in charge and I was able to focus on the important things in life without interruption from the two groups doing their best to butt into it.

The distractions of the real world—or my reality anyway—were just that, they were distractions keeping me from truly appreciating the simplicity of earth's spirit and elegance all around me. And, since mountain-top kingdoms and massive waterfalls were not to be found in San Francisco, I was determined to absorb every moment.

As Kelly once said, 'moments are fleeting. Take a picture in your mind and you'll never forget it.' She was right. Though I snapped at least a thousand pictures since arriving in South America, the living ones in my memory were the only ones to do this place justice. I'd never forget the fragrance of fresh water slicing through the humid dirt and sweet vegetation of this amazing oasis.

Unfortunately, all good things come to an end. All too soon we landed in Sedona and were trekking the paths through its mesmerizing red sandstone mountains and marvels.

The guys insisted on a side trip to the Hopi Indian Reservation. A friend-of-a-friend had mentioned the name of a shaman who was a *must-see* if they found themselves in the area.

From the outside, the shaman's house was a simple structure covered in cream colored stucco and surrounded by gardens of various plants, bushes, and flowers. A petite dark-haired woman with a pleasant smile welcomed us into the home and escorted us to a back room.

Upon our entrance, an elderly man stood up from his arm chair surrounded by shelves of books, herbs, a magnifying glass, and candles of all shapes, sizes and colors. Dried flowers and plants hung in bunches from the corners of the ceiling. The room itself was all white and decorated with simple oak furniture.

"Welcome, boys," he greeted Gabe and Justin who blocked me from sight unintentionally. "Nice to meet you. I'm Qaletaqa."

The guys nodded and shook his hand enthusiastically. As they stepped aside, Qaletaqa caught sight of me.

His eyes opened wide and his jaw dropped open.

"So it *is* true," he spoke softly. "The final cycle has begun."

I shook my head and raised my finger to my

lips, hoping he would stop talking.

He cleared his throat as Justin and Gabe turned their perplexed gazes toward me.

My finger quickly shifted from my lips to my nose, scratching it nonchalantly. I shrugged my shoulders and pretended not to understand Qaletaqa's allusion.

"What did you mean?" Gabe asked.

"The energy you bring with you carries a story, boys. It's a tale that's been told since the beginning of time across many great nations. The battle between the light and the dark. Your search for the ley lines and the healing plants might help bring an end to the fight between light and dark, life and death," Qaletaqa explained.

His wise, old eyes told a slightly different story as they rose to meet my gaze.

I smiled to acknowledge his assertion. He grinned and nodded. And thankfully, our little exchange went unnoticed by Justin and Gabe.

He went onto explain his own journeys through South America, Asia, Australia, and Polynesia in search of *the secret* as he called it. The shaman in each location told of similar, ancient methods for healing people with physical, mental or spiritual ailments. All of the ailments had a common source. They were born of the darkness—spirits and entities sent to wreak havoc and negativity on earth.

Gabe took extensive notes, while Justin continued the conversation with Qaletaqa about the possible correlation of earth energy on vegetation.

Qaletaqa mentioned that earth energy not only affected our physical plane but also had the power to open vortices—passageways to other dimensions or paths that defied our understanding of space and time.

"Can anyone access these vortices? Has anyone disappeared through them?" I interjected. Memories of instantaneous tunnel-travelling with CJ and the Bellatori jumped into my thoughts.

"Anyone can enter the space, but its effect depends on the person. We are not created alike. Our experiences are not created alike either.

"Travelling through the vortices is possible, I imagine. My people's legends mention it, but why bother trying to physically move through space when you can do it instantly here," he leaned forward and touched his finger to my forehead.

"How?" I begged for clarification.

"Your thoughts, your energy, you yourself are products of your mind. The mind is more powerful than we realize. The crossover between the physical body and spirit begins with the mind. The two are not separate, unattached beings; they are one with the ability to experience different things in different ways at the same time. Your mind—your soul—is eternal. Your physical body is temporary. Your soul seeks to accomplish its purpose endlessly. A little thing like a body or the constriction of time cannot stop it, but they can enhance it because they force you to experience a certain action and reaction.

"You will always rise above the limits to do whatever it takes to fulfill your purpose."

With his energy resting intently on me, the group conversation had shifted to a more personal tone as if I was on the receiving end of grandfatherly advice.

I nodded. "But what if someone wanted to use a vortex to travel instantly. Could they?" I pushed.

He smiled, knowing I must've witnessed this myself. "It depends on the person."

I nodded again. There's a reason my friends and I were able to use them. There's a reason that all the vampires, angels, and others were able as well. Perhaps, the connection wasn't so much with the supernatural, but that our spirits and bodies were more attuned to the spiritual dimension than here.

Gabe and Justin steered the conversation back on course and after a lengthy afternoon, we said our farewells to Qaletaqa and, as our first few footsteps walked along his front garden, we began discussing the quickest route to the airport.

"Wait!" Qaletaqa cried suddenly.

Worried, we spun around on our heels.

"Angel," he called and motioned for me to come back into his house.

I walked behind him into the entryway and sheepishly asked, "Yes?"

He grabbed my hand and turned it palm upward. In the center, he placed a small blue stone with gold flecks.

"My ancestors used turquoise to protect and heal. It will align you with the spirit world and balance or release the energy that is holding you back now. Pyrite—what you know as Fool's Gold—sparkles like the rays of the sun. Like the sun, it heals and gives you energy to accomplish anything your mind sets itself on. Keep it with you always, *Artemis*."

My heart felt light. I could feel Qaletaqa's soul; he was a good man, a pure man, and someone I knew I could trust. I smiled.

"Thank you, Qaletaqa. Truly, thank you. I'll keep it with me," I replied sincerely and slipped the pretty stone into my right pocket.

A few hours later we were en route to California's golden sunsets.

Justin had promised me a getaway, and a getaway I got. Aside from the near-death experience in Machu Picchu, life's realities were a million miles away. A vacation of discovery and natural beauty proved to be far more rejuvenating than scorching myself on a tropical beach somewhere.

Even more amazing was that my energy was completely in check. Surrounded by tranquility in the middle of nowhere filled me with energy, but I'd learned to build it, channel it, and ground it. I felt like a rechargeable battery with limitless storage capacity. One day when I'd need it, the energy would flow. Until then, I had a handle on it.

Gazing through the plane's oval window at the lush green Sierra Nevada mountain range far below, I smiled to myself. Without being smug or conceited, I was proud of my accomplishments. Somehow I figured out a way to compartmentalize my life.

Sadness, loss, and loneliness had a place in my head, but my heart was growing each day respective to my growing self-assurance and independence. I wasn't whole yet, but I felt good. For the first time in a long time, *I really felt good.*

Lying in my lap, I glanced at the keepsake children's poem that had been tucked behind mugs and stuffed animals at a gift shop featuring Native American trinkets in the Phoenix airport. The sheet of recycled, handmade tan and green paper eerily summarized the ancient creation "myth" that Qaletaqa mentioned:

High on Leader's shelf, sun and moon in a box were kept.

Leader said the animal-people were not ready for it yet.

The world was always dark as night, and

The animal-people really wanted light.

Coyote, sneaky and sly, could not wait.

He stole the box to change man's fate.

The animal-people knew coyote was wrong.

They argued and fought, but he was strong.

Tugging this way and pulling in that,

The box flew from its protective mat.

Spinning through the blank night, into the heavens it rose.

Its top slipped off and light burst forth, shining on the foes.

Sun, so warm and bright, burned like a fireball in day.

Moon, so cool and shy, glowed at night to light their way.

Leader punished coyote for all time.

Left to scavenge and steal, he looked for a sign.

For one day against the animal-people he'd find revenge,

And use the sun and moon, his punishment to avenge.

"Protect the life of all," Leader charged the sun and moon. "Selfish coyote wants to fight and will return someday soon."

Since the beginning of time, sun and moon shined bright,

Banishing coyote's darkness with their pure, loving light.

Could this be a final message from the Bellatori? It seemed to wrap up everything I had learned. I needed to protect people no matter what the cost to me. It was my job and the reason I was created. The thought was both invigorating and daunting. Glancing jealously at Justin, who was lightly tickling Gabe's ear with a napkin corner to wake him, I craved their carefree life. They were so lucky to have each other and life's basic responsibilities.

However, for the first time ever, I was beginning to feel peace around my purpose. If my gifts could help others and I could use them for good, then I could find peace within myself. Then, and only then, it truly wouldn't matter whether or not I was like everybody else.

Determined not to let the vacation end, Justin kept me occupied every minute of every day when he wasn't in class. I was usually up at the crack of dawn, but every day since we returned I had been sleeping till noon.

Justin's endless need to keep me moving was only partially to blame though. I felt like I was building and storing all of my energy at night. Since I learned to keep it from sucking the life out of those I loved, I didn't feel a need to gather and release it anymore.

"Saturday, promise?" Justin asked me on Monday night at the pizza place amid his friends' cheers during the World Series telecast on the flat screen behind me.

Biting my lip, I hedged. Was I ready for this?

"I'm not asking you to marry me," he laughed. "Just a date. Please?" he begged with a sweet, lost-puppy-dog-look in his eyes.

It's time, the voice in my head said. My heart felt torn. Loyal to CJ, bewildered by Rick, and disturbed by Diego—I shivered at the thought—I wasn't sure if I was ready for the world of dating.

It's time, the voice repeated. Who was I to question the almighty, and possibly insane, voice directing my actions?

Ignoring the confusion in my gut, I took a deep breath and jumped, "Ok. I'll go out with you," I swallowed nervously, "on a *date*."

"If you're going to treat this like it's the end of the world, then never mind. I don't want to force you to do anything you don't want to," he teased with a tinge of anger, which revealed his true feelings on the matter.

His patience was wearing thin. Why did it have to be all or nothing? Without Matt, Mark, and Davey—especially Davey—in my life, I was in desperate need of a guy friend, who was not interested in me romantically.

"I do want to," I urged. "I will go out with you," I added sincerely.

It was time. And a date wasn't marriage. It was just a date for two people to have a good time and enjoy each other's company. It didn't have to end with a kiss or anything else that would make me feel like I was betraying CJ.

Justin's lips curled into a blindingly white grin of pure joy. A knot of guilt tightened in my stomach. The Bellatori wanted me to have a normal life and I was trying. Yet, why did it have to feel so bad? Justin was kind and caring, and he was a genuine friend. Provided I didn't royally screw this up, I had nothing to lose with a little date.

The next day I crawled out of bed around noon and growled at the sun, which rudely interrupted my sleep. Slamming the room-darkening curtains shut, my feet wandered to the bathroom without guidance from my eyes, which were still closed.

The ring of my cell phone echoed down the

hallway as I started to head back. Running down the hall, I swerved into my room and ricocheted off of the door frame. Sliding on the hardwood floor, I reached for my phone on the nightstand and slipped, crashing onto my back. The phone slipped from my fingers and smacked me on my forehead. *Great...* This day was starting out splendidly.

Wincing in pain, I grumbled, "Hello," into the receiver.

"Well, hello to you too," the voice answered back angrily.

Familiar yet distant, I knew this voice. I missed this voice. Spinning upwards, I sat against the side of my bed and rubbed the back of my head.

"Sam?" I asked curiously.

"Come now, Angel. It hasn't been that long, has it?" she teased.

"Sam!" I screamed. "How are you? What have you been up to? What's going on?" I couldn't get the words out fast enough. I was beyond ecstatic. I was in heaven.

The Bellatori's rules prohibiting our communication were the farthest things from my thoughts at the moment. Sam bent the rules on more than one occasion; I was sure she figured a way around them now. And not a moment too soon. My chest expanded in euphoric happiness and hope.

"I can't speak for long. You know, with the Bellatori watching *everything*," she added disdainfully. "Did you receive my parcel?"

"Package?" I repeated, looking around my

room in case Kelly tossed it in here while I was gone or asleep. "No, I didn't. Why? What's in it?"

"Are you certain?" she asked. "It was scheduled to arrive this morning."

"Hold on."

Nearly tripping over my own feet in excitement, I rushed from my room and flew down the staircase. "There's nothing in the living room."

Glancing around the room with one hand scratching my head in thoughtful confusion and the other gripping the cell phone, there was only one other place it could be.

I threw open the front door.

"Aaaaaaaaaaaaaah!" I screamed in shock.

Chapter 19 – Surprise

Sam attacked me in a suffocating hug. Once I remembered to breathe, I opened my eyes to the most glorious sight in the world.

Fearsome in his spiky black Mohawk, black get up, and skull and crossbones tattoo encircling his neck, Cynan stepped forward and embraced me and his sister.

"Miss us?" Cynan asked impishly.

"You have no idea," I squeaked with joyful tears streaming down my cheeks.

Shoving Sam and Cynan aside, Mark squeezed me in his typical bear hug, which I'd longed for since the move to California.

"Nice to see you're wearing it," he smiled, fingering the marcasite cross hanging from my neck. "I thought for sure you chucked it after I left."

"You thought wrong," I corrected him happily. "It hasn't left my neck since you gave it to me."

"Has it kept the vampires away?" he whispered in my ear.

"Most of 'em," I quipped, ignoring the fleeting memories of Rick worming his way into my head.

"Well, no better time than now to try it out," Mark added, stepping aside.

My heart caught in my throat. On the bottom step, waiting for a break in the greetings, waiting for me, Matt stood hesitantly. My Matt. My vampire Matt.

Without thinking, I jumped down the stairs two at a time and nearly tackled him. His jaw tightened and body grew rigid as I got closer. Screeching to a halt, I stopped on the step right in front of him. I trusted him and I was willing to risk a vampire bite or two.

"You're here," I cried. I never thought I'd see him again.

His body may have died, but his sense of humility had not. He glanced down at his black Skechers and dark jeans, but when he turned his face to meet mine, he beamed. Unconsciously, I stepped backwards—a safety mechanism, I think.

For my sweet, friendly Matt looked positively, heart-breakingly beautiful with his pallid skin, messy strawberry-blonde hair, sparkling teeth, and jet black eyes. Deep, dark, bottomless black eyes.

Before I could get too worried, Mark and Cynan appeared vigilantly behind me on either side, willing to take out their friend to save me.

Last summer's self-loathing returned in a millisecond. Why couldn't I have taken his place? Matt was too good to deserve this fate.

Turning his head to the side, Matt gulped a long breath of San Francisco's fresh, sea air.

"I'm fine," he said to Mark and Cynan but paused hesitantly. "I *am* fine," he reiterated forcefully, trying more to convince himself than us.

The black dye of his gaze faded into the warm, loving brown I knew so well.

My lips curled into a smile. "May I hug you?" I asked him.

At the same time I said this, the memory of his new vampire skin burning beneath my touch played back in a painful instant.

He nodded. "We've been practicing," he smiled at his accomplishment.

"Yeah, I'm glad we're finally here so he can stop asking me for hugs," Mark said snidely, turning toward Matt. "Seriously, dude, I can only take so much man love."

Matt rolled his eyes at Mark and stretched out his arms to me. Without pause, I threw my arms around his neck as he very gently wrapped his arms around my back.

"I've missed you so much, so, so much," I cried. "Please forgive me for not protecting you. I seriously can't live with myself knowing I failed you."

"Angel," he sighed in a chiding tone, "you couldn't be everywhere at once and you can't always protect us. What's meant to be is meant to be. We're only responsible for our own destinies. Ok?"

I nodded somberly.

"Of course you're forgiven," he added. 'There was nothing to forgive in the first place."

I kissed him on the cheek and he sucked in a quick breath of pain.

The outline of my lips lingered in bright red on the side of his face. Closing his eyes and breathing deeply again, he concentrated until the mark disappeared completely.

"See? I'm fine," he smiled sweetly.

My left eyebrow arched doubtfully. "Really?" I asked in disbelief.

"Ok, it hurt a little bit, but I'm fine now," he stared intensely into my eyes. "Really."

I wrapped my arms around his waist and walked him inside.

"Ang, what the hell?" Mark bellowed from the kitchen a few minutes later. "Where's all the food?"

Cynan stood in the middle of the bay window admiring the white sailboats dotting the dark blue bay and the stark red bridge leading to the green-gold lushness of the Marin headlands.

"Obsessed much?" Sam asked, staring at the framed black and white sketches lining the walls around the fireplace. "You're feeding into his vanity. He'd love to know he's preoccupied so much of your thoughts," she said as her fingers lingered on Rick's eyes.

"Oh," she gasped in surprise, "was this CJ before he was CJ?" she asked pointing to the picture of Zach and me dancing at prom.

"Yeah," I responded. The minuscule moment in time seemed like a million years away.

"Hmmm," she muttered, "he's cuter as CJ."

"He's nicer too," I replied without thinking, though it was entirely true. CJ was far more caring and loving than Zach had ever been.

Laughing hysterically at Matt's impression of Mark's careless slaying of vampires last year, I was choking on a gulp of water when Kelly arrived home that evening.

"Oh," she said, her eyes narrowing in confusion and surprise, "I didn't realize you were having guests tonight."

She paused at the top of the stairwell, her gaze darting to each of my friends assessing them.

"Sorry," I giggled as I wiped the water from my mouth, "they sort of dropped in unannounced."

Kelly's eyes glanced nervously around the room.

"My friends from Wales." I pointed to the

largest of my pencil drawings on the wall.

"Oh," Kelly replied, nodding in understanding and feeling completely ill at ease.

"Everyone," I began, hoping to diffuse the tense and awkward situation. "Kelly has been my best friend for as long as I can remember," I said, wrapping my arm around her shoulders.

Sam bristled at my statement. I ignored her reaction. As much as I loved her, Kelly was a part of my human life—a part I treasured just as much as Sam's supernatural presence.

After a round of introductions, Kelly sat on the couch uncomfortably watching our every move. However, more often than not, her eyes remained unabashedly focused on Matt. Thankfully, she was so engrossed with his picture-perfect face that she didn't see the daggers shooting from Sam's jealous eyes.

This was the first time my world of normalcy was fully and irreversibly colliding with my secret life. When Mark met my family, I easily passed him off as a normal friend. With all of us together in one room now though, it was only a matter of time before one of us slipped up.

My eyes shifted to Matt who met my stare at the same time. Raising his eyebrow, he read my thoughts and shook his head in frustrated disbelief. He wasn't going to attack Kelly. I should have known better.

I mouthed, "Sorry," to him. My face burned in guilt for doubting him in the first place. Vampire or not, he was still Matt.

With game four of the World Series playing in the background, Mark and Cynan were debating whether or not baseball was a boring sport when Sam turned to Kelly.

"Don't you have someplace to be?" Sam said snidely.

Interrupting her gawking at Matt's perfection, Kelly blushed. The rest of us turned to Sam angrily. Matt stood and walked to the window with his back facing us. Clearly he knew this was about him and he couldn't do anything about it.

I could feel he wasn't happy. He was a vampire and, as such, everything about him enticed easy prey. Unfortunately, it was the nature of his unnatural self. Timid, human Matt would never have wanted this kind of attention and now he couldn't avoid it.

Realizing our annoyed glares, Sam clarified, "I mean, we interrupted your evening with our unexpected arrival. We don't want to impose," she laughed off her faux pas nervously.

Kelly glanced at her watch. "Oooh, Uri is waiting for me," she remembered suddenly. "It was nice meeting all of you, but I have to run."

She smiled at me awkwardly, grabbed her coat from the banister, and rushed downstairs.

After the door slammed shut, we glanced at each other.

"Thank God!" Sam muttered under breath as she collapsed beside Cynan on the couch.

"You could've been nicer to her," I said with

my eyes fixed on Matt's unmoving back.

"She bothered me," Sam answered bluntly with a dismissive wave of her hand.

"You can't keep Matt from everyone," Mark yelled from the kitchen. "Look at his undead hotness. You can't deny he's a nice piece of cold meat."

Sam's stare shifted from Matt's quiet stance by the window to her hands clutched in her lap. In the next millisecond, Matt was kneeling beside her.

He placed his hand on top of hers. "I love only you. You know that," he said earnestly. His glorious, almost glowing face pleaded sincerely.

Sam glanced into his earnest puppy-dog eyes and nodded sadly. "But you're perfect. I'm not. I never will be. I can't compete with that."

Mark pretended to vomit in the kitchen. "Please," he ordered.

The living embodiment of Snow White, a bouncy black bob framed Sam's angelic, pale, heart shaped face with nature's gift of unadorned ruby red lips. Walt Disney himself couldn't have imagined a more ideal model for the character.

Sam rested her head on Matt's shoulder as he caressed her cheek lovingly. They were an adorable couple. They belonged together forever. Though in that same thought, reality reared its ugly head. Forever for Matt meant an eternity; for Sam it was a matter of decades.

Suddenly, I felt Sam's pain. I may not have had CJ with me, but she was trapped in a relationship she wanted more than anything in the world. Only time was against her. Youth lasted only so long and Matt was destined to be twenty-one forever.

Cynan stared at me thoroughly absorbed in an unspoken thought. As I caught his eye, I managed to catch the flavor of the idea passing through his head.

Turning to face him, I looked at him perplexed. "You never mentioned why you're all here."

Mark returned to the room with a pizza and beer in hand. Sam and Matt shifted uncomfortably in their seats.

"Don't get me wrong. I'm thrilled you're here, but the Bellatori were very clear on our not having any contact with each other. Did they decide to give you an extended vacation?" I giggled anxiously.

My four soul-connected friends exchanged pensive glances, which only made the knot in my stomach squeeze tighter.

"Angel," Cynan began, leaning forward in his seat to place his hands over mine. He hesitated as he stared deeply into my eyes. "We're here to protect you. It's our duty," he reminded kindly.

"Yeah," I agreed, "but why *now*?"

The knot in the pit of my guts was about to spark a full-fledged anxiety attack.

The group turned to Matt expectantly. Apparently they thought if he delivered the news, I wouldn't be as upset, although that ship was about to sail regardless of the messenger.

Looking intently at Matt, I waited. Patience

was wearing thin.

In less than the blink of an eye, Matt was beside me on the love seat.

"We have to be here now," he began, clearly unsure of how to spill the proverbial beans.

"Again, *why*?" my tone was agitated.

An explosion of energy pulsated in my fingers and palms. The need to destroy something grew in intensity and was about to burst through my weakening attempt to control it.

Focusing on the floor, Matt took a deep breath. "Whatever happened while you were on vacation in South America had bad consequences."

"How bad?" I asked uncertainly.

"Rick escaped."

Chapter 20 – Past, Present & Future

The unrealistic hope for having fun and hanging out like normal people died only a few hours after everyone arrived. My friends were back, but they were standing guard 24/7.

I gazed emptily at the cold and foggy San Francisco Bay the next morning. My life lesson for independence morphed into nothing more than a prison with a view. Glancing at Alcatraz Island sitting in the middle of the bay, I knew exactly how its inmates must have felt—to be so close to life and freedom, yet so far away.

"Come on, Ang," Mark said as he sipped a cup of coffee. "S'not so bad, is it?"

Looking at him I felt the longing in my eyes convey my true feelings.

"At least we're with you. I thought that's what you wanted," he added with a bite into a bacon, egg, and cheese croissant.

"It is," I started, "but not like this. I thought we'd have more time."

In my head, I was damning Adam. "Why didn't the Bellatori just warn me or stop me?"

"They didn't want to scare you and they wanted you to learn on your own," he said matter-of-factly with a mouthful.

"If the situation's that bad, they could've said something," I added indignantly as a trio playing football in Marina Green Park across the street caught my attention.

Pressing my nose against the cold window, I studied the group more closely.

"Are you kidding me?" I spun around to face Mark. "Rachel, Steve, and Jack are here too?"

They were my first line of defense and protectors before I even knew I needed them. I met them at the youth hostel in London and they'd been following my footsteps from a distance ever since.

Mark shoved the last bite into his mouth and

placed his food-free hand on my shoulder. Crumbs dropped from his mouth as he rushed to explain, "It's either this or being locked away in the Bellatori's underground vault. We all agreed you'd enjoy this view better than cave walls."

Sam's footsteps echoed at the top of the stairs. Having just rolled out of bed, she resembled the bride of Frankenstein with her hair standing on end and her eyes still half asleep. Matt stood by her side, holding her hand securely in his. As they made their way downstairs, Sam plodded like a baby elephant compared to Matt's silent, graceful glide.

The new Matt was going to take some time getting used to.

"Yo, dude, why am I on watch at night if you never sleep?" Mark shouted to Matt.

"Just because I'm a v—," he stopped as Kelly emerged from the kitchen with a white frosted pop tart hanging from her lips, a thermos of coffee in hand, and books in her arm.

Struggling to stay balanced, she caught all of our guarded eyes resting on her. How much had she heard? How much did she deduce? Red flush painted her cheeks in embarrassment.

"What?" she asked uncomfortably with her teeth gripping onto the breakfast pastry.

"Good morning," the four of us greeted and smiled suspiciously in unison.

"Good morning." Her eyes darted around the room distrustfully. "Can I talk to you?" she directed to me as she ran past us, downstairs, and through the front door.

I shrugged in response to everyone's curious stares and followed Kelly outside. Out of the corner of my eye, Rachel, Jack, and Steve moved closer, poised to act in case of any threat.

The flat top of the thermos served as a tiny table for the pop tart she placed there carefully with her teeth to free her mouth to talk.

"How long are they staying?" she asked a little coldly.

"I'm not sure," I replied, feeling upset that she didn't like my friends. Perhaps I needed to redirect. "I may not be here much longer though either. We may go away for a little while."

Suddenly her angry façade fell and her eyes misted with tears. "You just got back."

"What's going on, Kelly?" I asked of my uber-independent, best human friend.

She sighed miserably. "Other than the fact that they're all a little weird—,"

I giggled nervously.

"—they haven't seen you in a year and you're more connected to them than you are to me. I don't know what's going on with you anymore. We're growing apart—"

"Wait a second. Are you jealous?" I interrupted.

She looked away. "Yeah, I guess. You're always with Justin and now they're here."

There are more important things going on in the world, I wanted to scream but managed to maintain my composure. The balancing act of human versus supernatural was growing exceedingly difficult to maintain.

To Kelly our friendship was important. I took it for granted…again.

"I'm sorry for being a crappy friend. I need to do a better job of being here for you," I promised and vowed in my head to make it so.

"I'm not asking for a lot, just some girl-time to talk," she added quietly.

"Promise," I said with conviction.

She smiled. "Crap, I'm gonna miss the bus," she said dashing down the stairs from the front porch. "Tonight?"

I nodded but wasn't entirely sure if I could keep my promise. Glancing at Rachel, Steve, and Jack served as a reminder that my time here was limited. I was about to leave reality again and, likely, wouldn't be back for a while.

A chill shot down my spine. I hadn't thought about dying in a battle against fallen angels, vampires and werewolves in a long time. Now that I was face-to-face with the possibility, cowardice returned full force even though I knew I was ready.

Thankfully, Justin was M.I.A. He texted my cell phone saying he was tied up in tests and projects and that he was looking forward to Saturday, which churned my stomach anxiously and guiltily. A blessing in disguise, his absence avoided the awkward introductions with my freakish, semi-human entourage.

For the first time, I realized I didn't want to scare him away, which meant one thing. I liked Justin. I actually liked him.

Later that day, as I sat on a grassy precipice in Land's End overlooking the ruins of the Sutro Baths' foundations, the ebb and flow of the frigid Pacific mesmerized my thoughts. Each wave washed over the broken, grey-brown cement walls and outline of the once grand swimming pool complex before sliding back out to sea.

"Why are you smiling like an idiot, Ang?" Mark interrupted the only content, peaceful thought I'd had in days and a happy recognition of my first step toward a life without CJ.

"Thinking about stuff," I said absentmindedly, distracted by Sam's balancing act on the crumbling foundation hundreds of feet below us.

"CJ?" Mark asked curiously.

"I thought you didn't like mushy conversations," I said, turning to face him.

"I don't, but you're not usually this quiet," he smiled to encourage me.

"What the hell?!" he exclaimed as a shot of lightning smacked the rock beside him shooting a cascade of shards into the stagnant pool of water below.

Cynan shouted up to us from the abandoned beach past Sam, "Fight?"

Always ready for an altercation, Mark bounded down the cracked, broken, and dirt covered remnants of stairs and rushed across the ruins to tackle Cynan.

"Oh my God!" I gasped as Matt appeared out of nowhere beside me.

"Sorry," he muttered apologetically. "Still getting used to being…different."

"It's ok." I patted his arm gently. "I'm just glad you're here."

Leaning my head against his shoulder, we watched Sam dance and twirl beside the rough waves crashing into the wall just beneath her.

"Does being so close to me bother you," I asked concerned. I'd already put him through so much.

"No," he replied emphatically. "You're not a dinner option at an all-you-can-eat buffet," he laughed.

"Besides, the energy on your skin and in your body would electrocute me even if I wanted to try."

Bundled up in a heavy jacket and long jeans, the cool fall temperature made my teeth chatter but had no effect on Matt who only wore a thin, red, button-down shirt. He preferred this weather now. Sunless skies and cold temps meant his skin wouldn't burn and decompose.

Thick fog blocked the sun from warming the freezing breeze twirling around us. I breathed the fresh sea air and groaned wishing I could've enjoyed it without worrying about the limited time I had left here.

"Tell me," Matt said slowly. "What does the air taste like? What does the ocean air smell like? I'm forgetting it all."

"What?" I asked unsure of what he meant.

"I can't smell the details anymore. Trying to breathe and smell and taste is hard. It's like I've got a stuffy nose. The only thing I can smell is blood. I can find you from miles away," he smiled, flashing his brilliant teeth at me.

"What does the air smell like?" he pressed.

How could I get beyond feeling guilty about his situation? His presence alone served as a never-ending reminder of my failure. Then again, I wanted him in my life, so I was going to have to embrace him as-is and make the most of his future. Still, if I could make it any easier for him, I would.

"It's pungent—like rotting fish at low tide," I fibbed.

"Don't lie," Matt barked. "Remind me."

Gulping a huge breath while Matt watched enviously, the salty air tingled in my throat. I began slowly, quietly. "It's fresh—not like the Atlantic Ocean's salty, fishy smell. The Pacific reminds me of drinking a glass of ice cold water. A hint of grass and sweet wildflowers linger in the breeze along with an undertone of the red dirt's dustiness. There's also a slight metallic flavor in the air, probably from the exposed pipes and beams in the ruins."

Content, Matt smiled, closed his eyes and leaned his head back. He breathed and tried to memorize what I'd said. "Thank you."

"How is it that you can smell blood but not

air?" I wondered aloud.

"Blood is all I want," he answered simply. "I suppose over time this will end. I know your scent, but you're potential food. The funny thing is that I don't need food or blood to survive, but I crave it," he growled at the thought before shaking it from his head.

"The stuff that kept me alive before—air, water, heat—is lost. I try to remember, but now they're just memories of memories. Actually, my existence as Matt seems to be slipping away too. Morgan says that when people die, their soul moves on and integrates back into the spirit world, where they don't really care about human names and concerns as long as our purposes are fulfilled."

"That's kinda sad," I said.

"Yeah. She thinks that I'm experiencing the "letting go" process here, since I'm between both worlds now."

Sadness for his sake clouded my thoughts. "What does the future hold for you now?"

He scoffed and shrugged. "I'm one of the eternally damned. There's no bright future for me. Although, I do have a job with the Bellatori for all eternity."

I followed his gaze to Sam.

"But what about Sam?"

The pain in his eyes melted away but was replaced with a longing I didn't fully understand.

"She gives me hope. When I'm with her, I forget what I've become. I can't imagine an existence without her."

"You're too good, too pure. I don't think you could be one of the 'eternally damned,'" I defended him against his caustic ideas. "Think about it. God created angels, even weird ones like Gaap—who was a vampire god of sorts. If that's true, he's one of God's creations just like you. I just don't believe that a good soul or spirit would be eternally punished."

"I don't have the luxury of playing the what-if game, Angel," he responded quietly. "There's no going back for me. I'm in the game and have to deal with the consequences."

"Which wasn't your choice to begin with!" I shouted. Matt was like my overprotective guardian angel. I would not let him give up.

His gaze steadily eyed Mark, Cynan and Sam carrying on and laughing on the beach below.

"Ever wish you were still…normal?" Matt asked hesitantly.

I couldn't help but chuckle. "Yeah, there's not much normal about either one of us anymore, is there?"

He grinned and nodded softly. "But do you ever wish that all of this would just disappear?"

I thought for a minute as I stared at the hypnotic undulations of the deep blue waves. "Yes. I miss Davey and I miss the easy relationship I used to have with Kelly. I guess in finding out who I really am, I've grown comfortable with the abnormal-ness of my life. It's not weird to me. I actually feel like I've found the place where I fit in finally. I belong with the supernatural and non-mainstream but I miss the easiness of being 'normal.' What about you?"

Matt stared at me thoughtfully. "I miss my family—my sister especially. I really want to visit them, but they can't see me like this. At least you're still human. I'm tempted to kill a person just so the Bellatori will kill me…"

A horrified gasp escaped my lips at his suicidal idea.

"Chill. I would never kill a human, but some days—the days when it's really hard to deny the thirst or when I can't go out into the hot sun with Sam—those days, I can't help but consider it. Whatever exists beyond here for me can't be as torturous as being torn between my natural instinct and knowing what's right."

Finally, I understood Matt. To me a vampire was no different than a human with the obvious exception of a beating heart. But, as we watched our friends chase each other playfully on the beige expanse of sand, an invisible veil separated Matt from the rest of us.

He was dead.

The thought tortured me the rest of the day and led to a pounding headache of guilt and regret. Matt was no more than a ghost with a body and, while that wouldn't make me love him any less, he was trapped between the living and the truly dead.

As promised, Kelly and I hung out after dinner, just the two of us. Everyone else headed over to Fisherman's Wharf to get their fill of touristy entertainment.

My protective, psychic thoughts were following Matt in an odd, mother-like panic. I'd periodically nod at whatever Kelly was saying; she was too involved in her monologue to realize I wasn't really paying attention.

Yes, I was continuing to be a crappy friend, but I also had worries.

"—Uri's taken me out every night for the past few weeks. We go to dinner, then he takes me dancing or to the park or to the library. We talk for hours. I really think I'm in love with him, Angel," she said, grabbing my hands as we sat across from each other on the couch.

I smiled. "I'm happy for you, Kelly. Really."

"I know he likes me. He keeps making plans for us every day, but I can't get him to plan anything long-term. I wanted to go skiing with him in Tahoe over Christmas break, but he keeps stalling. Why do you think he's doing that? Maybe he doesn't really like me." She gasped, "Do you think he has another girlfriend?" Kelly began hyperventilating. "I don't think I could deal with it if he's cheating on me. I've been so honest with him. I…"

"Kell," I interrupted and squeezed her hands to calm her down. "He's not cheating on you. If he had another girlfriend, he wouldn't be able to spend every spare second outside of school with you. Maybe he doesn't want to schedule anything long term because he lives in the moment. After all, you never know what tomorrow will bring, right?"

Her breathing slowed, and she nodded uncertainly.

"Have you seen the way he looks at you? His face is filled with complete admiration and adoration. I don't think you need to worry about anything," I added to make sure I pulled her off the ledge.

"You're right. You're right," she said trying to convince herself.

Her pants beeped.

Staring at her expectantly, she finally reached into her pocket and silenced her cell phone. A minute later it was beeping again.

"Just take it," I urged. It was probably Uri anyway checking in on her for the tenth time today.

"No. He's been bugging me all day."

"Who?"

"Dave."

"What does he want?"

She paused but gave into the argument raging in her head and blurted, "He wants to know how you're doing and what you've been up to."

"Again? But he still won't call me himself?" Fury overrode reason. "What an asshole!"

"It's getting super irritating. I hate being the middleman."

Kelly's fingers sped through her text response. Exasperated, she tossed the phone onto the coffee table.

"You're lucky," she said.

"'bout what?" I asked, though my eyes focused on the cell.

"I know you're sad about Zach, but at least you don't have any guy issues. They make life so complicated."

And she was right. I spent over a year ruing CJ's loss, trying to understand my weird fascination with Rick, and regretting how I treated Davey. How could I ever move forward with my life if I focused on the impossible and the past? The past was gone and the future wasn't here.

The time was now. Life was now.

It was time to move on.

Chapter 21 – Just a Date

Just past two on Saturday morning, I snuck outside in the cover of the midnight moon to the grassy field across the street. Rubbing my arms in a vain attempt to warm up through my heavy jacket, I stood on the field and stared at the last sliver of the waning silver crescent moon, which reflected dimly on the undulating black bay.

"CJ? CJ, can you hear me?" I called through my thoughts.

His warm embrace encircled me and his arms locked together on my back as he pulled me close.

"I love you," I cried in a whisper, wishing his

body and soul were actually with me, not his invisible ghost. "More than anything and forever, but…" My voice broke as the tears sped down my cheeks.

"But I can't hold onto you when you're not here."

Staring at our wedding band, I lifted my hand and placed it on his unseen chest. "As much as I love you and as much as this hurts, I have to ask you to do one last thing for me."

My breath quickened; hysteria was on its way.

"I need to live my human life and, as soon as it's over, I'll find you." With a hard swallow, I closed my eyes, but the rivers ran free beneath my lashes anyway.

"Please, CJ, let…me…go," my breath caught on the last word as I realized its finality. For the rest of this existence, CJ would merely be a wonderful, tragic memory.

His energy pulled away from my body. He held my hand and kissed the simple wedding band. Then his lips met mine. With my eyes closed, it felt like he was actually there in front of me.

All too soon, his energy faded away and I collapsed to the ground shaking and crying. Losing Zach once was devastating. Losing him as CJ was insurmountable but doable because I knew he'd be with me. Losing him for the third and final time gouged a permanent hole in my heart which, no matter what happened in my life, would be there till I died.

The morning sun glowed cheerfully, casting bright orange, pink, and golden yellow hues aglow on the walls of my room.

I groaned miserably. Part of me was already regretting last night's decision.

A cold hand brushed across my cheek.

"Oh," I gasped in surprise and opened my eyes to find Matt sitting by my bed.

"Feeling better?" he asked cautiously.

I nodded, then shook my head and broke down in another round of tears. "I said goodbye to CJ."

"Oh," Matt replied and wrapped me in a hug. "I'm sorry."

"I had to let him go," I whimpered and sat up in bed.

Matt rolled onto his back and watched me steadily.

A beam of sunlight escaped through the blinds and illuminated my wedding band. With a heavy heart, I unclasped my necklace from Mark, slid CJ's ring from my finger, and strung it onto the chain. Shaking from the sobs vibrating in my chest, my hands tried unsuccessfully to replace the chain around my neck.

Matt's frozen, yet agile, fingers caught the clasp and hooked it. "A new day, a new you? Wanna try?"

He jumped up from the bed without a sound and lifted me up by my hands. "Mark's been cooking downstairs. I guarantee a good laugh with whatever concoction he dreamt up for breakfast."

Thank God for great friends, I thought as Matt flew down our wooden staircase, dragging me behind him.

The day grew progressively better with each passing hour. I was at peace with my decision, knowing it was a necessary step for my heart to heal.

"Why won't you let us meet him?" Sam begged later that day as she applied a second coat of mascara to fully elongate my lashes.

When it came to beauty tips, half the time I had no idea what she was talking about. Having been away from her for so long, I'd forgotten how irritating she was when she treated me like a grown-up Barbie.

She added 'blush and bronzer to my pale palate' and then a quick sweep of lipstick topped with sparkling clear lip gloss.

"Aren't you finished yet?" I whined.

"No," she said emphatically. "And you didn't answer my question."

"Because I don't want any of you to scare him away. Owww," I complained as she pulled the brush through my hair roughly. She shrugged half-heartedly.

"True, our blokes are very protective and may hurt him, but I won't. Please let me meet him. I won't *say* anything. I only want to *see* him," she begged in her Welsh accent.

"No." I wasn't budging on this.

I wanted to ensure this very normal human activity was going to happen without any supernatural interference. It was bad enough Rick was on the loose hunting me down. Who knew how many regular, human nights I had left before he caught me? I wasn't stupid. It was only a matter of time before it happened. Escaping once was sheer luck. Escaping the second time was an absolute miracle. There was no chance I'd escape a third time.

On top of that, the Bellatori cleared my date with Justin, so I was going to be safe. I was sure the other protectors would be nearby anyway.

Getting ready for a date had never been as torturous as it was tonight. Not so much because of my emotional issues, but because Sam made sure to make it as physically painful as possible to punish me for not letting her meet Justin.

Mark whistled as I made my way downstairs in 4" heels, a black pencil skirt, and a fitted, silvery long sleeve top with black and red tattoo detailing.

"Wow, Ang, you're lookin' hot!" he exclaimed.

"You sound surprised," I replied sarcastically though inside I was completely self-conscious and sure he was only being nice to make me feel better.

"Well, yeah, you're always in 'comfy clothes.' His finger quotes emphasized mockingly. "Ya, clean up good."

"Thanks. I think," I muttered.

"You're beautiful," Matt complimented from his seat beside Mark on the couch.

"Yes, she is," Sam added, "thanks to me. Seriously, Angel, exfoliate and moisturize. It's not that difficult to remember."

"Can I go now? I don't want him to wait for me."

"Isn't it rude for him not to escort you from the front door?" Cynan asked bumping fists with Mark, who leaned forward in agreement.

"Not when I gave him direct instructions to wait in the car," I replied, happy and relieved I'd considered every loop hole my friends would surely attempt to exploit.

A car horn sounded. Like a shot from a gun, Cynan, Mark, Matt, and Sam jockeyed for the best position at the bay window. Using the opportunity to escape, I rushed into the cold night and over to Justin, who stood by the car door to let me inside.

As I reached him, he presented a bouquet that he'd been hiding behind his back. One deep red rose nestled in the middle of two dozen white ones filled the space between us. Closing my eyes, I leaned over to breathe in their delicious fragrance.

"These are beautiful! Thank you!" I rushed to acknowledge his kind gesture gratefully.

"You're looking lovely tonight," he whispered and smiled broadly.

My heart squeezed guiltily, but his honest eyes melted away the turmoil. Smiling, I turned and waved to our audience. Sam's mouth hung open speechlessly. Cynan stood staunchly with his arms folded. Mark winked and gave me the thumbs up—though I think it was because he approved of Justin's grey metallic convertible Corvette. Matt glared.

"Um, do your friends want to come with us?"

Justin asked hesitantly as our gazes turned to find their faces plastered against the window.

"Ahem," I cleared my throat. "Ignore them."

With the pulsating bass beat vibrating in our bodies and unable to hear each other talk at the club, Justin was determined to make me laugh and smile all night even at the expense of his looking completely uncoordinated with no rhythmic bone in his body.

Eventually, I cracked. I couldn't help it. The events of the day dissipated and were easily replaced by Justin's wisecracks and never-ending jokes.

"So, how am I doing so far?" he asked as we sat at the bar and I chugged a bottle of water. "Are you having fun?"

"You get an 'A' for effort and an 'A' for patience, but I'll have to dock some points for that shirt," I teased, drinking another sip.

"What's wrong with this?" he asked slightly offended, pinching the blue sateen material with pinstripes and staring at it trying to figure out how it was inappropriate.

I giggled.

"Nothing," I winked and dragged him back to the dance floor.

By one a.m. I could barely walk. Laughing about our non-stop dancing and the serious clubbers we offended by our mere, untalented presence, we inched our way to the car to avoid inflicting more pain on our feet.

As Justin inserted the key into the ignition, he turned to me. "Tired? Ready to go home?"

"Why? Aren't you?" I asked, still out of breath.

"Nah. I'm never tired," he winked.

"Did you have something else in mind?" I wondered curiously, cautiously.

"Only if you can keep your eyes open for a little while longer." He played coy. "Actually, it's something I want to show you."

"That sounds like the worst cliché come-on ever," I giggled.

"No come-on, I swear. It's just a place I know you'll like."

Hesitance made me pause, but I trusted Justin.

"Ok. Show me," I ordered.

The car sped along the nearly empty San Francisco streets until we reached the outskirts of town and merged onto 19th Ave. heading north.

"Taking me out of town?" I asked, arching an inquiring eyebrow at him and his intentions. "I thought this was going to be quick?"

He smiled deviously as he pulled the car to the side of the road and stopped in front of a gate along the top of a hill, which plunged into the bay below.

"Wait here," he ordered as he jumped out of the car and ran up to the gate.

The padlock and chains on the simple low bars of the red gate fell to the ground. Justin rushed back to the car and drove us past the entrance into a vacant parking lot.

"Are we allowed to be in here? Usually a locked gate means *keep out*?" I worried.

"We'll be fine," he grinned.

The Corvette screeched to a halt at the edge of a cliff. The blackness of the moonless, post-midnight sky was brilliantly illuminated by millions of white-gold "stars" shining from the San Francisco skyline. The jet-black waters of the bay were broken every few seconds by the spinning beacon from Alcatraz's lighthouse.

"Wow," I whispered.

Justin pressed a button on the dashboard and the convertible's top pulled back to reveal the Golden Gate Bridge standing regally behind us.

Words couldn't formulate in my mind. I was taken both with the view and with Justin's sweet gesture.

"You like it?" he asked uncertainly.

My head nodded on behalf of my speechless self.

He grinned at his accomplishment, but his eyes were filled with concern.

"What?" I asked.

"It's no secret. You know I like you, Angel," he began.

Uh-oh.

"And you know I'll wait for you," he paused.

"As long as you need."

Another pause.

"But, if you don't mind me asking, I was wondering about something tonight."

Not wanting to jump to conclusions, I stared at him and waited—not patiently—but waited for him to finish.

His eyes dropped to my left hand which rested in my lap. "Your ring is gone."

Unconsciously, my hand reached for the necklace to grab it.

Justin nodded. "I noticed. I was wondering if…well…if you're ready?"

How could I explain to him I'd never really be ready? Whether it was Justin or someone else in the future, they'd always be second to CJ.

"The city's lights are beautiful, aren't they?" I asked.

Justin's hopeful gaze turned speculative.

Instead of waiting for an answer, I decided to keep going. "San Francisco wasn't always here. The buildings and lights were built on the ruins of whatever existed before. Sure, it's gorgeous, but a fault line runs under the city. What we see is beautiful, but it hides a scary and dangerous place."

Justin waited, thoughtfully crafting his reply. "The lights weren't always here, but they're here today. They're breathtaking now. Who knows what will happen tomorrow? Maybe they'll be here; maybe they won't. And despite the unseen danger, it's nice to appreciate them and enjoy their life and beauty now."

"Yeah, but what about where it's been and where it's going?"

"That's a lot to worry about. How can you ever appreciate today, if you're worrying about what's been and what hasn't happened yet?"

"I just wonder if a little choice today will affect me forever."

"What do you mean *forever*?"

"Do you ever think about mortality or immortality?"

He shrugged. "A little."

"Well, I worry about how my choice now will affect my soul?" *Or soul mate*, I wanted to clarify.

"I wasn't asking you to make a life-long commitment," he laughed and then paused hesitantly. "But what if I did?" he asked beguilingly.

"What are you saying?" I worried.

"What do *you* think about immortality?"

"We all live forever. At least, our souls do."

He nodded in agreement and eased back into his seat to stare at the millions of stars flickering on the sky's navy blanket.

"I think love is what lasts forever. Have you ever wondered what it would be like to actually *live* forever? That would suck!"

"The thought crossed my mind once or twice,"

I laughed to myself nervously.

"Would you really want to though?" he grimaced. "That's a long time."

I considered the idea. Clearly I wanted to be with CJ. As an immortal on earth I'd never see him again. However, being a vampire would certainly have its advantages in the next battle. I'd be on an even playing field with Rick and the rest of the vampires and werewolves. While a vampire death of being stabbed, burned, and tossed into the sea certainly seemed painful and unpleasant, it wasn't impossible. I could manage to have myself annihilated and still find CJ so we could come back in another life and pick up where we left off here. Suddenly, the veil separating Matt from the rest of us seemed more like an advantage than hindrance.

"Yeah, I guess I would, but only if there were others like me so I wouldn't be alone."

He smiled. "I'd never leave you alone," he replied flippantly.

His blue eyes caught mine and an undeniable feeling sparked to life.

This was the moment I'd been dreading. I could keep delaying the inevitable and push away a great friend and potentially wonderful boyfriend, who was willing to wait for me to fix the emotional hurricane churning in my head and heart. Or, I could take the next, unsure step into healing my broken soul. CJ wanted me to be happy. He said he'd love me eternally. My soul loved him, but my human-self craved a love CJ couldn't give me any more.

As the new moon hid in the sky, this seemed

like the perfect time to start a new life and make new decisions without worrying about the past. The past was gone. Justin was here. He liked me, and I liked him. It wasn't the same as my feelings for CJ, but I did like him.

Staring in his eager eyes, I leaned toward him and closed my eyes in anxious anticipation.

Chapter 22 – A New Beginning

A cold, pulsating energy reached for me as Justin met my lips halfway. The spark exploded into a million tingles racing through my body.

He pressed his lips against mine more forcefully, hungrily and I was only too happy to return the intensity.

This is what I'd missed for so long. I craved this physical connection.

In this minute, I was just a girl; he was just a boy. Both of us were nervous; the hesitance in each kiss made that clear. But that vulnerability made Justin all the more attractive. CJ and Rick had an air of self-confidence in this area, which Justin lacked. He reminded me of what life was like before I met Zach and before my life delved into the insane and otherworldly.

Justin's lips gently kissed my nose and cheeks until he reached my ear. Unable to control his pleasure in the moment, he growled hungrily as he nibbled on my earlobe. The sound sent thrilled shivers racing down my spine.

Excited and eager, my energy wrapped around him pulling him closer. I squeezed my eyes shut for only a second to pry them from him. Killing my new boyfriend was not quite what I had in mind for a first date. I struggled against the natural instinct and pictured myself shoving the supernatural side of me into a closet and locking it away.

"Angel," he paused. His heavy breathing was magnetic.

"Yes," I gasped, hoping to get back to kissing as fast as possible.

He pulled back infinitesimally to look in my eyes. "I want you to know I love you. I don't expect you to ever feel the same way as I do, but I've loved you since the first time I saw you," he added with sincere and heartfelt fervor.

"Um, thank you," I muttered. It was a stupid thing to say, but I didn't want to lie and I was grateful for his honest acceptance of my broken self. "I like you, Justin. A lot. Really," I emphasized.

His needy eyes gazed into mine seductively. Charm, sweetness, and beauty collided at once making him positively tempting. I couldn't resist him even if I wanted to. There was no turning back.

Sighing in relief I pressed my lips onto Justin's giving into the pleasure of the moment. He pulled away only slightly, just enough to sweep my hair along the side of my head. His cold fingers brushed the length of my face and hooked gently behind my neck. Leading me to his lips once again, I melted into his embrace on this frigid, dark night.

Out of breath, I kissed him furiously. The

strength of his grasp on my neck and waist grew in matched intensity.

The pulsating energy from his lips tantalized me as it crept from my lips, along my jaw, to my neck. Running the tip of his nose from my ear to shoulder, sent a jolt of electricity through me, which I hadn't felt in a very long time. Each tiny kiss stretching along my neck radiated a static charge that felt like heaven on earth.

Without realizing what I was doing, I pulled his head closer into my neck. The harder the pressure, the stronger the charge, the better the feeling.

Rational thinking—what was that? All I knew was that I wanted him and I didn't want this moment to end.

With my arms wrapped powerfully around Justin, I felt his body tense up slightly as he pressed his mouth onto my neck with a ferocity that matched my desire.

And then he was gone. The pressure from his electric lips, the proximity of his body, the labor of his enticing breath pulled away from me in an instant.

Feeling slightly rejected and disoriented from the euphoria of the moment, I opened my eyes slowly.

Justin's body was pulled out of the seat and pinned on top of the trunk by a dark mass.

"Get off of him," I screamed, punching the attacker in the back. "Owww," I shouted in pain. His back felt like a slab of concrete.

Justin groaned and struggled under the

attacker's grip.

"Stop!" I shouted again and pounded the assailant's back with my fists.

As if my punches were nothing more than feathers, the massive figure punched Justin in the face.

"No!" I screamed.

The energy I reserved for vampires unleashed itself and punched through the dark entity.

Justin and the figure howled in pain. Justin lifted his head to face me.

I gasped in horror and lurched backward into the car door.

"Justin?" I whispered, terrified of the deep black eyes burning into my gaze.

A thin, glowing ice blue rim encircled his huge black pupils with vibrant crimson red rays piercing them. They were the same eyes, which first gazed at me through the window of the youth hostel in London. They were the unforgettable eyes of my vampire protector in Wales.

His gape overflowed with repentance, longing, and pain.

My own was just confused until the black mass turned to me.

I blinked twice not understanding who it was or how he got here. Guilt, sadness, and a new found level of torture I didn't think possible surged in my chest.

"CJ?"

Chapter 23 – No One

The neon blue of CJ's eyes was unmistakable. No one had eyes like CJ.

But these eyes were cold and heartless.

"CJ?" I repeated. The black mass of his body masked his face.

Without a word, the vivid, enraged eyes turned back to Justin. The mass began to take shape. Finger by finger, its hands came into sight first. The fingers locked solidly around Justin's throat.

Slowly, the black mist faded revealing his forearms, elbows, shoulders, torso and finally its head. A head of bronze and gold short wavy hair. The head of an angel. My angel.

"CJ!" I screamed. "Be mad at me. It's not his fault!" I grabbed at his arms trying to pry them from Justin.

Ignoring me, CJ growled angrily and banged Justin into the back of the car again. The echo of his head cracking the trunk's exterior reverberated in my ears.

"How dare you?" CJ hissed into Justin's face. "It's forbidden!"

"Not if she wants it," Justin struggled to say.

"You tricked her," CJ spat.

"She said it," Justin breathed, trying to rip CJ's fingers from his throat.

"I'll kill you," CJ seethed.

"Will you, brother?" Justin asked with blatant hatred.

"Brother?" I repeated in a breathless whisper, hoping I didn't hear him correctly.

Ignoring me, Justin continued. "The same blood boiling in my veins runs in yours," he fumed. "You're no better than me."

The words sunk into CJ's thoughts causing him to pause momentarily.

"But I'd never change her to make her mine." Then he snapped and punched both his fists into Justin's chest.

Thank God Justin was dead already otherwise the impact would've killed him instantly.

"Enough!" I shouted, throwing a ball of energy at the brothers.

Brothers!

CJ fell backwards and out of the car, giving Justin the chance to roll out from under his grasp and into my protective arms.

That, of course, did not improve the situation.

"Are you ok?" I whispered to Justin.

"You're going to *help* him?" CJ yelled at me. "Are you kidding?"

Ignoring his vicious tone, I repeated, "Are you ok?"

"Fine," Justin grumbled unhappily.

Not knowing when to quit, he jumped out of the car to confront CJ face-to-face.

"Please, Justin, don't," I pleaded as I knelt in the driver's seat. Not sure of how I'd intercede, I just wanted to be close in case I needed to protect either one.

"If you didn't abandon her in the first place—like you always do, I might add—she wouldn't've come to me," he sneered into CJ's still angry countenance, "but she did. She chose me, Cenweard. She. Chose. Me."

CJ swung at Justin's face, but Justin's vampire reflexes were faster and he ducked in time. He then tackled CJ, knocking the wind out of him.

"Don't make me hit the two of you again," I threatened.

They lurched to their feet and put a safe distance of a car length between them.

Emotional confusion clouded my thoughts. Happiness. Regret. Pain. Love. Anger. Defiance. More confusion.

"CJ," I turned to face him, still unsure if it was really him, "I said goodbye to you," I said urgently on the verge of hysterics. "How can I ever get over you if you keep popping in and out of my life? As much as it hurt to do that, I did choose Justin—," Justin beamed, "for now," I added to temper his enthusiasm. "What happened between us tonight, quite frankly is none of your business anymore."

"Really," he asked sarcastically. "And this isn't

my business?"

He reached his hand to my neck. The proximity of his skin to mine set my entire body ablaze a thousand times more powerfully than Justin. My eyes closed as the rush of memories from our past flooded my thoughts in an instant.

Roughly, he swiped his fingers up the side of my neck and held them up to my face.

Vibrant red dripped from his fingertips.

My heart cracked. "Justin?"

Looking slightly abashed, he stepped forward and reached for my hand.

CJ blocked his advance.

"Get out of my way," Justin roared at him.

"CJ," I glared.

Justin stared honestly and lovingly in my eyes, ignoring CJ's arm which was planted firmly between us.

"You asked for immortality. I was only giving you what you wanted, and I'd never leave you," he rushed to explain though it was hard to determine if he was telling the truth behind his blank, black-red vampire eyes.

The vampire burn was beginning to tingle around the wound in my neck. It wouldn't be long before death's infection reached my heart.

"Justin, I didn't know," I whimpered, backing up from him. "I didn't know who you were. It's not fair."

"But I'd help you. I'd stay with you. *I'd* never leave you," he repeated, glowering at CJ.

"I know you wouldn't leave—"

"Please," CJ shouted at me in disbelief, throwing his hands in the air.

Focusing on Justin, I continued, "But I can't after this. I would've been content just being your girlfriend. I didn't want anything else from you. I liked you the way you were, and the way I was. We can never get that back now."

I watched him steadily as all sense of hope melted from his handsome face.

"Immortality isn't a gift for you to give me," I added. "It's beyond us."

Justin's face hardened. The crimson rays piercing his pupils flashed angrily.

"You're taking his side?" he fumed.

"It's not about sides. It's about you *killing* me." My voice rose.

Before I could stop them, the energy tentacles broke free from my mental prison and latched onto Justin.

"I was giving you life," he roared.

The vampire virus burst with an explosion of fiery pain throughout my neck. My hand gripped at the wound as I swayed deliriously.

CJ grabbed Justin and flipped him onto the ground.

"I won't let the Bellatori have the pleasure of killing you," CJ said as he pulled a dagger from his pocket.

"NO!" I screamed in terror, trying to focus on their hazy bodies.

My energy managed to switch targets and ripped CJ off of Justin.

Justin's eyes flared with hatred at us and in the next instant he was gone.

Exhausted and giving into the pain I finally allowed myself to feel, I collapsed into the seat. CJ stood up unsteadily and leaned his back against the car door, avoiding my gaze.

Not knowing how to even begin explaining myself to him, I concentrated on the more urgent matter. Worried about what my fingers were touching, I sucked in a brave breath and felt the extent of the wound. Two thin semi-circles bled a steady stream down my neck and onto my silver blouse.

With each passing second that the infection spread, it grew stronger. As if it had its own heartbeat, the disease pulsated against my palm.

Squeezing my eyes shut as tightly as I could, I wished myself to get better. The energy which nearly suffocated both CJ and Justin only moments before was now distant and powerless. I couldn't rein it in to help me no matter how much conviction stood behind the wish.

Trying to focus on CJ through my blinking, hazy eyes, his body faded in and out of reality. Not sure if he was just a hallucination, I wrapped my arms around him and held on for dear life. He wasn't going anywhere without me tonight…or ever again.

"I know you're pissed and I don't care if you never want to speak to me again. I deserve that, but I need you to help me, CJ."

He turned to face me hesitantly, his presence crystal clear. Though his eyes no longer screamed in neon rage, they were still an unnaturally bright blue.

"Please," I begged. "Just take me back to my house. I can't drive. You can leave me at the curb and go back to wherever you came from. I won't ask you to stay. You deserve better."

Even as I said the words, my heart clung to the hope that he'd forgive me somehow. My prince charming was standing in front of me. He had to be a hallucination. I couldn't be this lucky to get him back right after I finally found the courage to let him go.

"It's not that easy." He shook his head irritably and climbed into the car beside me.

He didn't divulge any more information, and I didn't feel like I was in a position to pry. Having just made peace with letting him go, the wound in my heart was still fresh and bleeding. Tonight was supposed to be a new beginning. Instead, the lowest level of self-loathing and guilt I'd ever experienced just swallowed me whole.

I liked Justin. I trusted Justin. I enjoyed Justin. Why didn't I see what was happening? Was I that desperate? Or perhaps blind to the truth? After forging such a fulfilling connection, now our friendship was completely lost.

I doubled over in the car trying to catch my breath; whether this was because of my unsteady emotions or the vampire infection spreading through my system, I couldn't tell.

Add to this unavoidable reality that CJ witnessed our make-out session, I just wanted to disappear. My face burned in humiliation. I curled into a ball against the car door.

Wasn't it bad enough I asked CJ to go away? No, of course not, I needed to rub salt on his wound through a very public display of affection. The bile of shame rose in my throat. I wasn't going to make it home in time before I got sick.

CJ carried me through the front door and up the stairs into the living room where Sam, Cynan, Mark, and Matt's horrified, speechless open-mouthed gapes met us.

The mirrors around the fireplace reflected a tousled-haired me with a bleeding gash on the side of my neck. My pretty top now featured a macabre stain down one side. CJ's hair stood on end. His white shirt was ripped and stained with a black-red, oil-like substance, which I assumed came from Justin's nose and chest when CJ punched him.

Kelly stepped out of the kitchen with a glass of water in hand that slipped to the floor the second she saw us.

"Oh my God!" she screamed rushing over. "Are you ok?"

"Um, I will be," I glanced at Sam out of the corner of my eye and she ran upstairs to prepare her Wiccan vampire treatment.

"Where's Justin?" Kelly worried.

"He had to leave," I answered honestly.

Kelly's gaze shifted suspiciously to CJ.

"Hey Kelly," he greeted her as if he'd known her forever, which he had, but she only knew him as Zach.

Right after he said her name, he caught his mistake and shifted his weight uncomfortably as he set me down.

"And *you* are?" she retorted angrily.

"Kell, leave him alone," I begged. "I told him about you on the way home. That's all," I laughed off nervously.

She wasn't buying it.

"Angel, come here please," Sam shouted from my bedroom.

"I'll clean up," Kelly said still staring warily at CJ's back as he walked to the couch and sat beside Cynan.

With Kelly in the room, an uncomfortable and uncharacteristic silence befell my befuddled friends. They were dying to know what happened, but none of them could ask while she was around. The lone sound of Kelly banging cabinet doors as she searched for rags and a dustpan echoed in the still space.

The vampire infection began to spread. My fingers and toes tingled painfully. Teetering on each step, I pulled myself along the banister, hoping I'd reach my room. I glanced back once. Cynan and Mark watched CJ intently and curiously while Matt's eyes focused only on me.

He stood and walked as slowly as humanly possible up the stairs to meet me. Wrapping his arm around my shoulders, he pulled me the rest of the way.

Finally reaching my bed, I fell face first onto the super soft, pale blue, micro fleece bed cover.

"What happened?" Sam hissed as she wiped my neck with gauze soaked in a fluid that smelled so hideous I didn't want to know what it was.

"Justin was a vampire. He bit me—"

"I knew it!" Matt exclaimed, interrupting.

"—CJ saved me. End of story. Can you please hurry up? I can feel the vampire stuff crawling up my legs," I urged Sam.

The sensation felt like ice spreading through my veins, freezing me to death. In response, my body began to convulse in shivers.

She turned my head to the side to get a better view of the wound. Lighting a couple of white pillar candles beside my bed, she ignited the leaves of a St. John's Wort branch.

The fragrance sent Matt flying to the farthest corner of my room.

"Vampire repellent?" I'd forgotten about Morgan's cure for last summer's tattoo on my forearm.

"Sam carries it with her everywhere these days," Matt explained ashamed. He didn't need to say anything else. *He* was the reason she needed the vampire remedy.

Oblivious to us, Sam closed her eyes and began an incantation.

"How come you didn't know he was a vampire?" Matt asked. "Weren't you around him for the past few months?"

I thought for a moment. "I never really felt his skin. Whenever he touched me, it was always over clothes. In South America he wore gloves. He was always covered up. Tonight it was so cold outside, I didn't notice the difference on his skin. He had the human thing down to a science. Plus, San Francisco is the perfect place for a vampire—it's almost always overcast!"

"I wonder…" Matt's voice trailed off jealously, wondering if he'd be able to reintegrate into society.

"We'll help you figure it out," I assured him.

"Wait a second," I paused as my thoughts were catching up to me. "Why didn't *you* notice that Justin was a vampire?"

"You didn't let us meet him, remember?" he replied.

"Oh," I groaned through gritted teeth as the wound started to burn, counteracting the frozen numbness.

With her words swirling unintelligibly around us, Sam dug her fingers into my wound.

"You know, if you weren't saving me, I'd beat the crap out of you right now," I grumbled.

Eyes still squeezed shut, Sam smiled at me but

continued her whirlwind spell without pause.

Matt watched us intently and studied Sam's every move and nuance.

"Didn't you try to heal yourself?" he wondered aloud. "You manage to fix everyone else last year."

"I tried," I defended myself still wondering why it didn't work. "Oh God," I said with my heart sinking at the realization. "Just before he tried to change me, I convinced myself I wanted to be a vampire."

Matt dropped his head and shook it in disappointment. "*Why* would you want this?"

"It would make me equal to Rick. We could fight on equal ground."

"Angel, you're already more powerful than he is," Matt chided.

"But not in physical strength," I argued. "I want to be strong both in body and mind."

"Why can't you be happy with the talents God gave you?" Matt asked.

"Because I want to win this battle with the element of surprise," I defended.

"Is that all?" Matt asked suspiciously. "It wouldn't have anything to do with me, would it?"

I blushed.

"I saw it in your eyes at the Sutro Baths," he said. "You can't make up for what happened, and you can't protect me forever."

"I don't want you to be alone when we're all

gone," my voice dropped to a whisper.

"You've gotta stop worrying about me. My journey is meant to teach my soul. You are not tied to my destiny, Angel." The severity of his warning and sting of his rejection was palpable.

Despite what he said, I was tied to him, and one way or another I'd be sure to protect him even at the expense of my own life.

Winding gauze all around my neck, Sam secured the St. John's Wort flowers onto the wound. She tucked the end into the multiple folds and stepped back to examine her handiwork with pride.

"It's no wonder you couldn't heal yourself," Sam said as she gathered the gauze, scissors, branches, and remaining flowers from my bedspread. "Not only did you want what Justin wanted to give you, but look," she said, opening the blinds. "New moon. You're at your weakest."

I rolled onto my back. The soft pillows and fluffy comforter welcomed my body as the day's events spun around my head. Matt lowered himself gently onto the foot of my bed, testing how close he could come to the vampire repellent strapped to my neck, no doubt.

"Bugger!" Sam shouted. "Spilt the potion," she explained, staring at the damp spot on her shirt which began to smolder and burn a hole through the material.

Matt jumped up, reached Sam in a flash, and ripped the shirt from her body.

He stomped on the material and put out the

beginning of a promising blaze.

My hands lurched to cover my silent scream as I gasped in horror and jumped up at the shocking sight standing before me.

With only a black bra covering her torso, I could see what Sam had been hiding beneath her long sleeved tops and layers of sweaters.

The sight of her desecrated skin will haunt me till death. Countless criss-crossing crimson ovals filled with the super-pale, dull hue of dead flesh literally marked her delicate skin from her neck and arms to her waist. Some marks were larger and darker than others. A pale sheen illuminated the middle of each spot.

Shocked, I pushed up my sleeve. The outline and center of my tattoo matched all of Sam's.

The ovals were bite scars—the bite of a vampire.

"Are *you* a vam—" I began to ask her uncertainly.

"No!" she shouted and flew to my closet. The snap of clothes hangers echoed in my room until she emerged wearing a long sleeved red sweater.

In the next instant, Matt's embrace wound around her tiny frame tightly.

"I'm so sorry," he cried into her hair.

"Stop!" she yelled at him and pulled away to look in his eyes. She reached her fragile hand to his pale cheek, and said, "I love you. You love me. That's all that matters."

Sam stood on her tip toes, guided his cheeks

with her light touch so his lips met hers in equal intensity, if unequal in desire.

"Sam," he started, "You need someone better, someone who will never hurt you."

The pain in his gaze was crushing. My own eyes began to tear up.

"It's not like you did it because you wanted to hurt me or kill me. Besides, humans cause far worse pain," she explained carefully to him. "The heart hurts far worse than this and I can't live without you."

She gasped in worry. Apparently this wasn't a new conversation for them.

"Besides, it only happened during your transition phase," she continued. "You're beyond that now."

Closing his eyes, he shook his head sadly in disagreement. "What if…"

Sam threw her arms around his neck. "Me and you. That's it. No worries about everything else."

She kissed his neck until he gave in and smiled.

"Ahem," I coughed conspicuously in case they forgot I was still in the room.

Sam groaned, kissed Matt on the neck one last time and turned to me.

"How?" I begged, pointing to her now clothed torso.

Matt held her firmly by his side. Embarrassed, he avoided my gaze.

"Matt had a difficult time adjusting," she began slowly.

Involuntarily, my eyes opened wide.

"You haven't seen him in a year. The transition is a lot harder than he makes it appear." She glanced at him admiringly.

"In anger? Hunger?" I needed to know more.

"They're all from the first couple of months after he changed. The Bellatori helped him adjust and he's been fine ever since."

A vision flashed in my mind's eye of Matt sinking his teeth into her shoulder as she turned her back on him in Cynan's room where they nursed him back to health.

I shook my head to get rid of the thought and focused on Sam.

"—were from other moments," she continued.

"Other?" I asked unsure of what she meant.

"Other," she said, her eyes widening in hopes I understood without her having to explain. She blushed. "We got carried away."

"Oh," I breathed. After tonight's near miss with Justin, I understood completely. Kissing a vampire was—well there's no other way to put it—completely intoxicating. I knew what it meant to lose myself in the moment.

A half hour later, my hands mindlessly scrubbed a stained pot in the kitchen sink, while my thoughts were completely preoccupied by the horrifying sight of Sam's once perfect body, losing

Justin, and humiliating myself with CJ.

A chill of disgust shot down my spine as the realization hit me that I harbored a 'thing' for three brothers—three sons of my evil nemesis, Hadrianus.

CJ was on my side or at least I hoped he still was, but what if Rick and Justin wanted revenge for Hadrianus' death. After all, they were vampires like their dad. Somehow, CJ escaped that fate over-and-over again throughout the millennia.

Why was I so attracted to the brothers?

Cringe.

I scrubbed harder. Lady MacBeth's quote in Shakespeare's "MacBeth" echoed in my thoughts, "Out, damn'd spot! Out, I say." Like her, no matter how hard I scoured, guilt was corroding my conscience and making me sick—in the head as well as physically.

CJ and I were tied together in a way I couldn't explain. Our relationship seemed more like a necessary by-product of fate. It just had to be. I couldn't imagine my life without him. And now he was back. So, why wasn't I bouncing off of the walls in ecstatic joy? I thought I wouldn't see him again until I died.

Rick was the bad boy and there was something deliciously attractive about that little fact. He was capable of being sweet and chivalrous—my memories drifted to him draping his leather jacket over my shivering shoulders last summer on the set of his final movie. But he was equally evil and maniacal. While this terrified me, my infatuation overrode common sense and the need for self-preservation.

Stupid.

I flipped the pot over and began washing the food-stained bottom. What the hell did Kelly burn in this thing and why was I cleaning her mess while she was locked away in her room?

And Justin. My sweet Justin. We were such good friends and then I had to ruin it by agreeing to a date. If only I wasn't so desperate to find a romantic connection, I could've saved us both the pain of tonight's embarrassing and, for me, nearly fatal encounter.

Damn it!

"You know you're going to put a hole in the bottom of that pot if you scrub any harder," CJ laughed softly, appearing quietly behind me.

Silently, I rinsed the suds off and placed the pot in the sink rack to dry.

Thoroughly mortified that CJ caught me making out with his vampire brother, I couldn't turn to face him. Hanging my head and bracing myself against the sink, I began, "I'm so sorry, so, so sorry."

He scoffed and then sighed deeply. "Yeah, I wasn't expecting you to get over me so quickly, but—" he wrapped his arms around my waist.

I melted into his arms—his real arms, not the invisible touch I'd suffered through for over a year.

"—I wasn't here. You're free to date whoever you want even if it's," he paused and sighed again, "Justin," he finished painfully.

Spinning me around, he squeezed me in an

inescapable hug. "But now that I'm back, I want you to choose me," he whispered.

Tears choked my throat. "With you here, I can't imagine being with anyone but you," I cried as my tear-stained gaze finally met his glorious, deep blue eyes. "Can you forgive me?" I murmured, worried he couldn't, or even worse, wouldn't. As Zach, he had held a grudge for my far more innocent indiscretion with Davey.

"Angel," he said sincerely, lifting my chin and face to meet his eyes again.

My heart melted. "Say it again," I begged.

"What?" he asked confused.

"My name," I whimpered. "I've been dying to hear your voice for so long."

He smiled angelically. "Angel," he whispered and kissed my nose. "*My* Angel," he said emphatically and kissed my lips.

A rush of electricity ignited in my body. The charge darted through every extremity and exploded in my heart. Wrapping around his neck, my arms pulled him closer as my body fed off of the magnificent charge of energy our lip lock produced.

All of the love and longing I'd felt for him over the past year overflowed in this stolen moment that shouldn't have been. And yet, here he was. My knight in shining armor returned to save me again, even if it was from myself.

He pulled away slightly to look at me. Dazed and in a love-filled haze, we stared at each other.

Neither of us needed to say it, because we both knew it. We were together again and nothing could ever keep us apart—clearly, not even death, which reminded me.

"How did you come back?" I asked. "I thought the Bellatori owned you."

"So did I," he replied matter-of-factly. "But no one was going to intervene when Justin—" his voice trailed off as fury flashed across his eyes and the blue vein in his temple started throbbing.

I reached for his face and caressed his cheek with my cool touch to calm him.

CJ breathed deeply. "Anyway, they were just going to let it happen. I couldn't stand by and watch him kill you," he seethed.

"Did the Bellatori know he was a vampire?" I wondered.

"Of course they did," he said, pulling away from me to lean against the refrigerator.

"But then why would they let me near him?"

"Justin was working for them, but, like most vampires, he can't be trusted because he's caught between the spiritual world and the hunger of his living-dead nature."

"Heard that," Matt shouted from the living room having heard our conversation with his super-vampire listening skills.

"I said 'most,'" CJ defended.

"Why would they let Justin befriend me then? Why not an angel or someone else?"

"You had a slew of people or things," he said disdainfully, "looking out for you. Justin was a good choice because of his past connection to you and since he's a vampire, he can identify others pretty easily. Plus, he *is* an amazing soldier," CJ added reluctantly.

"Were there other vampires after me here?" I asked, suddenly worried.

"Yeah. Justin took 'em out before they got too close to you."

Feeling like the wind had just been knocked out of me, I braced the sink. The normal life I so naively thought I had over the past few months was all a set up. And Justin had been in harm's way because of me.

"Why would the Bellatori allow me to move to San Francisco if there's such a high concentration of vampires here?" I thought aloud.

"Maybe we're fearing the wrong things," Cynan offered logically, walking into the kitchen.

"Care to clarify?" Sam remarked snidely, popping up on a bar stool by the open window, separating the kitchen from the living room.

"Perhaps vampires are the least of our worries," he paused thoughtfully propping himself against the kitchen doorframe and running his hand through his long loose black mohawk. "What if the Bellatori's loyalty lies elsewhere?"

Every set of eyes turned slowly to face me, their bright gleams dimming to the furious darkness of their attack-ready gazes.

"But if we can't count on them, then who do

we trust?" I asked.

Cynan's stern black gaze flashed at me as he shrugged his shoulders dismissively. "No one."

Chapter 24 – Gets More Complicated

A series of loud bangs nearly broke down the front door.

Instantly, each of us readied for an attack. But who was waiting on the other side? Did the Bellatori hear our conversation?

"Isn't anyone going to get that?" Kelly yelled from upstairs.

We exchanged worried glances.

"Oh, for Pete's sake," Kelly grumbled and rushed down the stairs to the living room.

Cynan caught her before she made it to the stairs leading to the front door. He pulled her into the kitchen while I filed past him to the top of the stairwell with the rest of the crew on my heels.

Before I could go any further, the door burst open and a rush of wind blew into the living room.

Taking a few steps away from the frigid gust, I realized I was standing nose-to-nose with Gabe.

"What did you do?" he shouted at me.

CJ stepped between us.

Gabe stumbled backward. "How did you get here?" he asked confused.

"Back off, dude," Mike interjected pulling Gabe away from me.

"What happened?" Gabe repeated though his tone was slightly more subdued as he still stared inquisitively at CJ.

Conscious of Kelly's listening ears and needing to be discreet with my secret, I edited my explanation. "Um, Justin wanted to do something. CJ found us and intervened. That's it."

Gabe's eyebrows arched in speculation and his gaze shifted to CJ again.

"She's mine to protect. You weren't doing your job," CJ fumed.

"Like hell we weren't!" Ray exploded.

Standing straight and tall, CJ stepped forward intimidatingly, face-to-face with Ray. "Then where were you, when he almost—"

"Wait a second," I interjected and turned to the four linebackers before me. "You're one of us?" I hissed.

CJ leaned into my ear and whispered, "Angels."

"Not just any," Ray stated in a dignified manner.

I stared at them trying to figure out what level of holiness was taking up space in my living room.

"Come on, Ang," Mark barked behind me. "Michael, Gabriel, Raphael, Uriel—"

I gasped. "Archangels?"

Pursing his lips, Gabe sighed and nodded.

No wonder Gabe's patience was wearing thin with me. He was used to battling supernatural forces and here he was stuck babysitting an overly-emotional teen girl with raging hormones. Everything about Justin and his posse suddenly made sense.

"Why are you here then? What happened to Justin?" I blurted.

"He's gone," Ray said.

"What do you mean 'gone?' He and CJ got into a huge argument. He's probably just cooling down somewhere."

"Like you, we can feel people's energy," Mike explained in a hushed tone and sounding very regal. The surfer dude pretense was now gone.

Cabinets slammed shut and pots and pans shuffled in the kitchen. Cynan began speaking loudly about the importance and efficiency of an organized kitchen. We must've gotten too loud.

I hoped Cynan was keeping Kelly sufficiently occupied. I also hoped that Kelly wasn't freaking out at being alone with Cynan, whose Goth style, piercings and tattoos were a tad fierce.

"Except our sense is stronger than yours," Ray added to Mike's comment.

"We know where he is and how far he is from us at all times," Uri said level headedly.

"And right now, we can't feel him at all," Gabe finished.

"Well, it's not like he could've killed himself," I muttered. "Where else would he have gone?"

"If he got into one of the ley line vortices we found outside of the city, there's no telling where he'd end up," Gabe replied. "It's not just about Jay. There's something greater at work. Things are not as they should be…"

Gabe opened his mouth to speak, but Ray grabbed his arm to stop him and said, "We don't know where to begin looking, which is why we came here. We need to know what happened and that might give us an idea of where he would've gone."

I bit my lip and assessed their faces. They were earnest in their request and I could understand why they'd blame me for Justin's disappearance.

With my back facing Kelly so she couldn't hear me or read my lips, I muttered, "He wanted to make me like him. CJ fought with him to save me. I hurt him by choosing CJ, and CJ humiliated him in front of me."

The guys nodded in understanding.

A sudden thought popped into my head. "Hey, wait a sec. Why didn't the Bellatori tell you guys all this?"

Wordlessly, the angels exchanged minute glances with each other and vanished through the front door. Uriel paused and looked at Kelly.

Cynan released her from the kitchen. She ran to

Uri and wrapped her arms around his neck.

"What's going on?" she worried with fear in her voice.

Uri pulled her into a tight embrace, closed his eyes, and kissed her forehead. "Justin ran away. We need to find him before he does something stupid."

"Will you call me later?" she asked innocently.

My heart broke for her. She had no idea what was happening right under her nose or, more importantly, that she was dating an angel.

"I'll try," he said flatly. I could feel his unease at lying to her.

I glared at him and he caught my eye, nodding to me.

"Kelly," he began, "I'm not sure where Justin went. It may be awhile before I can see you again; I must find my friend. I love you. I truly and honestly love you…with all of my heart." He placed her hand over his heart and closed his eyes relishing the moment, memorizing it.

This wasn't a lighthearted see-you-soon farewell; it was a permanent goodbye.

He kissed her lips tenderly and rushed downstairs after his friends.

With the angels gone, the room felt lighter but a dark cloud of energy hung over us.

Kelly's tear streaked face turned to us.

I could feel her heart breaking. Uri was her first serious boyfriend. Seeing them together, I knew it was the real thing. There's no denying love when it's so obvious.

She spun around, ran upstairs, and slammed her room door.

Feeling ashamed, my shoulders hunched forward as I ignored my friends' stares and walked to the bay window to glare at the empty bay beneath the darkness of the new moon.

"It's not your fault," Sam offered, sitting beside me.

I shook my head angrily. Years of self-loathing bubbled to the surface. I twirled around to face the room.

"I've hurt every single one of you. It was never my intention, but my actions have directly or indirectly affected everybody here—not to mention my own family."

"Ang," Mark scolded, "you can't beat yourself up over this and wallow in regret. You need to realize that you always have the best intentions and move on. It's not like you sent Uri away on purpose to hurt Kelly."

"Cynan and Sam lost their dad because of me. Matt lost his life because of me. My dad is gone because of me, and my mom and family fell apart because of his death. I hurt CJ over and over again because of my fickle feelings. And all of the angels, vampires, witches and werewolves who died last summer, died because of who I am."

The anger throbbing through my veins was

about to unleash my sticky strings of energy. I fought to restrain them against the far easier will to just let them run amok and feed off of my friends.

"All of our decisions impact others," Cynan said wisely. "It's not restricted to you."

"The point is to make sure your intentions, goals and actions are always good," Matt added. "You can't control the outcome."

"I'm feeling a little offended, Ang," Mark quipped. "You've hurt everyone *but* me. I'm feeling left out," he smirked, placing his heavy arm around my shoulders.

I jabbed him in the gut and couldn't help but laugh. He always knew what to say to lighten the mood.

Cynan joined Sam in my room after our unsuccessful attempt to get into Kelly's bedroom to help her.

Sam and I were in the middle of going through her luggage when Cynan appeared in the doorway with a puzzled look in his eyes.

We stared at him expectantly. "Are you lost, brother dear?" Sam asked sarcastically.

"I was wondering what Gabe meant by finding 'ley line vortices?'" Cynan asked slowly.

I could almost smell the burn of the wheels spinning superfast in his mind as he tried to decipher Gabe's slip of tongue.

"Justin and Gabe studied earth's energy. Ley lines are paths of energy emitted by the earth. They thought ley lines connected different areas with high-energy frequencies like Machu Picchu or Sedona," I answered.

"Or Endymion Village?" Cynan speculated in an excited whisper.

Sam jumped off the bed to confront him. "The tunnels?"

He nodded. "I think we underestimated our home's location. The tunnels are enchanted, but what makes their energy so strong?"

"They're feeding off of the ley lines!" Sam exclaimed.

Cynan grinned.

"But the tunnels are tunnels. They're not vortices. They just connect different locations," I countered.

"But how quickly did you reach Scotland from Wales with CJ last year?" Sam asked.

"Pretty quickly, I guess."

"Exactly," Cynan said. "Vortices on ley lines must magnify speed—"

"By building on the energy stored along the paths and sucking more from the people who use them," Sam interjected.

Cynan nodded. "It propels people to their destination. What if there's more though? Bending time. Extra power."

"But wouldn't the Bellatori know all about the

ley line tunnels? Why would they have Justin and Gabe hunting for them through South America?" I thought out loud.

"Maybe they're looking for something," Sam offered, walking over to my window.

"But what?" I asked. "What could they possibly want or need?"

"Perhaps it's not the ley lines themselves but where they lead," Cynan said.

"They criss-cross around the world. Why start in South America?" I asked.

"Something there must tie them to the past or future," Sam added then turned to face me.

"What do you mean?" I stared at her dumbfounded.

Ignoring me, she continued to pace around the room deep in thought, her fingers tapping on her forehead. "The only thing they wanted more than anything last year was you, because you were the key to winning the battle. However, what if they're seeking something—or *someone*—else that can help improve their chances of winning the next one?"

"Person?" I mumbled as my thoughts raced back to the strange past life vision in the Temple of the Sun. I had been standing beside someone else.

"Oh my God! It *is* a person," I shouted eagerly at having figured out this piece of the Bellatori's puzzle. "It has to be. It's a person like me. In my past there was a man…"

"Who?" she interjected, hanging on my last

breath.

My shoulders hung low. "I don't know. I passed out before I reached that revelation in my vision."

"Great," she snipped sarcastically.

"Well, how was I to know the stupid vision was going to be important?" I shouted at her.

"Because everything you do and dream is significant," she snapped.

"Put the claws away girls," Mark laughed as he entered the room.

We shifted our glares to him.

"Seriously," he said, taking a step back. "We're on the same side, remember?"

I braced myself on the dresser, focusing on the pictures of my family and friends. Like the eye of a hurricane, my thoughts tried to make sense of the ideas surrounding the mystery person, which sped and swirled around me.

"Angel, isn't the Bellatori tied to your thoughts?" Cynan asked suspiciously.

"Not unless I want them to be," I smiled. "When I learned how to block Rick, I figured out how to block them as well. Actually, it might not be a bad idea for all of you to learn that too."

Cynan, Sam, and Mark exchanged knowing glances and nodded.

I began to tear through my disorganized

bookshelf where I'd strewn my library of sorts after the move.

"Ahh, here it is," I said, plucking the volume which Albert, the vampire bookshop owner, let me borrow permanently. Flipping through the pages of his family's diary furiously, I was looking for any indication of me or my other half in a past life. Suddenly, a pair of folded up pages fell from the book and fluttered to the ground.

Sam plopped by my side and opened the pages about the village's occupants from 1525, which she had stolen from Endymion chapel's archives.

Nomen	Propositum	Tempus	Adnotatio	Astrologia
Patrick Bertran	Natus	9 Ianiarius	Filius de John Bertran	∅
Patrick Bertran	Baptisma	23 Ianiarius	Filius de John Bertran	●
Margarete Pendragon	Natus	4 Julius	Filia de Christopher Pendragon	∅
APCE	Matrimonium	2 December		○
Artemis Pendragon	Mors	29 December	Filia de Christopher Pendragon	⊗
Sir William Endymion	Parricidium	31 December		⊃
Justin Bysshop	Absens	31 December		⊃

"Justin Bysshop," I said. There he was right in front of me. I should've known he was tied to me somehow.

"Do you think Justin is your other half?" Sam asked. "But the Bellatori already have him. Why would they need to confirm he's the one?"

"I don't know. Maybe it's not him. All I know is that I have two vampire stalkers, who happen to be brothers."

"Brothers with your boyfriend, don't forget," Mark added, making sure I was properly grossed out.

"Thanks for the reminder," I said as my stomach churned at the thought. I tossed the book back on the desk. Hurtling myself onto the bed, I buried my head face down into a pillow.

"Was it something I said?" Mark asked cluelessly. "The brother thing? I think that's kinda cool actually. How many girls can say they have a whole family of brothers and their dad chasing after them for thousands of years?"

"Oh God," I groaned into my pillow. I'd forgotten about Hadrianus' obsession with me.

"You need some girl time, Ang?" Mark asked perceptibly.

While he always seemed rather insensitive, he certainly had a radar for knowing when to clear out of a room in case the water works started.

I nodded into my pillow.

"Got it," he said, jumping to his feet from my

bed. "Let's go dude," he directed to Cynan. "Think they just ordered more pizza for CJ. He's been dying for real food."

The guys rushed out and Sam lingered by my dresser staring at the pictures lining it.

"Who's this?" she asked, picking up a purple framed pic.

I sat up to look at it. "Davey, Kelly, and me. We were best friends. In that picture we were hanging out at my house, like we did every day until…"

I drifted off thinking about the heartbreak I caused in that friendship as well.

"Till what?" Sam prodded.

"Till I started dating Zach seriously." Remorse filled my tone.

"Why was that a bad thing?"

"Zach hated Davey, and Davey didn't trust Zach," I sighed.

"Where's this Davey now?"

"Don't know. He's mad at me for stringing him along, which I actually did, so I can see why he hates me."

"That sucks," Sam said simply.

"Yeah, it does," I replied, realizing finally why I'd been missing him so much. "He was probably the only human who ever liked me as-is before all of this supernatural crap happened. He accepted me and truly just loved me the way I was. I think I've wanted to reconnect with him because of that. He was a good friend. I miss him."

Sam nodded. "He's cute too." She pointed to his messy brown hair, dark eyes, and gorgeous smile.

I smirked. "Yeah, he is."

Thinking of my best friend made my thoughts jump to my current ex-best friend, Justin. I groaned again.

"What?" Sam asked, plopping down beside me.

"Justin. How could I have been so stupid?"

"In what way? You made a few stupid choices."

Forever the unsympathetic shrew, I shouldn't've been surprised by her cold remark.

"That I didn't see he was connected to the Bellatori and, more importantly, that I gave into him."

"Let's not forget that CJ had to interrupt your snogging session."

"Thanks, Sam," I said sarcastically at the reminder.

"Well, at least CJ is back," she offered to ease the blow.

"True," I said unhappily.

"What?"

"I should be happier, but I'm not and I can't figure out why."

"You finally let him go, Angel," she said as if I

should've realized this. "You made peace with his death and now he's back. It's quite an emotional big dipper."

"A what?"

"Those things at amusement parks. You call 'em roller coasters, I think."

I nodded.

"Two vampires and an angel in love with you. Supernatural or not, that's quite a group of infatuated blokes chasing after you."

"Yeah," I said mindlessly, thinking about the evening's events.

"Have you given any thought to becoming a vampire?" I asked timidly.

She nodded, still not looking at me. "I've come close myself."

"Do you want to?"

"No," she said emphatically and turned to face me.

"Why not?" I asked curiously.

"Because it's not natural. Matt doesn't want this existence for himself and he surely doesn't want me to suffer the same fate."

"Then how will your relationship work? You'll get old and eventually die."

She nodded slowly. "But we always come back and hopefully he'll wait for me in each life."

"That's horrible," I muttered.

Sam's distressed eyes stared intently at me. Her unusually pale skin looked even more sickly than usual and dark circles marked her sunken eyes. This issue had clearly been affecting her for some time.

"I love him. He loves me. That's enough for now. Who knows what tomorrow may bring?" she said sadly, turning back to face the moonless night.

"I may change my mind tomorrow. I may die tomorrow. So, for now this is fine. I love him the way he is and he would never change me. Not to mention the Bellatori would kill him for doing so anyway," she continued. "Would you want to live forever?"

"No," I said, seeing her point of view.

"CJ?" Sam assumed astutely.

"Mmm-hmm," I nodded. I couldn't imagine a life without him. The year apart was bad enough, but an eternity away from him would be excruciating torture. For a fleeting moment, I pictured myself as a vampire killing someone just to have the Bellatori take me out so I could hurry back to CJ.

A clash of thunder echoed outside.

"A storm?" Sam asked as she glanced to the starlit, cloudless sky outside.

"We don't get thunderstorms," I worried.

"Angel!" Mark bellowed from downstairs.

Wide-eyed with horrified surprise, our breath caught. We lurched to our feet and raced downstairs.

Chapter 25 – Au Revoir

Tripping over the last step, Sam and I collided and fell into the semi-circle of our friends standing edgily in the living room.

"What are *you* doing here?" I asked as my gaze met that of our uninvited guest, who was lounging comfortably on my white couch.

"A 'thank you, Adam, for saving my arse countless times' would be nice for a change," Adam glared at me.

Taking a deep breath, I realized I could be a little bit nicer. "I'm sorry, Adam. Thank you for everything."

"There now. Was that so difficult?" he asked sardonically.

"No. It's just that you're usually the bearer of unpleasant news from the Bellatori. So, what is it this time?"

"Good news actually," he said, standing up and popping a red grape in his mouth from the bowl on our coffee table. "Rick has been captured again—"

My heart sank.

Giving me a glance of complete disapproval but otherwise ignoring my body's unconscious reaction, Adam continued, "—which means you are free to leave," he said, looking at everyone else.

"What if we don't want to?" Mark asked.

"It's not a request," Adam replied without feeling.

Sam huffed while Mark and Matt crossed their arms defiantly.

"When?" Cynan asked evenly though his eyes were not happy about this order.

"Immediately," Adam said, popping another grape. "These are really sweet," he remarked, ignoring his hostile audience.

"And me?" CJ wondered aloud.

"The Bellatori hasn't figured out your punishment yet—"

"Punishment?!" I shouted. "Where the hell were the rest of you? He saved me—no thanks to the Bellatori."

"Regardless, they'll collect him when they're ready."

Adam's gaze scanned the room. "Why the sad faces? I thought you'd be pleased to go home."

"We're family, Adam," I said and meant it with my entire being.

"Awww, that's sweet," he began, "but a foolishly human emotion."

I'd forgotten angels were totally cerebral. Entirely rational, they were level headed because they lacked the feelings, which drove human decisions.

Turning toward everyone, he said, "Angel needs to complete her training. She is unable to finish it if you are with her. It's imperative she not be distracted or assisted in this matter."

Cynan and Mark's fighting glares were seriously contemplating eliminating Adam on the spot.

"Any questions?" Adam asked, refusing to acknowledge their attack stance. "Well then, I'd best be on my way. Oh, Angel," he spun around to face me, "the Bellatori is proud of your progress. You're almost ready." He beamed his glorious smile, which knocked all the anger right out of my head.

And as I regained consciousness, he vanished.

"Prick," Mark blurted.

The next day, with their bags packed and plane tickets purchased reluctantly, we decided to grab a last meal of sorts before the separation sentence was imposed on us again.

My own lunch plate remained untouched as I stared in awe and disgusted curiosity at Matt who ordered four rare filet minions and was relatively imperceptibly sucking the blood from each slice and hiding the remnants of gray meat beneath a growing mound of mashed potatoes.

The bustling restaurant provided ample background noise to keep the Bellatori from eavesdropping on our hushed conversation in the corner booth.

"—but can we trust them?" Mark asked Cynan.

Sam pushed her salad plate beside Matt's to help hide the evidence of his bone-dry remnants of colorless steak.

"Until we have more evidence, we *cannot* take a stand against them," Cynan whispered across the table.

"It would be unwise to reveal our position prematurely."

Mark nodded unhappily but shrugged and shoved a huge bite of lobster into his mouth.

"What's wrong?" CJ asked me and pointed to my full plate.

"Thinking," I replied utterly distracted.

"We'll figure out the Bellatori. Don't worry," he reassured. His hand rubbed hypnotizing circles along the length of my spine.

"Something about it doesn't feel right," I murmured.

"Maybe you just don't want to be left alone again, Ang," Mark offered sincerely before grabbing a huge bite of steak between his teeth.

"I agree with Angel," Sam said suspiciously. "Something is off."

"Remember what Gabe said, 'There's something greater at work. Things are not as they should be,'" I continued. Leaning forward, I whispered, "We're pawns in the Bellatori's game."

Everyone nodded in assent and their eyes dropped to the table in worry.

"I still think the note matters," Matt interjected.

"What note?" CJ and I asked in unison.

Cynan shook his head. Sam rolled her eyes. Mark flagged the waiter down for another basket of fries.

"A few months ago, a handwritten note was delivered to the cottage. It said, 'The gods' reign of terror starts when the leader ends. And so begins the end of days.'"

"Come on, man," Mark whined. "That sounds like a superstitious prophecy from the bible."

"It's bloody rubbish!" Cynan moaned. "Someone is trying to scare us…"

"Or send us on a wild goose chase to take us off track. We're probably close to something and they want us out of the way," Sam added.

"Regardless of whether or not it's true, there's nothing we can do at the moment," Cynan stated. "We know what we need to find. Our best course of action is to continue investigating."

His voice lowered and he stared right at me and CJ. "No matter what their orders, we should all rendezvous in one month's time."

"What if we don't have a month?" I worried.

"Time is irrelevant," Cynan answered. "We'll never abandon each other—not even in death. We're bound together for eternity."

I forced a smile for his benefit. I just wasn't that hopeful.

Chapter 26 – Realizations

With Cynan, Sam, and Matt off to Wales and Mark headed back to New York, CJ and I were left alone to figure out our share of the Bellatori puzzle.

Endlessly

Lying on my bed with Albert's diary open in front of me, CJ's calm and glorious presence sat at my desk beneath the front window of my bedroom. With his back facing me, the sun poured through the blinds highlighting his blue-gold aura, which shimmered in a pearlescent hue.

Sigh. The light brown, short, wavy hair adorning his head shined in the sun's light like a built-in halo. He was beautiful. My heart tightened painfully in confusion. I wanted to be with him, but I was worried about the emotional fallout if the Bellatori ripped him away from me again.

Regardless of my personal feelings, the energy swirling around my room was filled with peace and love thanks to him.

"Angel?" he asked quietly with his head still buried in several books.

"What?"

"Can you stop staring at me and focus on the research?" he asked mockingly as he turned around in his seat to face me. "I can feel your eyes burning a hole in my back," he smiled.

"Sorry," I apologized, feeling my face burn in embarrassment.

He stood and walked over to me. Kneeling at the foot of my bed, his hand slid along the side of my face. The static electricity of his touch sent waves of energy through me.

"What is it?" he asked.

"What if you leave again?"

"I won't leave you," he said forcefully.

"You don't want to. I get that, but the Bellatori can make you. If they're already mad at what you've done, who knows what kind of vengeful punishment they'll come up with," I rushed to explain. "I'm happy you're here now, but I can't lose you again," I whimpered. "The pain, CJ, it pierced my heart. I can't risk hoping you'll stay now because tomorrow you may be gone again. I love you so much, but, if I don't protect myself, I may not survive losing you again."

Tears slipped from my eyelashes.

CJ caught them on his fingertips before they raced down my cheeks.

"I understand," he said sadly and kissed my cheek. His lips lingered there wishing I'd change my mind. A new wave of depressed guilt washed over me. Why couldn't I be like everyone else with average human problems?

Unable to withstand the muddled and clashing feelings fighting within me, I pulled away from CJ and sat up on my bed.

The wounded look in his eyes was too much to bear. "I'm sorry. Truly, I am," I whispered, "but I can't…" My voice trailed off.

There were so many things I couldn't do. Couldn't be vulnerable. Couldn't give into temptation. Couldn't reconcile the guilt around Rick and Justin. Couldn't be the girlfriend CJ needed me to be. The list was endless.

He nodded.

Loathing myself, I watched him return to his

stiff, wooden chair. His muscular, massive shoulders hunched over the desk as he immersed himself in the book about Endymion Manor.

"I'll be back," I said, desperately seeking an escape.

As I turned the key in the ignition, the Viper's engine roared to life, mimicking the hunger for speed and power pulsing in my veins.

I raced through the San Francisco streets and found myself heading west on Fulton dying to reach Ocean Beach before sunset.

Screeching to a halt in the nearly empty parking lot along the expanse of white sand and rough surf, I jumped from the car and ran to the water's edge. I kicked my white flip flops off of my feet and let the waves wash over them. Their undulating rhythm soothed the tension tightening in my neck and shoulders.

How could I be so powerful as an individual yet so weak and submissive in a relationship? Could these sides reconcile so I was powerful in both areas? Or was there an unwritten cosmic rule that declared constant conflict was necessary in order to be human? Why couldn't I just find peace? If I could kick the crap out of vampires and werewolves, why couldn't I figure out my love life?

Pathetic. That's what I was. So strong and self-assured when it mattered, but here I was allowing my messed up romance ruin all the healing and independence I'd gained over the past few months.

Several groups of witnesses were jogging on

the beach or playing with their dogs, so I couldn't let my energy surge through the sky.

Breathing deeply, I let the excesses drain through my feet into the sand, which provided a perfect tool for grounding me. All of the tension gripping me physically and emotionally diffused instantly leaving me feeling content. Not happy. Not sad. Just balanced.

When I got home, the amazing aroma of dinner lingered in the air as I opened the front door. CJ and Kelly were laughing and carrying on over a full spread that looked positively delicious.

Instantly, jealousy reared its ugly head. While I was busy grappling with the insane emotions ruining and running my life, CJ cooked a dinner—there's no way Kelly could've made it; she was an expert on frozen food—and was sharing it with Kelly.

"Oh, Angel," CJ started guiltily, "I wasn't sure when you'd be back so I made dinner."

Kelly was wiping tears of laughter from her eyes but avoided looking at me. "Thanks for dinner, CJ," she said, standing up and taking her plate to the kitchen sink.

"Stay, Kelly," CJ insisted, "You haven't had dessert yet."

A flash of rage burned my face.

"Thanks, but I'm full," she said, barely so much as glancing at me as she walked by.

As her footsteps faded away, I glared at CJ.

"What?" he asked stupidly.

"What?" I imitated. "I'm an emotional mess and you play all nice-nice with my friend, who hates me for whatever new reason at the moment? Are you kidding me?" I shouted.

"You're being completely irrational," he said, helping himself to another piece of roasted chicken and mashed potatoes.

"Don't you have any feelings? Or have you been around the Bellatori angels too long to remember what it's like being human?"

His eyes flashed angrily at me. "You left. I was hungry, so I made dinner. Thinking it would be completely rude of me to make dinner for one, I made enough for the three of us and a small army. You could lose the bitchy attitude and say 'thank you' instead."

Suddenly, he looked in my direction, "Unless…"

"Unless what?" I snapped back. I wanted to be right. I wanted to win this argument.

Turning back to his dinner, he continued, "Picture a violet light spinning around you counterclockwise—kinda like a hula-hoop running non-stop."

Even though I didn't want to, the second he put the thought in my head, I couldn't help but see what he wanted me to do.

Oddly enough, the little exercise made me feel better.

Taking a deep breath, I continued, "Sorry. And thank you for dinner. It just pisses me off that you can have a good time with Kelly. I want you to have a good time with me," I whispered, feeling like an idiot begging to be loved.

"You're the one keeping yourself from having a good time with me," he quipped. "I'm ready and willing whenever you are."

I slunk into the dining room chair beside him. "I'm sorry."

"While you were out, I actually came across a couple of things I think might help us," he said, switching subjects.

I looked at him hopefully.

"The tunnel we found in Cynan and Sam's backyard last year is actually part of a massive labyrinth that is connected all over the world. Albert's diary claims that some of the tunnels seem to move or at least propel its occupants faster than others. I think that ties into what Justin and Gabe found out about ley lines.

"If some of the tunnels run along those energy paths, it would certainly serve as a way for us to hide and move quickly from one location to another."

"Wouldn't the Bellatori know about those lines already though? And Aeterna Flamma for that matter?" I asked.

"Most likely," CJ answered slightly disheartened. "But the one thing they may not have learned is this: Wales, and Endymion Manor specifically, are at the heart of earth's main ley line."

"Was that in the book?" I exclaimed.

"No," he shrugged, "but it has to be the center point. If Aeterna Flamma's headquarters are located there and most of the Bellatori are stationed nearby, they must be feeding off of the massive energy waves emitted in the area. Take away the energy; take away their strength."

"Why Wales?"

"Why not?" he retorted. "Think about it. The Bellatori said they'll protect you anywhere you go, but it's not like San Francisco or Machu Picchu were paranormal hot spots. Wales is completely overrun with angels, vampires and werewolves. There's barely a human in sight."

"If you're right and Endymion Manor is the center for the ley lines, we at least know the starting point, but the lines can run in any direction from there. Better yet, what's the point of looking into the vortices other than to find new ways to escape?"

CJ grinned and raised his eyebrows.

"Oh my God, you think that it'll help us pinpoint the location of my other half?"

He nodded. "Can you stop calling him or her as your other half though? It's insulting. I'm your other half."

I beamed. "You're my *better* half. This other person is just another…"

I hadn't actually thought about what this other person might be. However, he could only be one thing if he was equal to me.

"God," CJ completed for me.

The enthusiasm I felt only seconds ago was replaced by terror. If that person wasn't aware of his powers yet, he would face the same risks I did last summer if Aeterna Flamma reached him first. If he was already using his powers, did he have the right frame of mind to use it for good or evil?

Watching the thoughts cross my expression, CJ said, "Now you know why we need to hurry."

I nodded. "So, we start with Endymion Manor, but where do we go from there?"

"Didn't Justin or Gabe mention other energy points?"

"Well, yeah, the obvious ones that I mentioned already, Machu Picchu and Sedona."

"What about historical locations?"

"I'm not following."

"We know our chapter in this battle began five thousand years ago in Greece. We can start there. It would help if we could remember the locations of our past lives. The past may offer clues to the future, since we seem to repeat it."

"This time it's different. I survived when I shouldn't have."

"True, but the past can still teach us."

"In that case Greece and the Temple of the Sun in Cuzco are high on the list of places to check. We can add Angel Falls."

"What about ancient civilizations? Rome, Egypt, Sumer, China?"

"Definitely."

"I also think you need to take a closer look at the book about psychic vampires. I marked a couple of passages I think you'll find interesting," he added.

I looked at him waiting for an explanation.

"Hungry now?" he asked instead with a wink.

Whatever the passage was, his reaction made me think it was going to be totally interesting and absolutely terrifying. Clearly, CJ wasn't going to tell me which.

After dinner, I rushed upstairs and jumped on my bed where the book was lying open. CJ noted the paragraphs with pink Post-Its just in case I missed the neon yellow highlighted sections.

> ...Psychic vampires tap into energy fields to feed their own need to grow healthier or stronger. The easiest and strongest source of energy is from humans. While psychic vampires are humans themselves, they are able to pinpoint strong energy fields and drain them— as is evidenced in figure 32.b below of a human's before-draining and after-draining aura.

> Most vampires of this sort are not aware of their latent urge to feed. They often lack something in their own lives, such as good health, and use energy from the stronger sources around them. Think of them like mosquitoes. They do not kill their life source; they just feed on them until they are full. Although, if the source remains spiritually

unprotected (see the appendix for methods of protecting yourself), the vampire will return again and again until the source is so weak that he or she is no longer of value.

Most psychic vampires do not know how to control their abilities. They are often easily identified as individuals with aggressive 'A-personality' types who are dominant leaders and tend to be surrounded by tired co-workers, friends, and family. However, once identified, these vampires are easily avoidable.

A word of caution: not all vampires are clueless to their needs or skills. Psychic vampires who intentionally manipulate their strengths and control their life draining talents around others are the most dangerous individuals alive on this planet. They are able to take energy far more easily and less reluctantly than they are to give it.

These individuals are often spiritually advanced and able to share healing energy through their extremely strong life force. They are a delight to be around when they are open to others. Yet, this is a frequently used device to lure energy food sources. These vampires do not need to be near individuals to affect them. They can kill others simply by establishing a mental connection and desire to use them as their prey.

Once the invitation to befriend their prey is accepted, a psychic vampire can access their victims in person or through dreams at night when people tend to leave their bodies and project themselves through astral travel.

The most perilous psychic vampires are those who see every being as a feeding source to build their own energy field and grow to infinite power. When they die, they can partner with demonic entities and often choose to remain in limbo, lingering somewhere in the void between life and death, to continue feeding off the weak and vulnerable.

Protection is vital to safeguarding you and your loved ones from these maniacal personalities, who may look angelic but resemble serial murderers in intention.

The mythical monsters of vampiric folklore are nothing but imagined nightmares compared to the very real and very much alive wolves in sheep's clothing walking amongst us every day...

"CJ!" I shouted at the top of my lungs.

His footsteps echoed in the house as he bounded up the stairs taking them two or three at a time.

Panting, he stood in my doorway, worry painting his expression.

I threw the book at him. "Are you kidding me?" I shouted.

"What?" he asked obliviously.

"As if I didn't have enough nightmares already! Now I need to worry about people who are more dangerous than our blood suckers!" I screamed.

CJ scoffed. "Not others, Angel." His

omniscient smirk irritated me and pushed my last button after a long day of ups and downs. My energy tentacles whipped out and enveloped him instantly.

He arched his eyebrows waiting for me to understand.

Memories from Endymion Manor flooded my thoughts.

'I can understand the whole thing between good and evil and even witches with unexplainable powers, but vampires? Everyone knows they're not real,' I had said to CJ.

'Well that depends on your definition of a vampire,' he replied.

'Do they run around sucking people's blood?'

'Depends on which ones you're talking about.'

'There's more than one kind?!' I screamed horrified.

That memory faded into the one of Rick when he babysat me during my rose petal bath before the battle.

'Part of being a vampire is being enticing to people. We attract our food. If we were repulsive, we'd starve,' he'd said.

'So your touch, your scent, your appearance are your tools of the hunt?'

'I guess so,' he said indifferently.

'Weird.'

'It's not so different from what you do,' he retorted.

'Me? I don't do anything.'

He growled in disgust. *'One day you'll figure it out and realize how many people have suffered because of you.'*

"Oh. My. God!" I breathed, feeling like I was about to lose my mind and dinner in front of CJ. "I'm...a...vampire?!"

Chapter 27 – Power, Fear & Blindness

"Took you long enough to figure it out," CJ laughed, plopping himself down beside me.

"Why didn't you tell me?" I asked belligerently.

"I didn't know there was a word for what you did. Besides, the rest of us are all so strong, I don't think we realize you're *feeding* off of us."

"Please don't say that again," I begged, thoroughly disgusted with myself. "I can't believe last summer's training was actually teaching me to become a...this." I couldn't bring myself to say the word.

"We weren't teaching you to become anything. We taught you to recognize what you are. And I thought you wanted to be a vampire?" he asked, alluding to my confession to Justin. "Now you know you are."

"It's slightly different from actually sucking blood from someone," I argued.

"Not entirely," he began and reached for my hand. His soothing touch vibrated peace through my worried thoughts. "Everyone has energy. Not everyone has blood."

It only took a millisecond for me to catch on to his innuendo. Vampires used other people's blood to gain energy, but they didn't have any blood of their own. People had both blood and energy and I had more concentrated energy than any other person.

"I can kill vampires by doing this?" I asked aloud in speculative wonder.

"You can kill vampires," CJ smirked.

My confidence soared. I tackled CJ in unrestrained happiness and we rolled off of the bed. As I lay on top of him on the bedroom floor, my hormones took over.

I wanted to kiss CJ. I wanted to kiss him like I'd never kissed him before.

"Ahem," he coughed, "maybe we should get back to our research?" he suggested, remembering my need for emotional distance.

"Yeah," I muttered feeling confused.

Thankfully, CJ was levelheaded. My rash motives had gotten me into tons of trouble to date. Hadn't I learned my lesson? At least CJ knew my limits and knew I'd regret this in the morning.

As I rolled off of him and he nearly ran from the room to escape me, I leaned against my bed and hung my head in my hands. What was wrong with me?

On top of my apparent lack of self-control, I

was now able to add another character trait that could win me the weirdo-of-the-year-award.

Psychic vampire. Seriously?

Perhaps that tiny little fact should've become abundantly clear when I nearly killed Diego and his friends without really lifting a finger or when Kelly always complained of being tired when she was around me.

While the thought of being a monster more terrifying than my blood-sucking counterparts was going to take some getting used to, an exhilarating sense of power catapulted me to a level of arrogance I'd never experienced. I could win any battle. All it took was confidence in my abilities, which had demonstrated themselves time-and-time again over the past few months.

By sucking the energy from vampires, I could kill them without having to go through the Wiccan process of stabbing, burning, and purifying them. But how would it work? Draining someone took longer than the Wiccan way.

Beyond my control, an evil grin spread across my face.

I wasn't just strong. I was a killing machine—a force capable of taking down the strongest vampire alive today.

Rick.

In that same maniacal thought, remorse squeezed my heart. As Aeterna Flamma's leader, killing him would significantly jeopardize the group's survival. It was no secret that I was the Bellatori's weapon to meet this goal. The bigger question was could I kill him if given the chance?

Walking to my window, I stared at the empty night sky.

I didn't feel an overwhelming urge to kill Rick anymore. Sure, he was deceitful, cocky, unstable, and incredibly strong, but none of those were reason enough to annihilate him. A seed of kindness and purity was still planted firmly deep down somewhere inside of him. Of that, I was 100% sure.

However, if the Bellatori required his death at my hand or if my friends' safety depended on it, could I do it?

I wasn't a hit man. I didn't want to be one.

And there it was. A vision played through my thoughts. Standing before Rick, the choice was mine. Dagger in hand, I stared in his eyes. My duty and loyalty were clear. The strength and will to follow through on my direct orders were pulsing in my fingertips.

But deep in Rick's eyes I saw a truth I was too scared to admit was real. That truth meant that both my feelings and purpose weren't as black and white as I wished they would be.

"Angel?" CJ's soft voice asked from my doorway as the morning sun peered through my windows the next day.

"Oh," I groaned.

"Tired, sleepyhead?" he laughed.

Tired? Yes. But the groan came from guilt, confusion, and a general irritation with my stupid self.

Propping myself on my elbows, I opened my eyes to find CJ's carefree smile turn to a frown.

"What happened to you?" he asked.

"What?" I replied concerned, jumping from my bed and rushing to my dresser's mirror. Dark circles under my eyes and a greenish gaunt tint made my face look more like a Halloween mask of a zombie.

"The last time I looked at the clock it was about five thirty this morning," I said, falling back onto my bed and pulling the covers over me.

"The vampire thing is still bugging you?" he asked.

"Yeah," I muttered with my face covered by the blanket.

I didn't want him to see the uncertainty on my expression, because it wasn't so much my being a vampire that was bothering me. It was the disgusting yet obvious revelation about my celebrity vampire that kept me from closing my eyes and dreaming about him. He almost caught me in South America. Though Adam said the Bellatori imprisoned him again, I wasn't entirely secure in that. Since he somehow had access to my thoughts, the more I thought of him, the more likely it was I'd lead a path for him straight to my front door.

"Enough!" I moaned to myself.

"What'd I do?" CJ asked confused.

"Not you," I groaned. "I can't get Rick out of my head."

In a flash, the covers flew off of my face and body. CJ sat beside me and touched my head with the back of his hand to assess my temperature. His warm hand slipped to my jugular where he counted my pulse.

Worry creased lines across his forehead.

"Stop," I ordered. "I don't deserve your pity."

"It's not pity," he clarified. "I wonder if they found a new way to get to you. We knew they could read your thoughts and track you, if you didn't block them. They can also impact your emotions. They have to know your strength has grown. Maybe they'll affect your health instead to try to kill you."

"Rick would never do that," I blurted before thinking.

CJ scoffed. "Why don't you see he's manipulating you? You're not thinking rationally because he's in your head already!" he seethed while pointing to his temple, which was throbbing with an angry blue vein.

My gut told me CJ was lying, but my brain considered it. If Rick could manipulate my thoughts—after all, he was able to manipulate his appearance, it was a very real possibility that he planted these seeds of infatuation and longing for him too. What better way to get to me than to have me reject the one person who died to protect me time and time again? If I left CJ, I would be vulnerable, and Aeterna Flamma could easily over power me.

"Sorry. You're right," I muttered. "You're

right," I said a second time trying to convince myself.

The corner of CJ's mouth pulled into a strained smile. "Let's get outta here tonight. You need to relax and I'm sick of staring at the four walls downstairs." Looking at me tenderly, he caressed my cheek.

The energy from his fingers was addictive. I didn't want him to let me go.

"How 'bout I pull something together and we have fun later?"

My nose and eyebrow pulled upwards speculatively. Zach's version of fun rarely matched mine. I hadn't really been in the real world with CJ, so I could only assume he was still attached to his human interests from his life as Zach.

CJ laughed. "I swear no car shows, concerts, or football games. Ok?"

Slightly relieved, I sighed and nodded.

Having slept till three in the afternoon, I didn't have to wait long before CJ's night of fun. Dressed in a long black skirt and long sleeved, fitted pale purple woven sweater, I left my shoulder length hair down— an odd feeling and sight since I preferred the ease and organization of a ponytail.

A quick smear of red-tinted lip gloss added a bit of color to the pale, green glow of my eyes and cheeks. Unfortunately, the color was dark enough to show through a few dabs of pressed powder. As I was about to hook the marcasite cross necklace from Mark around my neck, the light glinted off of my wedding ring from CJ.

CJ was back. He loved me. Did I need to agonize over the future when I could live for today and appreciate every second we had together? The agony of losing him again would be unbearable, but I'd be far more upset if I wasted the little time we had together now.

As I slipped the ring from its lonely home beside the cross and onto my finger, the tinkle of the chain echoed the cheerful happiness overflowing in my heart.

CJ was the right choice. I had no doubt. He was a part of me in a way that no one else was. I didn't know the right words to explain it. I just knew that we felt like two sides of the same coin. Same but different.

Despite looking like a recently resurrected corpse, the dresser mirror reflected something I hadn't seen in a long time.

Peace. Contentment. Happiness.

A picture of a Renaissance-costumed Zach and me at a Halloween party stood less than an arm length's away from me on the dresser. Our simple, naïve joy seemed a lifetime away. He would always be a part of that future whether in this life or the next.

And in that reassuring thought I found both the comfort and confidence to embrace him and my fears of losing him again.

Emboldened with a full heart, I nearly skipped to the stairs. The soft chords of an indecipherable song played softly from Kelly's room. Taking a deep breath, I thought I'd try to speak to her again. She couldn't be mad at me forever, right?

Tied up in knots, my stomach seemed more nervous for this confrontation than my logical thoughts. Three quick raps. If she didn't answer, I'd leave her alone until she was ready to forgive me.

Having lost Davey was bad enough. If she didn't forgive me, what would I do without both of my best friends? My only normal friends.

The white door slowly creaked open. A flash of Kelly's blonde hair caught my eye as she spun around and walked back to her bed where she laid down and hugged a picture of Uri to her heart.

The air in her room hung heavy with despair and negativity. Afraid to venture any closer, I leaned against her doorframe and glanced around the sterile white space.

The only color in the room came from a picture of the Virgin Mary holding the baby Jesus on the wall behind her bed. The facing wall was plastered with prayer cards and pictures of angels, including the archangels.

A dim ray of light from the late afternoon sun illuminated the three short, white candles lining the small, white oak cabinet in her prayer corner. A simple, dark wooden crucifix hung on the wall just above the foot-tall statue of Jesus. The blue and black scapular of St. Michael the Archangel was draped around Jesus' arms.

The urge to confess my reality and her connection to the archangels became overwhelming in this moment. She was so close to God's divinity and yet she didn't recognize the pure energy and spirit surrounding her every day she spent with Uri.

Without looking at me, her strained, tired voice said, "It hurts so bad." Her red, tear-filled eyes turned to me. "I can't believe he's gone," she sniffled.

"But Uri's leaving has nothing to do with you. You have to take comfort in that."

Kelly's sad eyes transformed into a murderous glare.

"Justin left. They're friends. They want to help him. Case closed," I continued despite her spiteful stare.

"Yeah, and Justin left because of you—" she said angrily.

"Yeah, because CJ kept him from assaulting me!"

There was no way she was going to survive this escalating argument. My energy bounced in and out of me tangibly. It was becoming painfully difficult to keep it from grabbing Kelly.

My invisible vampire arms wrapped around Kelly. I wanted to pry them away but a slightly stronger part of me didn't care.

She gasped.

And my energy sucking tentacles disappeared.

"Are you ready to go?" CJ whispered in my ear. His arms enveloped my entire upper torso from behind. Apparently, he was blocking me from murdering my friend.

Turning my face into the crook of his neck, I breathed his scent and energy deeply. Like my own personal talisman, his angelic presence radiated a magical power that erased every bit of rage.

Kelly grimaced at us.

"In a few," I replied to CJ. "Stay nearby," I whispered, hoping I wouldn't need him to intervene again. "Just in case."

He nodded and walked to the end of the hallway.

With CJ so close, it was easy to remember that no one else's opinion mattered but ours, and it was easy to see what really bothered Kelly.

"Kell, I'm sorry you're going through this, and I know exactly what it feels like. It sucks.

"As for Justin, I really liked him, but finding a good connection with someone doesn't always happen in the most logical way. I miss Zach and Davey and Justin, but I'm happy now. Even though I haven't known CJ as long as them—," she didn't need to know the truth, "—he likes me for who I am, broken pieces and all. Just the way Uri loves you."

Her skeptical stare remained steadfastly silent.

"I'm sorry Uri isn't here right now, but at least he will come back as soon as he can. Zach never will and I need to move on with my life."

"Then why are you wearing the wedding band again? If you're getting over Zach, why would you put it back on?" she argued astutely.

Good question. I paused grasping for a reasonable explanation. "It's just a symbol that I can love Zach but move on with my life too. I can have both."

"Humph," she grumbled unhappily.

"Please don't be mad at me, Kell," I begged. "I'm sorry that the Justin thing led to this mess. I never thought you'd get hurt by it," which brought me to my point in a round-about way, "Listen, I may be going away soon…"

Her eyes opened wide, curious and questioning.

"I may go on a vacation to visit Sam, but I'm not sure when the plane tickets go on sale. It might be a quick last minute getaway. Maybe you could go home during that time too."

She sighed in relief.

"I've been dying to go back," I continued. "Besides, I'd like to do some research while I'm there."

She nodded.

"Are we ok, now?" I asked timidly.

"Yeah," she muttered. "I'm sorry."

"I'm sorry too."

I walked over to her bed and gave her a quick hug. "Believe me. I know what it's like to lose someone you love. It's hard to see things clearly."

But was I seeing clearly? I had a nagging suspicion I was missing something hidden in plain sight.

Chapter 28 – A Moment Too Soon

Sunset's warm, orange-gold glow over San Francisco Bay seemed more than a little magical. Like the living embodiment of a Renoir or Monet painting, the fading sun cascaded deep amber hues across the steel city structures. Sea gulls floated effortlessly on the Pacific jet stream, which propelled sailboats across the choppy surf toward their safe harbors.

The view was breathtaking. However, as the sun slipped behind the Marin headlands, I was beginning to regret wearing a skirt. My legs were numb against the frigid breeze. Standing behind me with his arms holding me securely against the rail of the ferry, CJ blocked most of the wind spinning wildly around us.

"Like it?" he shouted in my ear over the whipping wind.

I nodded and smiled at him.

"Where are we going?" I asked curiously and slightly worried. Zach would surprise me with things he wanted to do. He really didn't have a romantic bone in his body.

CJ laughed. "It's a surprise," he winked.

I gave up trying to figure it out and savored the moment.

Content in his strong, warm arms and wishing the moment would last forever, we absorbed the beauty of our surroundings from the ferry's top deck until it slipped into the dock at Tiburon. A sleepy town situated directly across from San Francisco, it paired the bay's rich hundred-fifty year past of trading and railroading with the modern world's rich and famous. It was a refuge from the hectic pace of city life.

As we descended the gangplank, I glanced at CJ in twisted fascination and curiosity. In response, he smiled a beaming wide-toothed grin which caused my knees to buckle.

Chuckling under his breath, he caught my elbow to steady me. "Glad to see I still have that effect on you. I was beginning to get worried."

"Why?" I asked. "You know how much I love you."

"Do I?" he asked. A sudden flash of pain crossed his expression as we walked toward the town's Main—and only—Street.

"What do you mean?" I asked defensively.

"Come on, Angel," he sighed. "You almost let my brother turn you into a—" he glanced around to make sure no one was listening, "vampire," he whispered, "and your heart skipped a beat at the sound of my other brother's name. It's a little hard not to wonder who has your heart today."

I curled into his chest and stared in his eyes earnestly. "It's you. It's always been you."

He smiled and sighed again, content with my assertion.

"So, where to now?" I asked as we reached the crosswalk.

Endlessly

Pulling my hand gently and beckoning me with his finger, he led me down Tiburon's block-long Main Street before stopping about twenty paces away at a restaurant with a neutral coral terra-cotta façade.

"After you," he motioned for me to enter the tiny patio area enclosure ahead of him.

He gave his name to the host, who led us upstairs to a completely deserted balcony overlooking the Tiburon pier, Angel Island, Alcatraz, and the San Francisco skyline not to mention the majority of the navy-black bay.

After we were situated at our private table, I studied his face, bewildered by his every move so far this evening.

A roaring grumble and bang ripped me from my romantic daydream and my head spun around to assess the danger hiding in our midst.

"Chill," CJ laughed. "It's just the patio heater," he motioned to the reddening fixtures lining the ceiling.

"Oh," I muttered embarrassed.

"Angel," he began sincerely, "we've been through so much together. You have nothing to be ashamed of. It's hard not to think about when they're gonna pop out of the walls next."

Myriads of thoughts swirled around my brain. Trying to pick just one to focus on was about as easy as finding a diamond in a mountain of cubic zirconia.

"It's just that I'm not used to this." I motioned between him and me.

"What do you mean?"

I leaned forward and said softly, "Acting like normal people."

He grinned.

"It's been so long and last year we were completely absorbed with the battle—"

"Which was hardly normal," he scoffed.

I nodded.

"So, where do we begin?" I asked, worrying if our relationship was only successful under high stress, death-defying situations.

"How about you tell me what you've been up to over the past few months since you moved here?"

Taken aback, I blurted, "I thought you could see my every move?"

He sighed. "I *did*—until you moved here."

"Why?"

Tilting his head to the side, he said, "Because I really didn't want to watch my brother get his groove on."

"Oh," I nodded, feeling my face blush a hundred degrees deeper.

"So, tell me, what's been going on?" he asked, tossing a garlic sautéed prawn into his mouth.

I began to tell him about Diego until he nearly snapped the table in two when he pounded his fist into it. At that point, I switched tactics and focused on my adventures in South America with Justin though he didn't seem too surprised by this tale. He was probably keeping a closer eye on me than he wanted to admit.

"What about Kelly?" he asked eventually.

"What about her?"

"How's the living arrangement with holy mother church?" he grinned, taking a swig of his bottled, local microbrew.

It was my turn to smile. "Fine. I thought you were beyond the petty arguments?"

Zach and Kelly shared a mutual disgust for each other. Apparently, death didn't change that sentiment.

"I can tolerate her more easily, since I don't see her all the time, but my God, did you get a good look at her room? She could be canonized a saint today!"

"She needs to perform miracles for that," I reminded him.

"I'm sure she could qualify without that," he muttered sarcastically, staring off toward the darkening bay.

"CJ," I whined, "be fair."

He rolled his eyes.

"Living with her has been…refreshing?" I squinted.

He arched a disbelieving eyebrow.

"Well, it has been," I defended. "She's not like the rest of us. Even if she and I have had our share of challenges, it's nice to be around normal people."

"Normal?" he argued, shoving a stuffed mushroom in his mouth. "She was never normal."

"She's honest, trustworthy, good-hearted, and a better friend than I could ever be," I argued, standing up for her, and then sighed. This wasn't an argument I'd win. I couldn't change his perspective. "Can we change the subject?"

He shrugged. "What do you want to talk about?"

"Definitely not Kelly or any aspect of our double life," I paused, wondering what we could talk about. It'd been forever since we had the chance to speak like regular people, I'd forgotten how. "Um, you could tell me about what you've been thinking about since you've been d—away—" I corrected as the waitress placed our entrees on the table.

He concentrated intensely on cutting his chicken parm. "You."

"That's bull," I called him out. I knew when he was lying because he refused to look me in the eye.

"Honestly?" he asked, glancing at me. "Food."

"What?" I asked, slightly offended.

"People never appreciate things until they don't have them anymore," he replied and took a bite of pasta. Closing his eyes, he savored the aroma, the texture, and every bite until he swallowed it.

I, however, was insulted. "Did I at least fall anywhere near food on the list of things you missed?"

"Of course you did," he winked. "Right behind cappuccino and Mediterranean grilled fish."

"Huh?!" My temper flared.

"I can't believe you're even asking," he retorted. "I thought about you constantly. Every time you wished me to be with you I was there and not being here hurt as much for me as it did for you. I would've given anything to come back to you."

"How did you, actually? I thought you couldn't return."

"Usually the Bellatori hovered near me constantly. After you returned from Machu Picchu, they were thrilled with your progress and that Justin had helped settle you down."

Stopping his fork in mid-twirl between his fingers, he bent it in half.

"You seemed to be in control of your energy and generally happy. The Bellatori backed off their vigilance. I didn't agree. I never trusted Justin and knew he'd try something if he'd find the chance."

"But how did you come back? Did you have a body there? I thought you were dead."

"I don't know." His eyebrows furrowed as he thought about this technicality. "I wished it and kind of jumped."

"Jumped?"

"It's hard to explain," he paused. "Remember when we traveled through the vortices. Time and space were irrelevant. It's kind of like that. I mean, that's how the angels travel back and forth too. Our bodies in one dimension adjust to fit in the other. Besides, it's our souls which really matter and those aren't affected by dimensions."

I was vaguely aware my mouth was hanging open as my brain tried to process this. "But you're technically dead," I whispered. "How—" my voice drifted off.

"Zach's body *is* dead," he clarified. "It's like when they sent me back last year. I didn't come back as Zach. This body is much closer to who I really am or what my soul looks like, I guess."

"What? You're losing me here," I said.

He leaned forward and began to explain in earnest. "When each of us was created, our souls were made to look a certain way. When we're born into our human bodies, our souls take on the genetic appearance of our human parents."

"Oh," I nodded finally starting to get it. "So, this is what you really look like?" I wondered aloud.

Devastatingly handsome with eyes in which I could easily get lost, he radiated a magnetic charm and subtle peaceful glow.

"Pretty much," he smirked. "You like it better than Zach?"

"Uh, yeah!" I answered confidently. "Zach was cute, but no human compares to you like this!"

Though he lacked the wings of other angels, he was one of the spiritually elite and it showed in his physical appearance.

He grinned arrogantly, which immediately reminded me of my pathetic human state.

"Why exactly are you attracted to me?"

"You're beautiful. Never doubt that," he said seriously, reaching across the table to caress my cheek. "But once you die, it's the souls' connection you desire. It's a human thing to be attracted to physical appearances."

"So, I'm ugly as a human?" All of my insecurities rose to the surface.

He rolled his eyes again and eased back into the leather bound chair. "You're perfect inside and out. Whether you look like a princess or a one-eyed, one-legged pirate with no teeth, I love you just the way you are," he grinned sincerely.

Somehow, I doubted that, but it sounded good. "I love you too."

Trying to read my eyes to see if I was telling the truth and whether or not I was ready to drop the subject, CJ sighed and shoved another bite of chicken into his mouth.

"What's heaven—or wherever you were staying—like?"

Washing the bite down with a gulp of beer, he said, "It's a lot like here. People have jobs but there's no money, fighting, evil, politics or anything that would create unrest or competition. Everyone's equal, content, and completely peaceful. It's nice."

"Nice?" I repeated. "Heaven is…nice? Not spectacular, breathtaking, or amazing?"

He squinted. "Are you trying to pick a fight with me?"

"No," I replied defensively. My thoughts

drifted to my idea of heaven and all those who had passed on.

"Did you see my dad?" I asked apprehensively.

CJ smiled sweetly. "Yeah, he's much *nicer* to me now." The smile turned into a full grin.

To put it mildly, my dad had issues with Zach. Then again, he *was* my dad. It was to be expected since I was his first born daughter. No one was good enough in his eyes.

"He still loves you more than anything and he definitely keeps an eye on you," he paused uncomfortably, "more than you'd probably prefer."

"Why?" I asked worried about how much Daddy was actually aware of.

"He's pretty much always with you, ready to intervene when needed."

"He saw the Justin thing?" I asked nervously. "Oh my God. He saw us making..."

I didn't want to finish the sentence. The thought of having an audience during my most private of moments was making my stomach churn.

"If you don't want him there, just set up boundaries and tell him when it's ok and when it's not. Ghosts don't care about the things that embarrass people."

A shiver shot through CJ as I'm sure he pictured my dad spying on us, while our hands and lips were all over each other last summer.

I wondered what it would be like to be dead and not enjoy the sun's warmth or taste food.

Considering how much I liked both, death would suck. There was no other way around it. Maybe that's why I kept coming back here—not so much to fight a battle for good, but to eat. A pathetic thought, but it was a real a possibility considering my affinity for comfort food and sweets.

"You're too quiet," CJ interrupted again.

"Eating," I said, pointing the fork to my mouth as I chewed a mouthful of pasta.

He laughed wholeheartedly. "That's what I've missed!"

"What?" I asked, trying not to lose a crumb. The gnocchi was too delicious to waste.

"You just being you!" he exclaimed. "Who cares about being proper or about the other things we have going on?! This is the Angel I've missed."

He reached for my hand and his eyes ignited in unrestrained passion.

"Seriously?" I mumbled as I tried to swallow a bite that was far more than I could chew.

"Yeah," he smirked. "I think you need more ordinary days."

"What d'ya mean?" I asked taking a sip of ice water.

"You've been so obsessed with this shit that you've forgotten what it's like to live," he reprimanded. "There's a lot of life left to explore and the damn Bellatori are always in the way. I say we enjoy every second we have left. What do you think?"

I grinned. "Sounds good, but we do have a job to do."

"We'll research during the day and go out at night. Movies tomorrow? San Francisco Ghost Tour on Saturday night? Did you go to Yosemite?" he paused. I shook my head. "We can go there for a few days next week. It'll tie into the ley line research anyway. It's time to pull you back into the world of the living. What do you think?"

"As long as I'm with you, I'm in," I beamed. CJ would keep me so busy I wouldn't have time to dwell on Justin or the Bellatori. Plus, as long as I was with CJ, I knew I'd be safe. We were nearly equals in strength. We could protect each other.

"What movie do you want to see?" CJ asked, interrupting my thoughts as the server cleared the table.

"I don't know. What's out? No sappy love stories and no stupid guy movies with lots of explosions and naked women. Are there any action adventures playing?"

"I'll check," CJ said simply. He smiled at me. "Happy now?"

I nodded. "Absolutely," I grinned. "You make me feel...human," I whispered. "A date with you today and tomorrow and for the rest of our existence is all I want. I want to blend in and be like everyone else. I don't want to think about being special every day of my life."

"Oh, you're *special* all right," he smirked playfully implying I wasn't entirely right in the head.

"Thanks," I stuck my tongue out at him.

We both exploded in unrestrained laughter.

Staring through the misty windows at the starlit sky and crescent moon, we cuddled on the blue pleather clad seats of the ferry's main deck. The bay's surf had become a little choppy, but the night ride was perfect otherwise since we were the only ones on board.

Before long, we were standing in my living room and staring at the bay, reminiscing about our third first date. Firmly planted behind me, CJ wrapped his arms around my waist. Our pulsating energy created a positively addicting combination, which I didn't want to leave for the cold loneliness of my bedroom. But if I stayed, I was afraid of what I might let happen especially since Kelly left a note saying she'd be out late. Apparently, Uri made good on his word and came back.

"Well, goodnight," I forced myself to mutter eventually as I twisted around in his embrace.

"Goodnight?" he groaned. "Not yet," he begged, kissing my nose.

I pulled back knowing it wouldn't take much to convince me to stay.

"But CJ—" I moaned.

"But what?" he whispered.

"This won't end well."

"Why not? I thought we're ok now," he pulled back slightly to gaze in my eyes. The hypnotizing blue of his irises was impossible to refuse.

"Angel, I've wanted to hold you for so long. Please," he paused to kiss my cheek, "Please. Let's enjoy the time we have. Don't worry about losing me. Not tonight."

"I'm not afraid of losing you," I hesitated shyly. "I'm afraid of not being able to say 'no' to you tonight."

He grinned, knowing he'd won the battle. "I won't let it get that far." He kissed my ear and slipped to my neck, not so subtly avoiding the cold, dead spot marked by Justin. "Just a kiss…or ten."

And I was lost to him and our desire.

CJ kissed my lips tenderly, but that wasn't good enough for me. I pressed my mouth against his with such force he stumbled backward. Wrapping my arms around his neck, I pulled him close. He wouldn't get away from me tonight. The Bellatori would have to pry my cold, dead fingers from CJ's body if they wanted me to let him go.

Our energy exploded through the room with waves of energy bouncing off of the walls and ceiling. The white pearlescent candles lining the fireplace, tables, and wrought iron wall sconces lit automatically cascading their warm yellow glow around the room.

My arms and legs wrapped around CJ sucking him into my inescapable grasp. Grumbling in pleasure, he didn't seem to mind as he took a few steps backwards, and we crashed onto the couch.

Pinned beneath me, I pressed my body against his and kissed his neck. Sliding my fingers through his hair, they slipped down to his navy blue shirt and unbuttoned it to expose his to-die-for sculpted chest. My lips worked their way south across his clavicle to his pecs.

Angel...

"What?" I muttered through my mouth's tentacle-like suction.

"I didn't say anything," CJ panted.

Angel...

In a haze, my head darted up from my dessert.

"What is it?" he asked as the black passion of his eyes tried to focus on me.

"Didn't you hear that?" I asked, looking around. It was clear as day—in my head anyway.

"Angel..." the voice echoed aloud this time.

Defensively and with superhuman speed, we shot upright.

And there he was.

Reflected in every mirror and surrounded by a pallid army clad in black, Rick smiled sinisterly.

Chapter 29 – Home

CJ wrapped his arms around me protectively as an evilly, chilling breeze began to swirl around the room.

We tried to step through the mini black tornado and got zapped as if we'd touched an electric fence charged with lightning bolts.

Caught in the middle, I turned to CJ. "What do we do?" I cried fearfully, hoping he had an answer.

His voice stayed strong for me though his eyes matched the worry in mine. "We'll get out of this. Don't worry."

"Let's go!" a third voice shouted behind me.

I spun around to find Adam's frazzled and terrified presence there.

"Adam!" I screamed overjoyed and threw my arms around our savior appreciatively.

We began to fade from the living room, but something was missing.

"What about me?" CJ's horrified voice asked echoing as if he was shouting through a tunnel.

Adam and I reappeared in front of him again.

"They're not after you," he blurted. Adam's blue angel eyes, though brighter than CJ's, burned intensely.

"I'm not leaving her," CJ roared and ripped me from Adam's grip.

"Owww," I complained painfully. The steel

grasp of both guys was far stronger than any human's.

"Angel..." Rick's voice echoed all around us as the tornado closed in.

"If you come, they'll find both of you," Adam rushed to explain. "You'll doom her. Her path isn't meant for you." Adam's severe rebuke only emboldened CJ's determination.

"I will not leave her side again," CJ snapped.

I placed my hand on Adam's arm. "Please," I begged. "I won't go without him."

Adam was mad, but he caved. Sucked into a vacuum-like vortex, we hurtled through a dark tunnel. Periodic flashes of white, red, and green light illuminated our faces highlighting Adam's determination and CJ's distrustful speculation.

We lurched to a sudden halt and suspended momentarily mid-air before crashing a half a dozen feet into what felt like a gravel road.

"Where are we?" I asked instantly.

"Doesn't matter," Adam spoke in the darkness. Only the neon blue of his attack-ready eyes shone through the blackened outdoor surroundings. "Come on." Holding my hand firmly, he led me forward.

I reached frantically behind me till CJ grasped my free hand.

Frigid wind blasted through us, dropping the temperature slowly until it felt like we were trudging through a meat locker. My teeth chattered uncontrollably and broke the deathly, heavy silence around us.

Numb in the cold, I was vaguely aware that my feet were having a difficult time moving forward. They slowly began to sink into the sludgy ground.

"Adam!" I screamed terrified.

He yanked on my arm nearly ripping it from its socket and pulled me free. CJ jumped over the spot to avoid the same fate. The sound of my shoes being swallowed by whatever almost ate me shot a shiver down my spine.

Barefoot, frozen, and scared, CJ pulled me into the cradle of his arms and we hiked forward as the space around us felt like it was beginning to tighten. I huddled closer into CJ's grasp which squeezed me protectively.

The encroaching walls of whatever tunnel we were in made it impossible for CJ to carry me any further. He set me down gently. Ignoring the pain cutting into my feet with each step, I worried more about the claustrophobic passageway. I could barely move forward without the wall's jagged coldness scratching and ripping my clothes.

Here we were—running again. It was only a matter of time. We knew that, but destiny caught up to us all too soon as it always did.

I lost track of our direction knowing only that we wound up, down and around countless paths and through several doorways. I hated being blind.

Adam hesitated.

"What?" CJ asked.

"Shhh," Adam ordered. I heard nothing.

"Oh," CJ muttered.

"What?" I asked turning to him.

"Voices," he mumbled, "in the distance."

"We're not far. We should make it," Adam whispered.

The tunnel widened slightly and darkness gave way to the light of an ivory candle with a gold flame about a hundred feet in front of us.

Adam sighed in relief and quickened his pace along the smooth slate floor, which soothed my bleeding, sore feet with its cold temperature.

My stomach twisted in knots. Dropping Adam's hand, I clenched my waist hoping to contain its contents.

CJ wrapped his arms around me. "You ok?"

"Nervous," I whimpered.

He nodded but focused on Adam's back. CJ's energy wasn't filled with the confidence I was used to sensing. We were both scared.

Three arched heavy-looking wooden doors stood regally across from the single candle. Carvings adorned the center of each door. The first contained Artemis' symbol of the full moon and two stars. The second bore the symbol of the witch with its waxing crescent, full, and waning crescent moons. The third featured an elaborate sun peeking out from behind a crescent moon with multiple overlapping rays reaching from its center.

"The three moons," I muttered and stepped forward to touch the image.

CJ's hand grabbed my shoulder. "What?"

"The three moons," I repeated. "I remember it from somewhere."

"That's not entirely comforting, Angel," he said. "Why do you remember it?"

"I don't know," I snapped, frustrated with myself. "I just do."

Our heads turned instantly toward the echo of approaching voices. They had to be close because I heard them myself.

"We don't have time. Let's go," Adam blurted and pushed open the creaking door with Artemis' symbol.

Rushing to hide from the entities who were gaining distance, we stumbled into pitch blackness and closed the door behind us. Reaching my arms forward blindly, a rough wall of stone and mortar met my fingertips.

"There's gotta be another door or something here," I muttered and felt my way around. "Here!" I exclaimed quietly.

With a quick push I fell through the opening into an immense opening of a room covered in black marble—floors, columns, walls. Torches lining the walls provided the only source of light in this otherwise dim yet rich space.

Adam's vivid blue eyes darted around uncertainly. His shirt was ripped to shreds from our adventure. I glanced at CJ who was likewise assessing our surroundings. His shirt, still hanging wide open from our earlier escapade, revealed his chest which bore countless bleeding scratches.

My own clothes hung in tatters. The black skirt looked like it was eaten by a paper shredder and my sweater more closely resembled an unraveled ball of yarn. I ran my fingers through my hair, which stood on end in a frizzy mess.

I turned back to Adam.

"Where are we?" I demanded.

"Welcome home," a devastatingly enticing voice echoed sweetly as its owner stepped into the light from the shadows of a marble column across the room.

My heart stopped.

Chapter 30 – Alliances

So often I'd dreamt of this very moment. So many different ways I'd imagined it. After all the fearful anticipation, here it was finally—a nightmare come true.

Appearing as gloriously as in the dreams he haunted, Rick took a step forward and materialized two feet in front of me. Wearing a loosely fitted light green shirt that complemented his eyes, he looked every bit the celebrity he was before his unexpected disappearance.

CJ jumped between us and stood nose-to-nose with his brother and worst enemy.

"Please," Rick scoffed in his delicious British accent. "Have you forgotten where you are? You can't protect her alone."

"I'll die to save her," CJ seethed.

"And you shall," Rick answered simply before shoving CJ aside. Two vampires appeared out of thin air to restrain CJ.

Rick's Greek god like nose, high cheekbones, and strong jaw line were perfectly complemented by a curly mess of dark brown curls with golden highlights. His deep emerald eyes beckoned me.

Squeezing my eyes with great difficulty, I envisioned a wall of protective energy surrounding me. Perhaps I should've spent a few more days practicing instead of playing over the past few months.

"Don't close your eyes," Rick requested gently. Hesitating, he stepped closer and reached for my face.

Running the back of his fingers along the length of my cheek, the electrical current from our bodies burned, sending shockwaves through both of us.

He grinned in painful pleasure.

"You're sick. You know that?" I groaned in disgust, but I couldn't ignore the elated feelings resonating within me at his first touch. I prayed CJ didn't hear my stuttering heart.

Ignoring my bitter comment, he continued, "I've waited too long to see you again."

"What do you want this time?" I ordered.

Endlessly

"We're not fighting. There's no battle…yet, anyway."

"You," he said perplexed. "It's always been *just* you."

"I'll kill you!" CJ growled as he tried to wrestle away from the four vampires holding his arms.

"How did you do this?" I asked as his army of vampires materialized from grey-black vaporous masses throughout the room behind him. "I thought the Bellatori caught you again."

He smiled deviously as only an angelic devil can. "I have my ways," he glanced toward Adam.

"You!" I fumed at being taken in by his charade.

"You haven't been introduced properly," Rick said beckoning Adam to stand by his side. "Angel, meet Adam Darius, my oldest and most loyal friend."

Adam smirked.

I took a rash step forward and wound my arm to punch him out in one hit.

Too fast to see or realize what happened, in the next instant I was locked in Rick's restricting hands.

"But you're an angel!" I shouted at Adam.

"Come now, Angel. Appearances aren't always as they seem. You should know that by now," Rick warned. "He works for me."

"This whole thing was a set up?!" I exclaimed angrily.

"Almost," Rick replied pensively. "The

Bellatori always interfere," he sighed matter-of-factly and let me go. "But that was easily remedied this time," he peered out of the corner of his eyes diagonally behind me.

My vampire savior stepped from the shadows.

"Sorry," he muttered guiltily.

"Justin!" I cried. "How could you?"

"Vampires are emotional creatures unlike heartless angels, whose loyalties rarely change. It didn't take much to convince Justin to save you from CJ," Rick explained.

At the sound of CJ's name, Justin's eyes flashed murderously in crimson.

With Justin and Adam working as double agents, the Bellatori most likely had no idea about what happened to me and CJ tonight. We were trapped and our luck had run out. There wouldn't be any miraculous rescues tonight.

CJ and I exchanged pained glances.

"Cheer up," Rick said without a care. "It'll all be over soon."

He extended his smooth hand to me. "Come, dear," he cooed as if we were an old married couple.

CJ's expression twisted in jealous agony.

A tear slipped from my lashes as my eyes met CJ's. I shook my head in a sad, unspoken apology, closed my eyes, and slipped my hand into Rick's patiently waiting grasp.

We walked side-by-side through hundreds of

undead. A howl from the room's perimeter set off a series of joyous cries from the werewolf contingent.

CJ's captors dragged him along behind us. As the crowd parted to let us pass, their crimson eyes began to glow vividly and a low rumble echoed through the group.

Timid and, quite frankly, scared out of my mind, my eyes dropped to my hand clasped inside Rick's grasp. My blood from the night's misadventures stained Rick's pale white palm and my fingers. Terrified of this unfortunate and life-threatening development, I stared at Rick to gauge his reaction.

His hungry red glare smiled forebodingly. "You smell delicious," he said seductively.

CJ growled. I shot him a warning glance, but it was too late. His eyes were determined to kill Rick. This signaled a battle cry of sorts for the other vampires who crouched forward ready to attack him at Rick's command. The blood dripping from CJ's chest didn't help our situation either.

If Rick wanted me, he was going to get me and everything that came along with me. Concentrating, my energy expanded inch-by-inch, foot-by-foot. I didn't want to give away just how strong I could be, but I was going to make this as uncomfortable as possible for him.

Seemingly immune to the pain, Rick grinned as his hand began to smolder and the skin around his fingers turned grey-black thanks to the infection I inflicted, which was working its way up his arm forcing an instant decay.

"I admire your determination. It won't help you tonight, but it's admirable nonetheless," he sighed, raising my hand in his ashen bony grip to meet his lips. The kiss he planted on the back of my hand sent a radiating surge of electric shocks up my arm and through my body, which twitched spasmodically.

"I hate you," I spat vehemently.

"No you don't," he retorted confidently.

"I do," I asserted, though it was more for my benefit than his.

His manipulations had to end. They *were* going to end tonight.

"Keep saying it and one day you may actually believe it," he replied, pulling me up a flight of a dozen black marble stairs.

My free hand fumbled in my pocket, searching for the one thing that had been glued to me since my trip to Arizona. I gripped the small piece of turquoise and pyrite from Qaletaqa. It was a stone of healing and power. Gripping it tightly, I prayed with all my might to channel the universe's strength in this moment.

At the top of the landing, which extended infinitely into the darkness, a black marble semi-circle table with thirteen seats overlooked the room below. Still holding my hand firmly despite the growing appearance and stench of decomposition radiating from his arm, Rick turned me around to face the crowd.

The vampires struggling with CJ stopped at the bottom step. Thousands of vampires closed in behind them leaving a thin semi-circle around the trio.

I'd never seen so many undead and their hairy pets gathered in one place. They must've been present at least year's battle, but being focused on my own goal I didn't realize the enormity of their side. Most of the audience wore black cloaks with their hoods dropped. Looking like a gathering at the U.N., the vampires and werewolves came in every shape, size, and color. However, the sea of red and silver eyes reminded me they shared a solidarity that humans couldn't. They fought for Aeterna Flamma and there would be no changing their minds about that.

"We have a decision to make," Rick said like a dictator riding the high of victory.

The massive room provided excellent acoustics so he didn't need to shout. Besides, vampires had hearing like bats.

"At long last, the key to our power is in our hands, and, fortunately for us, her sole protector decided to accompany her here. We have two options. Kill them and keep the Bellatori guessing about their whereabouts while we search for the stronger god among us or imprison them and use them as a bargaining tool with the Bellatori."

Standing straight and confident, Rick's eyes scanned the crowd. Gorgeous to behold, he exuded a magnetic charisma which would make it difficult for even the most powerful angels to argue with him. Knowing he could make people see and believe what he wanted, I had a slight advantage in realizing the power he had over his followers.

Without sound, a thin, tall, statuesque, blonde female vampire stepped forward to the bottom step.

Her unmasked hatred of me was evident in her icy glare.

"Kill them," she spoke succinctly and without hesitation.

Rick sighed in annoyance, though I was the only audience to this brief slip of his true character. No one else heard or noticed.

"Lilith, let's not let personal vengeance get in the way of the greater good."

"Lilith?" I asked, staring at her more closely. "Lilly?"

She sneered but otherwise ignored me. She was CJ's betrothed in the distant past and my snobby, self-centered roommate from the youth hostel in London last year. I knew both sides were keeping an eye on me, but until this moment I hadn't realized just how close.

"Fine," she seethed, holding her head high arrogantly. "She's the cause of our endless fight. Save Cenweard for the Bellatori," she smiled seductively at him, "and kill *her*." A grumble of assent rolled through the crowd.

"No!" Justin yelled from the back of the group. Rick's murderous glower silenced him immediately.

"Lilith, nothing will ever make me choose you," CJ scoffed. "I didn't five hundred years ago and I sure as hell won't today. Killing Angel won't make me like you."

Embarrassed, her scathing gaze at CJ made me want to protect him, but I was distracted by the hundreds of others focused only on me.

Seeing my death sentence in the ocean of hungry eyes, I instinctively squeezed Rick's hand in terror. Imperceptibly to the crowd, he squeezed it back and a feeling of reassurance flowed through me. Hopefully, he'd be kind enough to make me feel that my death would be a blessing and not a torturous end. One look at Lilith's ravenous determination told me death at her hands would be more gruesome and painful than anything I could ever imagine.

Ignoring Lilith and CJ, Rick turned to everyone. "We heard from Lilith. Will anyone else offer a suggestion?" Though his words sounded very democratic, his tone dared anyone to challenge him further.

"To maximize our assets, we will keep them as prisoners…for now," he added menacingly, looking directly at CJ.

"And let him escape again?" Lilith cried. A look of desperation crossed her eyes.

"Again?" I begged of Rick, yanking my hand out of his. What else had he orchestrated that I so naïvely believed?

Clenching his fist, he stretched his arm and watched the tendons, veins, and skin reform. He turned to me to explain.

A flash of movement in the crowd distracted me from Rick.

"No!" I screamed, but it was too late.

Lilith firmly implanted her bite in CJ's neck.

"No!" Rick echoed.

I threw my energy at CJ, but it only caused him to writhe in pain. Lilith was extremely powerful and her infection worked instantly.

Rick released a burst of energy through his palms and sent Lilith soaring through the air until she smacked a marble column and fell limply to the ground. He rushed beside CJ to keep the other vampires away from him and the widespread crimson river flowing from his neck.

Staring in horror at the scene unfolding before me, I realized too late that without Rick by my side, I had no protector. In a millisecond, Lilith was standing maniacally in front of me with CJ's bright red blood dripping from her ruby lips.

My invisible shield shot into place. It was now or never. Each stringy tentacle of my energy wrapped around Lilith until it felt like we were embracing each other.

She lurched forward to bite my neck, but her teeth got caught in my shield. Trying to pull free, my invisible arms of energy pulled her closer feeding off of her strength. Each pulsating heartbeat of mine sucked a wave of frigid energy from the she-devil.

The surge forced Lilith's thoughts and emotions through me until I began to feel her venomous hatred toward me and CJ. Despite this drawback, my own power grew with each breath and thought.

Lilith's struggles weakened against my grip as I fed off of her, wanting to suck every ounce of her so-called life.

Suddenly she was gone.

Rick held her limp body in his arms as Justin spun me away from her and bound my arms and body against his.

"Adam!" Rick motioned him over to CJ's convulsing body.

Free from Lilith's threat, I fought against Justin's hold wanting to rush to CJ's side.

"CJ!" My voice echoed in the cavernous space.

His chest heaved in frantic attempts to catch a breath, but the air itself was choking him as life slowly slipped away.

"Take him," Rick ordered Adam.

With a final foreboding look at me, Adam lifted CJ in his arms and disappeared.

"No!" I roared as my arms of energy knocked Justin away and lurched toward Rick and Lilith's almost dead body.

I stalked toward them allowing my Medusa-like feelers to expand powerfully around me.

A lone howl in the distance interrupted my concentration and my eyes slipped to the crowd.

Their eyes no longer red and silver, the muted gazes of a horrified audience met my killer glare.

Good, I thought. *It's about time they realize they aren't invincible.*

I turned back to Rick and felt my lips curl into a self-assured conqueror's grin. His arrogant mask of certainty didn't falter.

Howls roared deafeningly and in a split second I was trapped in blinding blackness beneath a horde of vampires and their snapping teeth.

𝔈𝔭𝔦𝔩𝔬𝔤𝔲𝔢

Two days passed since Adam betrayed us. Or, more accurately, it was two days since I regained consciousness. The waxing moon was about half full so I must have been comatose for a while.

Worried about the extent of the vampire's attack, I examined my entire body in the first few minutes after waking. The only hideous vampire marks were Hadrianus' tattoo on the inside of my forearm and the oval bite on my neck from Justin. I still didn't know who rescued me or how I got to this room. Of course, not knowing these details only added an extra element of unease and uncertainty to my already disgusted thoughts, which ran a mile a minute, inventing scenarios of what may have happened.

My head pressed against the freezing glass panel of the lanai door in CJ's old room high inside the front right turret of Endymion Manor. Surrounded by CJ's ancient belongings generated an acute sense of guilt. Life meant nothing without him and I would've gladly sacrificed mine to save his.

My memories were doing their best to torture me as they replayed Lilith's attack on constant loop. On top of that, being clueless as to what happened to CJ since then was slowly driving me insane.

I groaned in self-disgust.

The clouds parted and the moon's rays peered

through, illuminating the sterile white limestone veranda. A very small part of me rejoiced in nightfall. It not only meant another day was over, but I was getting closer to whatever end the Bellatori Dei or Aeterna Flamma planned for me.

For five thousand years the cool glow of the nearly full moon filled me with energy and power, and now it was a painful reminder that I just wasn't good enough or strong enough to protect the people I loved.

Yet, the starlit night sky and moon provided a tranquility which the glare of daylight eroded. Its dark presence reminded me that my past was filled with far worse ends. CJ's past and present, however, were a different story.

Overwhelming feelings of fury, remorse, blame, shame, love, and more anger flowed from me uncontrollably. The emotions clashed throughout the room leaving behind a negative charge, which only magnified my misery.

Since I awoke in my prison, I hadn't seen another soul—living or dead. No one visited me yet somehow three elaborate meals appeared on the bedside table every day usually when I was in the pure white bathroom or gazing longingly at the freedom just beyond the lanai's French doors.

The freedom I yearned for dreadfully was so close and yet so far out of reach. I wasn't afraid of death anymore. Matt and CJ faced far worse fates than me and, despite what both would say, their deaths were a direct result of my existence.

Five hundred years ago, I fell from the precipice a few feet from this door. Death came quickly then. It could again. There was only one complication. While the doors could open, I was unable to leave. An invisible shield kept me from placing my foot onto the porch.

Kicking, screaming, and punching it did no good except to frustrate me and hurt my arms and legs.

Day two of my hunger strike progressed nicely so far. They could take everything away from me, but I controlled this. And while this wasn't an honorable option, it was an option and the only one I had.

The ghostly reflection staring back at me in the window was marked with deep black circles under her eyes, which fell flat and no longer sparkled with life's color. Her ashen, weak, and hopeless expression haunted my thoughts. Did I really want to die this way?

With the moon lined up directly overhead, it must've been about midnight. A couple more weeks of this and it would all be over. Hopefully I wouldn't give into temptation; the food's aroma was sinfully enticing.

Weakness set in. Combined with a forced lack of sleep, I could put myself out of this misery sooner.

At the bottom of the manor's hilltop vantage point, the old-fashioned, black wrought iron street lanterns lining Endymion Village's main street had turned off for the evening. However, the pub was still active. Then again it was the only hang-out for the villagers. A smile cracked through my depressed state as I remembered Mark leading a group of locals in drunken renditions of drinking songs last year.

Periodic flashes of light flickered in the dense forest surrounding the manor's immediate vicinity and in the distance. I wondered if Sam knew what happened to us yet or whether the Bellatori even cared enough to save us.

The Bellatori.

How much did they know? Did they realize Adam was a double agent? They probably didn't otherwise they would've intervened earlier.

The damn Bellatori. All of my lessons were for nothing. I wasn't able to use anything I'd learned, except my most hideous and hidden talent. Considering its strength and evil nature—after all it only manifested after I killed Hadrianus, so a part of his energy must've been living in me—I wanted to murder Lilith for what she did to CJ. The worst part was that my vampiric tendencies took over. I felt no remorse whatsoever for this passion-fueled vengeance. After all, she was dead already.

Despite all of my rambling musings, the most important lesson was the one revealed that night. No longer would I be a naïve and trusting girl. I would trust no one. Never again.

Turning around, I leaned my back against the cold glass door. It numbed the pain pounding through my heart to my soul.

The candlelit room glowed cheerfully and highlighted every corner, which I'd memorized during last year's captivity. My eyes slid to the bed where a fresh set of red-black-white plaid PJs made of the softest material I'd ever touched had been laid out for me. It remained next to the pristine white ankle socks and untouched comfy dark purple crushed velvet yoga pants and long sleeved white cotton shirt which was adorned with silver studs in the shape of a fleur-de-lis. Rick always claimed he knew me well and the casual wardrobe he selected clearly confirmed this tiny detail.

Another pang of regret and disgust washed over me. Pressing my palms to my forehead, a guttural wail screeched through me. I slid to the floor and curled into a ball allowing the grief of losing CJ again consume me.

I let my guard down when I knew this was the only end for us. This soul-crushing pain was an inevitable result of opening my heart again and now I had to suffer the consequences. Picturing CJ either turning into a vampire or a truly dead human didn't ease my anxiety over his fate.

To make matters worse, my psychic abilities and all of my strength were completely gone in this room. I couldn't even replicate Sam's first lessons to generate a basic electric charge between my hands. I was no more skilled or special than any of the unassuming humans touring Endymion Manor's grounds each day.

My last psychic thought was more of a memory when I woke. The little arctic fox I dreamt of eons ago reappeared in my lonesome daydreams. The twinkle of his gold-green eyes provided a beacon surrounded by thousands of eyes—hungry, thirsty, blood-red eyes. Trapped by heartless, crimson eyed monsters, my dreams suddenly made sense. I wasn't chasing the vampires. I was running to them. *I* was the arctic fox. Would I be able to cunningly manipulate them or was I destined to become one of them?

Unable to help myself or anyone else, I was left alone to my irrational and desperate thoughts. And each time a memory of CJ's voice or touch popped up unexpectedly, it sparked another round of sobs. Faced with over forty-eight hours of this, my eyes were sore and my head ached. I cried so much that I literally had no tears left to cry. The sound of sobs still shrieked from my throat, but the salty rivers no longer streamed down my cheeks.

My current cries faded into periodic hysteria.

"What's wrong with this chair or a soft bed, perhaps?" his evil voice asked as he appeared out of nowhere.

Too weak to argue, I stayed curled up on the floor. "Hate you," I muttered without looking at him.

Ignoring me, he continued, "Had I known you preferred the floor, the least I could've done was provide a bed fit for a dog."

Turning my head to glare at him as he reclined in the plush black leather arm chair—the only new addition to the room since last year—I wished him dead. Unfortunately, my wishes were worthless at the moment too.

"A royal dog," he corrected flippantly, knowing he was irritating me.

"Go away," I grumbled, curling into a tighter ball as another episode of nauseous guilt constricted my heart.

He leaned forward in the chair to stare at me. "You look horrible."

"Great," I grumbled sarcastically.

"You smell worse," he noticed, scrunching his nose in disgust.

Drawing from the bottom of their reservoirs, tears slipped from my eyelashes and pooled on the polished wooden floorboards beneath my cheek.

"Aren't you cold?" he asked, standing up and walking over to the bed.

He returned a nanosecond later and tucked a white quilt around my blood-stained, shivering frame which still wore my tattered, filthy clothes from the other night. Crouching, he paused to assess me.

I refused to look at him and focused on his dull black dress shoes instead, which happened to be eye level.

"What do you need?" he asked cautiously.

"Someone to kill you," I blurted.

CJ was right all along. Rick wasn't to be trusted. I should've listened to CJ.

He sighed in exasperation. "Anything else?"

"Information."

"Like?" he encouraged.

"What happened?"

"I saved you from becoming the main course at a vampire feast," he answered sarcastically.

"Why did you bother?" I muttered lifelessly.

"Because you're worth more alive than dead,"

he explained simply as if I should've figured it out on my own. "And I assumed you'd want to live to see CJ again."

"He's alive?" A burst of hope sparked a glimmer of sunshine in my dreary world.

"Yes," he whispered unhappily. "Well, sort of," he clarified.

"Vampire?" I assumed.

He nodded.

A whimper escaped my lips.

"Still, while he's alive, you'll always have hope…and love," he choked on the final word.

"Why are you being nice?" I worried suspiciously.

"Can't I be nice?" he asked innocently.

"No," I replied emphatically. "What do you want?"

Moving as quickly as a—well, as quickly as a vampire—he lifted me in his arms and carried me to the bed with white gossamer curtains. Placing me gently in the middle, he leaned over me and caressed my forehead and cheek.

Too weak to swat him away, I argued pathetically, "You can't have me."

"I know," he said longingly. "I just figured the bed would be more comfortable than the floor."

I smirked. "What do you want then?"

"In no particular order, I'd strongly prefer you bathe, eat, and sleep."

He lifted the silver dome from my dinner plate.

"Seriously, Angel, this is such a waste. No one eats human food in the manor. The chef made this especially for you."

"To poison me?"

He rolled his eyes. "To feed you."

"So, you want me to eat and sleep?"

"And bathe. Please remember that one," he quipped.

"And bathe," I repeated acerbically. "And why should I do anything you ask?"

"Because I can give you what you want." He arched an evil eyebrow knowing he had me.

My mind raced with the possibilities. CJ. Freedom. My family. Sam and my friends. Finding my other half. Eliminating Rick and the rest of his twisted army. The list was endless.

Curled onto my side, I stared emotionlessly at his deceitful emerald eyes. "At what expense?"

"That will depend," he answered.

"On?" I waited impatiently.

He paused and leaned in closer to me until only a couple of inches separated his lips from mine. The energy radiating from him was both chilling and inviting.

"On you," he answered seductively.

Endlessly

His steady gaze did not waver.

"I'm here to offer a trade."

www.ingramcontent.com/pod-product-compliance
Lightning Source LLC
Chambersburg PA
CBHW021436240626
47153CB00001B/173